Whatever Happened to Will

Jerry Moorman

Published in the United States of America by
Raven Books
Grand Junction, CO
www.ravenbooks.net

© October 2015
ISBN 978-0-9963990-3-6
All rights reserved.

Grand Junction, Colorado

TABLE OF CONTENTS

INTRODUCTION

Is this book a work of fiction? Without a doubt, it certainly is and a product of the author's rather bizarre imagination.

Does that mean it could never have happened? I'll let you decide for yourself after reading the following.

In 1949, when I was less than a year old, my parents were encouraged to commit me to an institution, from which I would never return home. You'll find a striking similarity with the novel's protagonist.

You see, I had polio plus a fractured skull. Doctors postulated I would be severely mentally retarded and physically bedridden. Thankfully, my parents said no and I remained with my family.

As I grew older, I was exposed to several government experiments made without consideration for the health and welfare of participants.

First, I received the SALK POLIO VACINE with monkey virus. It was in 1960 that an NIH scientist named Bernice Eddy discovered that rhesus monkey kidney cells used to make the Salk polio vaccine and experimental oral polio vaccines could cause cancer when injected into lab animals.

Later that year the cancer-causing virus in the rhesus monkey kidney cells was identified as SV40 or simian virus 40, the 40th monkey virus to be discovered. (Shorter, e. 1987. *The Health Century*)

Sadly, the American people were not told the truth about this in 1960. The SV40 contaminated stocks of Salk polio vaccine were never withdrawn from the market but continued to be given to American children until early 1963, with full knowledge of Federal health agencies

Second, as a young boy, I spent a year in an institution for polio children. Visitations by parents were severely limited and sibling contact totally prohibited.

Research on separating and isolating a child from his family is well documented. It certainly did not contribute to a well-adjusted child. After the experience, I never totally reacclimated to my familial culture.

The government had nothing to do with my placement in the hospital. It is included only as an explanation of certain behavioral characteristics manifested because of such isolation.

Third, as a young college student, I went through psychological assessment for handicapped students at my university. My memories of it are sketchy at best. Other memories of that time period are very vivid. At the time, I thought it pretty innocuous; now, I'm not so sure.

Fourth, as a young adult, I was given the infamous Swine flu vaccine which never went through the required government vetting process for new drugs. The result was neurological damage for many who took it. It was an experience that very nearly cost me my life and still has lingering side effects today.

During the 1950's through 1970's, an agency of the government, the CIA, was conducting extensive Mind Control Research. Much of it was directed at methodology for creating the perfect Manchurian Candidate or more parochially stated, perfect assassins: ones who could do the deed, but never be connected to the government.

If you'd like to learn more about this subject, spend a little time and search ***The CIA Mind Control Projects*** to satisfy your own curiosity about whether or not these research projects really existed.

Chapter 1
Separation at Birth

The year was 1949; the place, Mobile, Alabama. A handsome young couple was sitting in the doctor's office listening very somberly to the family doctor's update on their nine-month-old twins.

"Justin is a very healthy little boy. William is another story, however. The constant crying the last three months had me stumped at first; then I called a friend in Birmingham who specializes in childhood diseases. I thought I had figured out the problem but wanted a second opinion.

"I explained William's symptoms in great detail: the crying, lack of basic motor skill development, the inability to crawl or pull up, and the seeming lack of basic social interaction with you and his brother.

"My Birmingham colleague confirmed what I suspected. William has polio."

Both parents gasped and immediately directed their attention to Will. The mother began to cry as the father softly asked a question. "What does that mean, exactly? Is he going to live?"

"It's impossible to know at this point. There are three types of polio infections:

"**Subclinical**: Approximately 95 percent of polio cases are subclinical, and patients may not experience any symptoms. This form of polio does not affect the central nervous system (the brain and spinal cord).

"**Non-paralytic**: This form, which does affect the central nervous system, produces only mild symptoms and does not result in paralysis.

"**Paralytic**: This is the rarest and most serious form of polio and produces full or partial paralysis in the patient. There are three types of paralytic polio: spinal polio (affects the spine), bulbar polio (affects the brainstem), and bulbospinal polio (affects the spine and brainstem).

"William has paralytic polio. From observable symptoms, it is most likely he has bulbospinal polio affecting his spine and brainstem."

The doctor tried to maintain eye contact with the father, even though difficult. "The child will no doubt live; but for how long, it's difficult to foresee. With the lack of physical and emotional development of the child, though, it will not be much of a life. I predict the child is and will continue to be severely mentally retarded. If he survives, he will be an extreme burden on your family.

"That's not my biggest concern, though!"

With tears in their eyes, the parents looked at each other and then back at the doctor. They anxiously waited for him to continue.

"My biggest concern is for Justin. I don't know how much you know about polio, but it's a nasty disease. It's highly contagious and has no cure. It's amazing Justin has not been infected."

The mother immediately picked up Justin and backed away from Will. Her voice was shaking uncontrollably. "What should we do? I don't want to lose Justin, too."

As both parents stared at the doctor, he responded. "I have a suggestion."

…leaving home

Three days later, an ambulance arrived at Mobile General Hospital. Identification revealed it to be from the LAKEVIEW ORPHANAGE AND HOSPITAL: A HOME FOR SPECIAL CHILDREN.

A baby boy was transferred from the hospital's isolation ward to the ambulance. His patient file identified him only as William. Across the front of the manila file in large red letters was printed POLIO PATIENT: TREAT ACCORDINGLY.

The parents told family and friends Will had been placed in a long-term hospital. Two years later, Will's death was privately communicated by the parents and a small private service held.

To the world, Will no longer existed!

Chapter 2
Several Years Later

His name is William Parker. It used to be William Hunter, and before that, it was William something else. He just didn't know what. Friends call him Will. He's 17 years old and free for the first time in his life.

Currently, Will is cruising east out of Miami at a respectable 65 miles an hour in a stolen Camaro. A Miami drug dealer is unconscious in the trunk.

As he tried to find a small private airfield, some background, on how he got into this predicament, is probably in order.

Will grew up in an orphanage for kids who, for one reason or another, could not be adopted. His reason for being there was polio. When he was born, people knew little about polio except that it was a very communicable disease with devastating physical outcomes.

Will's outcome was surprising to those familiar with the disease. At first, doctors gave him little hope. He was diagnosed as severely mentally and physically retarded. At about five, astounding everybody, he started walking.

He also began to demonstrate above-average intellectual achievement. By the time Will was twelve years old, he had endured several surgeries to correct physical problems with his left foot and ankle.

Other than a slight limp, Will appeared normal to those he encountered. Being close to normal, but not quite, was where his real problems started to develop. It was during that phase of Will's life, he first came into contact with law enforcement. There was a small misunderstanding with three classmates resulting in their stabbings.

Shortly thereafter, Will was transferred to another institution.

Chapter 3
The Orphanage

As a baby, Will's birth parents gave him to the LAKEVIEW ORPHANAGE AND HOSPITAL: A HOME FOR SPECIAL CHILDREN. He figured that was better than being left on the side of a country road like a mutt dog no one wanted.

Years later, he broke into the orphanage office one night and took a look at his file. It didn't reveal much other than him being picked up at the Mobile General Hospital in Alabama. The only identification received was his first name, William.

The file stated he would be known as William Hunter since Hunter was the next surname on an approved list of usable names for orphans. Approved by whom? He would never know.

The file was sketchy with only very basic information recorded on a yearly basis indicating overall physical condition and intellectual achievement. IQ test scores were also recorded.

One thing confusing in the file was a yearly rating on a 1-10 scale. It was titled *Potential Usability*. Will's first year he was rated 1. The score began to increase when he was 6 and went up every year. It appeared as 10 from the age 12 on.

The orphanage was not really a bad place like you might think. There was an isolation ward where Will lived until age six. Afterwards, he lived in the boys' ward. He was scheduled to live with boys his own age through about 18. At 18 everyone aged out of the orphanage and left. What happened to them was anybody's guess.

There was also a ward for babies and a separate girls' ward. Since Will had never known a different life, it was home, the only home he had ever known.

...

As orphanage kids reached school age, they were bused to the local schools in a moderately sized Virginia community close to the orphanage location. At school, Will soon learned those kids from the orphanage were not considered real people. Since each of them had some physical and/or mental disability, they were regularly referred to as gimps, retards, and any other degrading term that could be associated with their disability.

Don't misinterpret this, though; not all the kids were cruel. Many were kind and considerate of the differences. Even the kind ones, however, had a tendency to avoid orphanage kids if possible.

Knowing no other environment, it was years before Will realized the taunts and insults weren't directed to all students, just to those from the orphanage and a few select others.

Before long he started retaliating. After Will figured out he was smarter than the taunters, the realization started to alter his personality. He no longer accepted the verbal abuse as normal; he soon started responding to them. Mean and degrading comebacks to the bullies became his modus operandi.

A typical taunt directed at Will might consist of, "Hey, if it isn't gimp with a limp. Move retard."

His typical response would be to embarrass the bully with something like, "Better than being a chimp with a dick that's always limp."

It didn't take long for the feeble-minded bullies to figure out a price had to be paid for verbally harassing Will.

After a while, however, the taunting by Will's classmates progressed from mere verbal abuse to physical. It had all started in math class.

Because he was taking math at two grade levels above his grade level, classmates were mostly tenth graders; Will was an eighth grader. Three of the boys in the class were already starters on the high school football team.

Winston was a star linebacker weighing in at 190 pounds. The other two were defensive tackles. Mickey weighed 225 pounds and Tim about 240. They were really cocky because of their athletic skills. Usually, if you saw one of them, the other two were not far away. Winston was the leader of this anemic little brain trust.

After the first few tests, it became painfully obvious the three young men's skills resided outside the math arena. Because Will's test scores were the highest in the class, he soon garnered their attention.

Winston always did the talking for the trio, with the other two handling the smirking and belly laughs. During one class, when the teacher returned graded papers following a very difficult test, he congratulated Will on a perfect score.

The teacher then gave the trio their papers. He suggested if they wanted to continue on the football team, their grades had to improve. All three became very interested in studying their shoes.

Later, on the school's playground, the trio became very interested in Will. Winston swaggered up with a smirk on his face. Tim and Mickey were on either side of him. "Well, look guys. It's the gimp geek orphan math nerd. Think you're smarter than us, huh?"

A small crowd was gathering to watch the show. "Well, that wouldn't take much. Your combined IQ's wouldn't equal the losing score you guys had at Friday night's game."

The trio all had confused looks on their faces. As Will turned to leave, he smiled at them. "I'll leave you guys to ponder that math problem."

Winston was quicker to deduce the insult. "Grab him, Tim." Tim quickly engulfed Will's thin frame with his meaty arms and lifted him off the ground.

Winston was grinning. "What now, smart guy? Anything cute to say?"

Will smiled. "Well, Timmy, I'm probably the only guy at school you can catch. You certainly weren't able to catch anybody Friday night." Several students laughed at his comment.

Timmy threw Will violently to the ground. He was poised to kick him when a teacher interrupted their little fun session. After that afternoon, the physical bullying of Will continued with gusto. It seemed as if every time he looked up, one of the trio was shoving him into a locker or pushing him down.

He did his part by constantly pointing out their achievements in math class or mistakes made on the football field. Will knew his saving grace was the trio's fear of being kicked off the team if they really hurt him.

The other students at school watched the socio metric interactions as if the boys were actors in a great drama. Since Will wasn't really getting hurt, no one seemed to be concerned. He knew, however, the whole situation would reach critical mass once the football season ended. That was coming up the very next Friday.

Will knew any constraint shown by the three bullies would be replaced with all out mayhem very soon. He wouldn't stand a chance against three brutes the size of these. An edge was what he needed, literally.

...

The orphanage was set well off the main road about 10 miles from the center of town. Situated on 15 acres, it was pretty much self-sustaining. Staff consisted of medical personnel, orderlies, and cleaning staff, plus a grounds crew. The medical staff consisted of a part-time doctor, three nurses, and a psychologist.

The entire grounds were surrounded by an eight-foot-high brick fence. The fence was a beautiful work of masonry designed to keep people either in or out; Will often wondered which.

Orphans were not prisoners behind the walls; they were able to enter and leave the building as they pleased during daylight hours. Orphans were, however, always escorted when leaving the grounds. This was obviously for their well-being.

For almost 13 years, the orphanage had been Will's home. Very few of the orphans knew anything different. To Will's knowledge, the only children accepted were babies. All others went elsewhere.

As far as chores, all children had work assignments as their limitations allowed. Because Will was more able bodied than others at the home, he was assigned to help the groundskeepers. They also doubled as handymen around the place when things needed repaired.

With his work assignment, Will had access to all buildings, including a well-equipped workshop.

With the football season quickly coming to an end, he chose a day to complete his work duties a little slower than usual. Will wanted to be finishing up as the grounds crew left for the day. When he saw the last of them driving through the gate, Will headed toward the shop to return the hedge clippers he had been using.

To deal with the trio of bullies at school, he needed a weapon, something that might scare them into leaving him alone. The problem: there were no weapons allowed at the orphanage. Great care was taken by all staff to make sure anything that could be used as a weapon was locked up.

Will stood stoically looking around the shop. All woodworking and metalworking tools were locked behind a wire mesh screen. Even if he could get his hands on such a tool, its absence would be noticed at a glance by the staff.

No, he needed something concealable under his shirt that would pass muster as a scary weapon. Some type of cutting device seemed the best option. But what could he use? Will continued to scan the shop.

He was about to give up his quest when he came to the painting equipment. Covered with tarps, it wasn't used much this time of year. An idea jumped into Will's head as he moved closer. After digging under the tarp for a couple of minutes, Will found what he was looking for.

He stood holding a fairly rigid paint scraper in his hand. The scraper blade was about six inches long, three inches wide, and thick enough to have very little flex in the metal. Perfect!

Moving over to a grinder, Will began working on the blade. The grounds crew had taught him how to sharpen shovels and hoes on the electric grinder a couple summers ago. He now transferred that knowledge to the scraper.

By design, a paint scraper is not very sharp and has a wide flat front end to facilitate scrapping. Will started the process of converting the scraper into a crude dagger. The process proved far easier than one would have thought. A couple more days of after-work sessions and the dagger was ready.

His final check was to see if the knife was sharp enough to shave his arm; it was. Next, Will made a basic sheath from thin cardboard and duct tape. Securing the new weapon inside his pants over the right hip, he pulled his shirt over it and headed back to the main building.

...

Will was working a new math problem in class the Monday after the last football game. The new math procedure was requiring enough concentration he didn't notice the teacher leaving the room.

He also didn't see Winston, Mickey, and Tim leave their

desks and come his way. Will's first indication of their presence was when the sunlight coming through the window was blocked by their combined bulk.

Glancing up, Tim was the first one he saw. "Sneaky, Timmy. Too bad you weren't sneaky enough to catch any opposing players Friday night."

Timmy's leg was now brushing against Will's shoulder. Will moved slightly so he could look up at him. "Back off some, Timmy; it's my foot that doesn't work, not my nose." Even his buddies laughed at the comment.

Tim grabbed the shoulder of Will's shirt. "Real funny, gimp. How about I break your nose, then you won't have a problem."

About then, the teacher came in the door. "Anyone in here other than William finish the new problem? What about you three scholars?" He was glaring at the trio of bullies. "If not, get back with it; we still have a few minutes left."

Will's hand absently reached behind his hip to check and make sure the knife was still there. Today was the day; every warning bell in his body was going off. Maybe he should concentrate more on his environment than school work. Right now all he had was a polio leg limp; he didn't need it accompanied by a broken leg limp.

After school, Will made every effort to avoid the football stars. It just wasn't meant to be. As he got within sight of the bus back to the orphanage, his feet suddenly left the ground.

Mickey and Tim each had a meaty hand under an arm as they carried him behind a large utility shop. Will and the bullies weren't alone, though. It looked like every other kid from the orphanage and half the rest of the student body was trailing behind. Obviously, the trio had bragged about what they had planned for Will.

Once out of sight of the teachers and any other adults, he was unceremoniously dumped on the ground. Struggling to get on his feet, Will felt the sting of Winston's backhand slap knocking him back to the ground. He was standing over Will smirking.

As if on cue, the three boys backed a couple of steps back from Will's position, allowing him to stand up. They had used the pause in action to rip off their shirts. Several young girls were giggling and pointing at the boys' chiseled bodies.

Will placed his hand on his right hip and feigned discomfort as he tried to step away. "Okay, boys, I surrender. Although our match-up is close, I feel the three of you have a small advantage. You do know the definition of advantage, don't you: lead, gain, benefit, that sort of thing?"

"You are one stupid gimp, Hunter." Winston looked around for support from the crowd.

Several voices called out for him to leave Will alone. Another yelled, "Someone get a teacher."

Winston's face had started to redden; apparently, he had not anticipated support for Will. Another student from the orphanage even stepped forth to help support Will. He was met with a strong push from Mickey.

"Back off retard or you'll get the same as him."

Winston was now standing in front of Will with Tim on one side and Mickey on the other. "I tell you what, Hunter; you tell everybody how you've been cheating off me all semester in math and how stupid you really are and maybe, just maybe, I won't hurt you too much." Winston turned toward the crowd to acknowledge the laughs of a few fellow jocks.

Will's hand was now under his shirt pretending he was massaging his upper hip. "Look, Winston, I don't want any trouble here. You guys obviously don't like me and I don't like you. Why don't we agree to just try and avoid each other? Wouldn't that be easier than me embarrassing you more today?"

More laughs came from the crowd but not from the jocks.

The three bullies spread out into a semicircle as they moved closer to Will. In their minds, he would probably put up about as much defense as a tackling dummy. It never crossed their minds he might resist; after all, they were almost 700 pounds of muscle and Will was 150 pounds of gimp.

Will knew Winston would come at him first; it was his play. The other two were just along for the fun. Will's entire demeanor was now changed. The boys were no longer going to play with each other.

Someone was about to get hurt. This thing was going down. "Winston, please don't do this. It's just not worth it. Let me get on the bus and we can live to be enemies another day."

Winston inched closer. "Too late to beg, gimp." He glanced quickly at his two friends and made a slight head gesture.

Will was scared of these three beasts, make no mistake about it. But he would be damned if he let them bully him anymore. His fingers were now wrapped around the grip of his homemade dagger.

Winston exploded toward Will. Pure instinct caused Will's hand to come quickly forward and up. The power and speed of Winston's charge plus the quickness of Will's instinctual response created quite the synergistic strike force.

Before either of them knew what happened, the knife was buried up to the handle in Winston's chest. If it's true a person's spirit floats around in the air as death overcomes the body, then Winston was floating and cussing the smart-mouthed gimp who just killed him.

Will, of course, was not thinking any of these thoughts. There were still two thugs about to bash in his skull.

As he twisted the blade and withdrew the knife from Winston, Will detected movement to his right. He swung the knife in a backhand fashion toward Tim, who had his head lowered and was charging like a bull. The slashing motion hit him high on his right neck and continued downward opening the big vein in the side of his neck.

Will had stepped forward as Tim charged and thus avoided the painful encounter the other boy had planned. Will caught a brief glance as he passed behind him. Blood was squirting from Tim's neck; he was obviously out of the fight.

By this time Mickey was on Will wrapping his big arms around his smaller opponent's body. His strength was unbelievable as he squeezed Will's body while lifting him off the ground. Obviously, his mind had not yet registered the knife in Will's hand.

He grunted very loudly while squeezing Will to the point of unconsciousness. Will could smell his breath as Mickey clutched his entire upper body in a death grip. Both of Will's arms were pointing toward the ground as he fought for breath.

His last conscious act was to raise the point of the blade to Mickey's lower abdomen. He had a sense of falling backward as unconsciousness engulfed him.

For Will, the fight was over. He would later be told the

whole thing lasted less than five seconds.

…

Will woke up a day later in the local hospital. Within an hour, the Chief of Police and what was probably the department's only Detective were at his bedside. Will looked up at the Chief who was standing the closest. "Hi, William, I'm the Chief of Police and this is my Detective."

He acknowledged the Detective with a head movement. "How are you feeling?" Without allowing Will to respond, he continued. "You suffered a concussion during the fight and passed out. Can you tell me what happened?"

"I'll tell you what I remember. The three guys who jumped me are in my math class. They've been bullying me all semester by calling me gimp, retarded, and other bad names. Their main problem, other than my physical issues, seems to be because I'm good at math and they are not."

"Before yesterday, were there any physical altercations between you four?"

"Well, that would be dependent upon your definition of between. Most of the semester, they have taken turns pushing me down every chance they had. I never fought back until yesterday."

"Why yesterday and not before?"

"A couple of weeks ago, their taunting turned the corner away from harassment and began progressing toward serious injury. They pretty much promised me that after football season ended, they were going to seriously mess me up."

The Chief was listening carefully to William; not just to what he said, but how he said it. "Are you a senior, William? I figure you are because of the way you phrase things. Couldn't you have persuaded the three younger tenth graders without fighting?"

"Chief, I speak well because I study hard and pay attention in school, not because I am older. I'm an eighth grader; the three guys are all older than me. That didn't stop me from trying to talk Winston out of the fight, though, even if he would not listen.

"After Tim and Mickey physically lifted me by my arms and forcibly carried me behind a big shed, I tried to reason with Winston. If you haven't figured it out, he is the leader of the little bully gang, with the other two doing what he tells them to do. I tried, Chief, right up to the point when Winston charged me. There were a large group of observers, just ask them."

The Chief was obviously taken by surprise. "So, you're what? Maybe 14?"

"That's right, 14."

"Tell me about the knife, William. Where did you get it, and where did you learn to fight like that?"

"I made the knife out of a paint scraper. I don't know anything about fighting; it just kind of all happened. Whatever I did was instinctual; I certainly never did it before. I made the knife after they started getting more serious about hurting me.

"I intended to use it to scare them. After the last football game, I brought it to school. You know the rest. By the way, what happened to the three of them? How badly are they hurt?"

The Detective moved closer to William. "What do you remember about the fight, William?"

"I remember Winston hitting me with the back of his hand as soon as Tim and Mickey brought me around the shed. They dumped me on the ground; I struggled to my feet; and Winston slapped me.

"I struggled to my feet again and between insults from Winston, I tried to talk him out of fighting. There are probably 50 students that heard the verbal exchange. Then I saw Winston give Tim and Mickey a head signal just before he charged me.

"Since an altercation seemed inevitable, I had put my hand on the knife under my shirt. As Winston charged, I brought the knife in front of me for defense. Before I could do anything, Winston's body collided with mine. His momentum must have caused him to get stabbed. I certainly made no overt action to stab him.

"I immediately sensed Tim closing in on me from the right. I made a slashing motion toward him, hoping to discourage him. He apparently was closer than I thought; the knife cut him around the face. I didn't know where, but I did catch a glimpse of blood.

"About then, Mickey tackled me from the left. I ended up in a bear hug. The last thing I remember was a loss of breath and pressure on my chest as we fell to the ground. Then I woke up here. How badly were the guys hurt?"

The Chief was talking again. "We'll get to the boys later. As hard to believe as this whole situation is, it matches all the witnesses' statements. Witnesses stated that everything happened so fast, they never saw the knife until it was sticking out of Mickey's stomach. The entire altercation lasted between three to five seconds.

"As to the three other boys, Winston died almost immediately from a stab wound to the heart; Tim bled out at the scene from the carotid artery being sliced open; and Mickey died earlier this morning from a stab wound to his lower abdomen. Apparently, Mickey's weight drove the knife into him when you two fell to the ground."

William exhibited an expression of total surprise. "I am so sorry for their families. Hopefully you realize I never planned for this to happen. I just intended to scare them."

The Detective looked on with his own brand of surprise. "You're sorry for the families? What about the three kids laying in the morgue; aren't you sorry you murdered them?"

"Well, Detective, the way I see it; those three kids, as you referred to them, intended to do me serious harm. If I were in the morgue, I don't think they would have any real sorrow for me. If not dead from their acts, I would, no doubt, have ended up spending months in the hospital. I'm sorry if I can't muster up remorseful feelings for three egotistical jocks with sociopathic personalities."

The Chief intervened. "That's enough. Detective, forget what William just said; he's still under sedation. William, if you really feel like that, you might want to keep it to yourself."

William immediately realized the wisdom of that advice and decided to change the subject.

"Chief, what happens to me now? Will I go to jail?"

"I doubt it, William. All the witness statements support your side of the story. Also, the school principal and your math teacher already told us about the instances of physical bullying. We also have to factor in that you have several physical limitations caused by polio.

"Add that to the fact there were three 10th graders against, what I just discovered is one 8th grader, and your fear was certainly justified. I doubt any jury could be convinced you were the physical aggressor against about 700 pounds of football players.

"In my opinion, if anybody is to blame, it's the school for not taking your complaints seriously. As to you having a knife, hell, half the kids at school are farm kids. If they have on pants, they have a knife.

"No, William, I think you are not to blame for a very bad situation. You are also very, very lucky. Remember that, if you are ever bullied again. Next time might be different."

...

The next two weeks were a blur. They started with the District Attorney ruling self-defense in the three homicide cases. He and his staff joined with the school staff to try and prevent this ever happening again. They would start by formulating a plan to stop school bullying. *Good luck with that*, William thought.

Of course a large segment of the local community blamed the whole thing on all the 'gimps' and 'retards' out at the orphanage. But, as with many such situations, there was little action and a lot of talk.

To appease the community group, however, the elected School Board decided allowing a murderer, even a self-defense murderer, to remain in school would be an impediment to learning. William Hunter was expelled permanently from the local school district.

An even bigger problem for William, however, was the other orphans. Even though he had not been charged in the homicides, to them, he was a murderer. They were afraid to be around him; most of the boys in his ward refused to sleep with him in the room. His bed had to be moved to a converted storeroom.

Many of the staff were also concerned. They acquiesced

to any request he made, obviously out of fear. Who knew what he might do?

The orphanage psychologist spent several hours of therapy with William. The psychologist and the director of the orphanage then spent considerable time discussing options for William. It had become agonizingly obvious; he had to go.

He was 14 years old yet he could no longer attend school. Staff members were intimidated by him; other orphans were afraid of him; and if he went to town, he was likely to be attacked. The only option that made sense was for William to leave, but where could he go with his history? The Director said not to worry; he would handle everything.

Chapter 4
Military School:
The Evolution Begins

The next day, a van arrived at the orphanage. Signage identified it as being from the Niños Perdidos Military Academy (Lost Boys). Niños Perdidos Military Academy, known in its local area as the "Delinquent Academy," was in the western mountains of Virginia, about 30 miles west of Blacksburg.

William was instructed by the orphanage director to pack all his belongings and be ready to leave within the hour. When questioned about his destination, William had simply been told he was headed to a special school for boys like him. *Boys like him;* he had wondered what that meant.

The Academy had been established in the late 1940's by anonymous donors. It occupied a little over 5,000 acres of heavily-wooded, mountainous terrain dotted with a few flat meadows. The buildings were situated in one such area of about 50 acres.

The campus was surrounded on all sides by a six-foot, chain-link fence. Very prominent signs warned the public to keep out.

Access to the Academy Campus was through a very sturdy steel gate, manned 24/7. Nothing about the Academy encouraged drop-in visitors. Most who had ventured close reported the whole place emanated an intimidatingly hostile vibe while projecting an air of secrecy and danger.

None of these things escaped William's attention as the van cleared the gate and started up a narrow mountain road. He had no idea what to expect. To his memory, William had never been farther from the orphanage than the daily trip to school and a few trips to the community hospital. This trip of several hours had been, at one level, quite an adventure; at another, it was a nightmare.

Since he was a boy who had killed three classmates, William suspected this place might be really bad. Probably some sort of jail with other boys who possessed homicidal impulses. It was certainly isolated enough to protect the general public.

The van navigated a series of road switch-backs before entering an area of dried grass and weeds with numerous trees dotted about. During the warmer times of year, it was probably pretty with grass and wild flowers. This time of year, though, it just looked unreceptive and depressing.

Several structures were passed as they continued. William thought he recognized two of them from things he had seen on television: a shooting range and an obstacle course.

Up ahead he could see a large, barn-type structure, a big three-story log house, and several smaller structures. One of the smaller structures was surrounded by a high fence topped with some sort of barbed metal.

The fenced structure reminded him of dog enclosures he had seen in town back at the orphanage, only the dog enclosures seemed friendlier. He would learn later it was designed for boys like him who were too messed up to fit in, even here.

The van parked in a gravel area to one side of the house. The three men who had accompanied him in the van escorted him into the house. He was taken through the front doors and down a long hallway to an area in the rear of the house.

The room where he was taken had no window and the door was locked by his escorts. One of the men returned shortly with a set of green army fatigues, underwear, socks, and military boots. "Here, put these on. We got the sizes from your file. Please change now; I have to watch to insure you have nothing concealed on or in your body."

William noticed the language used by the man was much more polite than his demeanor. "I don't need these army clothes; I have clothing of my own. Would you please bring me my stuff I brought?" William could be polite also.

The man smiled in a very unpleasant way. "About now, all your stuff is being thrown in the incinerator. Here at the Academy, we give you everything you need. If we don't give you something, you don't need it. Understand?"

William did not understand. "Are you saying that my clothing, my radio, all my personal things have been destroyed? What kind of school is this? It sounds more like a prison. Who's in charge of this place? I never said I wanted to come here."

The guard gathered William's discarded clothing and laughed as he left and locked the door behind him.

For the next three days, William was locked in the room. He received water but no food. The only luxury, if it could be categorized as such, was a small toilet in the back corner of the room. He had to sleep on the floor without benefit of a mattress or any type of blanket to keep him warm. They were, without a doubt, the most miserable days of his life.

What kind of place was this? Was all this related to the dead classmates? Was he in some sort of secret prison? Even though William pondered these questions and his situation, he didn't worry about it. These people had something in mind or he wouldn't be here. He just sat on the floor and calmed his body. Because of the pain associated with polio, he had mastered the technique long ago.

On the afternoon of the fourth day, the same man came for him. "Okay, let's go."

They walked to a room down the hall and stopped. "There're clean clothes and a shower behind the door. You've got ten minutes."

Ten minutes later, William and his escort walked toward the front of the house and up the main stairway to the second floor. On the second floor, they entered a small elevator that took them to the top floor. Directly across the hall from the elevator was a large, heavy-looking door.

The escort pointed at the door. "Go in there. And mind your manners. Insubordinate behavior comes at a heavy cost around here."

William entered and closed the door behind him. A very pretty older woman smiled up at him from her seat behind a plain desk. "Hello, William. The Dean of the Academy is waiting to see you. It would be in your best interest to be polite."

That was the second time in less than a minute he had

been warned to be nice. He didn't have to be hit over the head. Obviously, he would have to go along to get along.

"Thank you very much, ma'am. How should I address the Dean?"

"I suggest Dean or Sir. He will be as polite as you. Don't forget that. Just go through that door." She had pointed to the door offset from her desk.

"Thank you, again." William gave her his best smile.

William went through the door. He was very careful to quietly close it. He smiled at the man behind the desk. "Good morning, Sir. I was informed you wished to see me."

William maintained eye contact as the man behind the desk looked up and smiled. Obviously, smiling was required on this floor.

The smiling man rose and came around the desk, extending his hand toward William. William stepped forward and shook the Dean's hand in a moderately firm fashion. The Dean motioned for William to take a seat in a high-backed leather chair. He opted for a similar chair in front of William's.

William waited for the Dean to sit before he did. The man smiled slightly at the polite gesture.

"You have very good manners, William. Did your parents teach you that?"

"No, Sir. To my knowledge, I have no parents or family of any type. Good manners were a requirement at the orphanage where I was raised."

The Dean had been told that already. He was just letting the young boy talk. He wanted to verify what the orphanage director had told him about William. The communication skill of the young boy certainly pointed to a strong and capable mind. "How were your accommodations the last few days? Did the conditions frustrate or upset you?"

"No, Sir. My assumption was that all new boys receive the same treatment. Other than no food, I was not hurt in any fashion. The exercise was obviously some sort of test. I hope I didn't disappoint you with my performance."

"How did you manage without food? Most boys start complaining very loudly about the second day."

"Well, Sir, you are, no doubt, aware that I have polio and have had it since infancy. With polio, most kids also have some level of chronic pain. Either you learn to use your mind to control the pain or the pain takes over. I taught my mind to control my body."

"Does that always work?" The Dean seemed genuinely interested.

"No, not always. It depends on the level of pain. Sometimes it's too severe to control; on those rare occasions, I manage it. I don't control it, but neither does it control me." William smiled. "Over the years, we have become friendly adversaries. As a matter of fact, I sometimes refer to pain as my old friend."

"Let me ask you something else, William. Your grade reports in school show all A's. Is that how you make such good grades, by controlling your mind?"

"Well, Sir, in my opinion, learning is about the ability to concentrate. Concentration occurs when one eliminates distractions. For me, the ability is a positive side-effect of the polio-induced pain. The fact that I wasn't able to run and jump and move around for the first few years of my life didn't hurt either. In those days, I could do little else than study. Those habits stuck."

The Dean took the opening to change the subject. "Speaking of running and jumping and other physical things, how are you now?"

"If you were to see me standing before you sans clothing, you would see a six-foot, 150-pound, 14-year-old boy. Everything you would see is normal except my left leg. It is somewhat atrophied at about two-thirds the size of my right leg.

"I will never win any awards; however, I can run away if need be and jump as high as any kid as long as I go off the right leg. I must admit, though, that in the past, I have counted more on stealth and trickery."

The Dean uttered a somewhat questioning laugh. "Is that how you killed your three classmates, by trickery?" He was very interested in William's response.

"No, Sir. I used their arrogance and the fact they could never conceive, in the wildest of their imaginations, a gimp with polio could best them. Also, the mentality of bullies won't allow them to believe the weak would resort to physical retaliation. They seem to think they have a corner on that market.

"I didn't go to school that day with the intention of killing three football players. But, when I saw the look in their leader's eyes, I knew the knife would have to be used to do more than scare them."

"How did you feel after killing the three boys? Do you feel sad; do you wish you could take it back; do you have nightmares and trouble sleeping? What has been the impact on you? "

"Sir, I believe the polite thing here would be to lie. Would you like for me to be polite or impolitely tell you the truth? Somehow, I think what I tell you will impact my stay here. With that said, I have been warned that being impolite to you might not be in my best interest."

The Dean laughed heartily. "You are an interesting young man, very intuitive and direct. So, as to your dilemma, whenever I ask you a question, now or in the future, the polite thing is to tell me the truth. Telling me the truth will always be in your best interest."

"Thank you, Sir; I won't forget. Now, to your series of questions, all the yes/no questions can be answered with a no. There has been no psychological impact on me. The three bullies were hurting people who could not stand up for themselves. They got what they deserved.

"When I was being interviewed by the psychologist at the orphanage, she asked the same type questions, only a lot more. After spending several hours with her, I'm convinced she considers me a sociopath with homicidal tendencies."

The Dean was staring intently at William. He had never encountered such a person. Immediately, he knew William would do exceedingly well at the Academy or be a major pain in his ass. "Are you a sociopath with homicidal tendencies?"

"No, not in the traditional sense. I believe I am a person with sociopathic tendencies who is capable of homicide. The difference being that I am capable of empathy and feelings for other living beings.

"I came to this conclusion after reading a book on psychology. Most sociopaths are born with the condition. I believe I was normal until the polio burned a hole in my brain and started its unique form of destruction.

"The polio obviously made me the way I am. I am neither normal nor sociopathic; I am something in between."

The Dean was stunned; he hoped it didn't show on his face. "William, I think you will fit in fine around here."

"Sir, if I may ask, what is here? What am I expected to

do?"

"Here at the Academy, you will be trained in all areas of the military. You'll learn to fight in many different ways including armed and unarmed. You'll be taught orienteering and wilderness survival plus the skills of collecting intelligence and acting upon same. You will continue your academic education with the addition of military strategy and languages.

"William, in the next two years, you will become a man uniquely prepared to excel in the military service. Most of our graduates go on to military careers. A few select graduates receive further training and pursue careers outside the military.

"All of our boys here are lost boys like you. Each was a ward of an institution like you. Also, like you, they have no family. Every boy got into some serious trouble requiring him to be removed from his institution. We are the institution of last resort. We don't give second chances here. Screw up and you're done. You will be legally emancipated and on your own. Most who have tested us ended up homeless on the street.

"We are, however, first and foremost, a military academy. If you follow the rules and give us 100% effort in all areas of instruction, you'll be fine. The majority of our student cadets spend two years here, graduate with a high school diploma, and enter the military." The Dean paused and looked at William.

"Sir, in two years, I'll be only 16. How does this work for me?"

"William, we have never taken a student under 16. Your orphanage director encouraged me to make an exception for you because of your above average intellect and the serious nature of your trouble. We also have never taken a physically-challenged student. The government entity that funds us likes consistency, not exceptions.

"So, to appease them and not have exceptions in our records, you are now 16 years of age and injured your leg in an accident. Your name is now William Parker. Your friends call you 'Will.'

"Do you understand everything I have said, Will? Of course, all this is confidential and between only us. Even the staff won't know. With your size and intellect, you can easily make the deception. Is any of this a problem for you?"

William knew he had only one response if he wanted to stay here. He didn't want to end up a homeless street kid. He had seen television about such kids. "No, Sir. I, Will Parker, understand it all. With any luck, perhaps my injured leg will get better here.

"And, Sir, I will not let you down. You won't be sorry you accepted me. Thank you very much."

...

As if by magic, the man who had brought Will to the Dean appeared. "Come with me, Cadet. You will call me Sergeant White." Will and Sergeant White left the house.

Will followed one step behind the Sergeant in silence. He took the time to process what he had learned from the Dean. Basically, the Academy was a place for serious juvenile delinquents and functioned as a quasi-prison. The first three days without food were obviously designed to convince boys this was a serious place.

If being denied food wasn't enough, being turned into a

military robot was sure to get your attention. The question begging an answer, though, was why they accepted him. With the physical limitations of polio, Will could never pass the military physical. There had to be more to this place.

Sergeant White, who happened to be white, led the way into one of the larger outbuildings. "Okay, Cadet, this is your new home. On the left is the kitchen. It feeds everybody at the Academy twice a day, breakfast at 5 am and dinner at 6 pm.

They passed a large open room with probably 30 beds. "That's the second-year Cadet quarters. Next are the head and showers. And last are the first-year Cadet quarters. Sergeant White entered the room. It looked much like the second-year room.

The Sergeant stopped by a bed in the rear of the room. "This is you; your fatigues and gear go in the locker at the front of the bed. No personal items of any type are allowed first-year Cadets.

"Stay here until the unit returns. Do not venture beyond the head. The Unit Cadet Commander will orient you to the unit. Since you are about three months late, you'll have some catching up to do. Pay attention to your Commander and do what he says."

Will had a couple of hours before he figured the unit would return. He used the time to study every inch of his quarters. Twenty-one of the beds in the room were made up and the room was neatly squared away. Will took note of the fact that his bed was a distance from any of the occupied ones. He knew he was not a part of the Unit. He'd have to earn his way in.

Will passed some time by making up his bunk. He had nothing to square away but the clothes he wore. All in due time, he figured.

He sat on the floor with his back to the wall and waited. This should be interesting

The other cadets came running into the first-year quarters at 5:45. They looked exhausted and about to collapse. Fighting their fatigue, they all undressed and headed for the showers. Five minutes later, most were back and changing into clean fatigues.

Will continued to sit on the floor as his new colleagues hurried to get dressed. Detecting movement through his peripheral vision, he looked up. A large, angry-looking cadet was headed his way. Will stood to meet the obvious threat at eye level.

"Don't eyeball me, boy! Stand at attention!"

Will stood with his arms loosely at his sides. He gave the big kid his best shit-eating grin.

"What you grinning at, boy? You look like some kind of retard with that stupid look on your face. Wipe it off or I'll wipe it off for you." The boy violated Will's personal space by stepping toward him until they were nose to nose.

While sitting and waiting for his fellow Cadets/Vicious Juvenile Delinquents to show up, Will had visualized how the first encounter might go. He didn't believe they would gush with happy greetings and welcomes to the school.

He figured he would be tested from the git-go. Over the years at the orphanage, he had witnessed numerous fights and had been involved in his share. Always being slow to anger, Will talked himself out of most fights or embarrassed the other kids with his intellect, much like he had done with the three football bullies.

When that didn't work, he had fought. He was slow to anger, but when he had become angered, he fought like a crazy person. He had never put a label on his fighting style until he was reading a military strategy book a couple of years ago.

The book's author had labeled what Will was doing as "violence of action." Basically, "violence of action" means that when you attack, you do it as quickly and as violently as possible; not stopping until your opponent was overwhelmed and defeated.

No doubt, this was a time for violence of action. Will looked up into the eyes of his aggressor. Wasn't hard, the bigger boy stood flatfooted with his legs apart only about two inches away.

Will smiled at him again. The boy's face flushed as his big hands grabbed Will by the shirt and violently shoved him against the wall.

Not hesitating, Will drove his right knee into the aggressor's groin with enough strength to lift the bigger boy off the floor. The knee was followed by four fingers driven into the boy's eyes with lightning speed.

Before the boy's brain registered either source of pain, Will grabbed his opponent's Adams apple in a vice grip and proceeded to try and dislodge it from his throat.

At the same time and in one single motion, he spun the bigger boy and pinned him against the wall. The move was followed by two more powerful knee shots to the groin.

As the would-be bully began gasping for breath, Will released his grip and let the boy fall to the floor. Will concluded his violence of action with two very hard kicks to the ribs.

Will backed away from the boy on the floor and turned to find the rest of the first-year cadets staring and pointing at him.

One was rushing toward Will and shouting at the same time. "Stand to, Cadet; stand to."

Will held both hands in the air signaling the universal sign of surrender.

The Cadet stopped and stooped down to check on his fellow Cadet writhing in pain. "What the hell did you do to him?" Turning toward the group he motioned at the injured boy. "Bob, you and Jim get Jeb over to the infirmary. Joe, go find Sergeant White and tell him what happened. Come on! Hurry up and get moving!"

Pointing a finger at Will, he angrily spit out a command. "Stay right where you are. Who are you; what are you doing in our quarters?"

Will gave the young man who was, no doubt, the Unit Cadet Commander, a more engaging form of his smile. "I'm William Parker, your newest Cadet. Sergeant White brought me here and assigned me a bunk about two hours ago. Assuming you're the Unit Cadet Commander, I've been awaiting your arrival and instructions since.

"I apologize for this incident, but where I've been lately you can't allow a guy to brace you like that without a response. I'm very slow to anger and if he had kept his hands off me, we would still be talking.

"According to the Dean, this academy is full of boys who have committed serious offenses against society, myself included. This is our last stop before ending up on the streets or even worse, that fenced-in building I saw.

"I don't want to screw up; however, I am under no misconceptions about my bunkmates here. I will never start trouble; you have my word on that. With that said, though, I will not allow anybody to lay hands on me with bodily harm in mind.

"I promise you I will go along to get along, even with that hulking mass I just met. Your Cadet rules and those of the Academy will be followed as long as everyone else follows them.

"With that said, what would you like me to do, Sir?" Will did his best to stand at attention.

The Commander was shocked; first by the highly intellectual verbal abilities of his newest Cadet; and second, the ability of the new Cadet to go through his toughest Cadet with so little effort, while seemingly calm.

"Cadet Parker, our rules prohibit one Cadet from laying hands on another except in self-defense or training. Even though not privy to the rules, you did not technically violate them. Cadet Miller was the aggressor, that much is clear. Most people in the room witnessed him approach and grab you.

"Even though your response seemed a little harsh, it was not a breach of rules. We'll continue this discussion after dinner."

The Unit Cadet Commander turned to the group and made a circling motion with his index finger and pointed toward the mess hall. Everyone double-timed out of the room, including Will.

...Dean's office, two hours later

The Dean responded to the knock on his door with a single word, "Enter."

Sergeant White approached the desk and casually took one of the chairs. "We have a situation in the Cadet One group. It involves our continual bad boy, Cadet Miller, and our newest Cadet, Parker."

"Don't tell me Miller has already assaulted Parker. I swear, if he did any serious damage, I'm going to put him in the cage for six months and then on the streets. In the few months he's been here, he's been more trouble than all the rest of his group combined.

"Obviously, my comments to him have fallen on deaf ears. What did he do?"

Sergeant White laughed out loud, causing the Dean to send him a curious look. "He's up to his usual M.O. trying to intimidate the guys with his size. Cadet Parker proved to be a bit more difficult to intimidate, though."

The Sergeant spent the next few minutes giving the Dean a blow by blow account of what the Unit Cadet Commander had provided.

"And where is Cadet Miller right now? I want to have a little talk before he goes to the pen."

Stifling yet another laugh, White continued his report. "He's been transported to the hospital in town for emergency surgery. Parker messed him up bigtime."

The Dean's mouth was open. "Really? That's interesting. What did he do?"

"First, Miller's trachea was severely crushed. Our medic had to do an emergency tracheotomy to keep him alive. Secondly, both corneas in his eyes are severely scratched. And if that's not enough, two ribs were broken with one puncturing a lung."

The Dean was smiling and sitting forward on his chair as if he didn't want to miss anything. "Is that all?"

"It is, if you don't count his balls kneed so far up inside, the medic thought he might need surgery for them too.

"Just before I came here, I talked to our medic again. He went with Miller to the hospital. He says the Docs at the hospital are confident the kid will live, but his recovery will take a couple of months.

"What do you want me to do with Parker? You want him punished?"

"Punished? Hell, he just reinforced everything I thought about him. What did the Unit Cadet Commander say about Parker's demeanor after the fight ended?"

"He said Parker apologized to him, if he had broken any rules. The Commander said he was very, very calm like they were discussing the weather or something.

"He's convinced Parker will not cause any trouble as long as no one else tries to attack him. He said he thought he had the whole situation under control and Parker would do just fine. He also said the whole thing was started by Miller when he grabbed Parker.

"The Commander added that he did not think Miller was a good influence on the other Cadets and would not lose sleep if the injured boy never showed up again."

"Okay, then, let him handle it, Sergeant. But keep a close eye on Parker. I'd like a weekly update on him for the next two months."

...

After that night, none of the first-year cadets ever heard from or about Cadet Miller. Most thought Will had killed the bully. Most didn't care one way or another. Miller had been a nuisance from day one and to a person, all the Cadets were glad he was gone.

Will prospered at the Academy both physically and academically. He learned and developed skills that most people could never even imagine.

Keeping his word to the Unit Cadet Commander, Will never had another serious altercation and grew into a role model for the other Cadets.

46

Chapter 5
Two Years Later

Will had been waiting for almost two years for an answer to his question, "Why was he here?" He figured it wouldn't be much longer now. Of the 21 Cadets with whom he started, seven had been converted to homeless teens on the street; ten had already been accepted into the military; and the last four, including him, were in a state of limbo.

The last two years had been interesting for Will. The academic side of things had been fairly easy. Finishing first in his class, Will had excelled in foreign languages, military studies, math and science. Other studies had been more of a challenge.

Orienteering and wilderness survival had been easy intellectually; however, the physical aspects had pushed him initially. He soon discovered, though, that these physical skills, like most others, were manageable for him. It didn't hurt that he hit a growth spurt after the first six months. Will was now 6'2" and weighed 190 pounds.

The training in collecting intelligence and acting upon it were very exciting. Practicing and perfecting those skills required the Cadets to spend considerable time in a big city. Will soon discovered he could survive as well in a large urban environment as he could in the mountains of Virginia.

Then there was the area of his training that had not been on the initial list, the Academy's Armory. Many people think an Armory is just a place to store weapons. Over the past two years, Will had learned there was much, much more.

After working 30 hours a week for the Armorer over the past two years, Will could break down and repair every weapon they had, and they had plenty. He had also begun to modify and even design weapons. The Armorer told Will he had a "God-given talent" with anything that went bang or blew something up. In addition to the aforementioned, he had also become quite skilled in the use of handguns and long-range rifles.

There was, however, one area where Will had little success: teamwork. If there were ever an activity that could be done alone, Will did it. Constantly, the sergeants had screamed at him to become a part of the team. He always smiled and said, "Yes, Sir," but soon returned to his loner ways.

All in all, though, Will had enjoyed his time at the Academy. As the Dean had informed him early on, "Give a 100% effort and you won't have a problem."

Will practiced the mantra in everything he encountered, with the possible exception of teamwork. Because he was respectful and gave his all in required duties, Will was liked and respected by the other Cadets and the instructors.

Will did not, however, feel any gratitude or loyalty to the

Academy. He knew, deep in his soul, these people wanted something from him. The past two years had been preparation for something. He was not surprised then, when Sergeant White came for him late the next Friday afternoon. "Cadet Parker, the Dean requests your presence in his office immediately. Double-time it; he's waiting."

Will headed off at a trot for the Dean's office. After running up the steps to the third floor (no elevators for Cadets), he took a moment to catch his breath and smooth out his fatigues before entering. The same pretty older woman (Mrs. Green) smiled at him. "Hi, Will. The Dean said to send you on in." She made a motion with her hand signaling the same door he had entered almost two years ago.

Will, once again, entered the room and softly closed the door behind. Standing at attention, he smiled at the Dean. "Good afternoon, Sir. Sergeant White said you wished to see me."

Other than the initial meeting, Will had not spoken to the Dean during his time at the Academy. He had noticed the Dean observing his fellow Cadets and him on numerous occasions, but no contact had been made.

"Well, look at you, Will; you've grown into a sizeable specimen." The Dean looked down at an open file on his desk, no doubt Will's.

Will remained at attention feeling the Dean's comment didn't need a response.

"At ease, Will. Come over and have a seat." Interestingly enough, the two occupied the same chairs as before. "How have you been? You're looking very fit."

"Thank you for asking, Sir. I have enjoyed my two years at the Academy. The instructors have seen to my fitness."

The Dean smiled, "I bet they have. According to your files, you are one of the stronger Cadets. Your leg has slowed you in some activities, but you still out-performed half your fellow Cadets. That's really quite amazing. To what do you attribute that, Will?"

"Laziness, Sir."

The Dean looked on with puzzlement. "Laziness? Please explain what you mean."

"Well, Sir, when I last spoke to you, you emphasized that if I gave 100% in everything I did, I would have no problems. I took you at your word, Sir, and I have had no real problems.

"It was apparent to me early on, though, that not all Cadets took your advice. Many gave only the amount of effort necessary to keep the instructors off their backs. I, therefore, profited from their laziness."

"I see what you mean. That laziness had a high price for many of them. They either found themselves homeless on the streets or facing a hand-to-mouth existence as a grunt in the military.

"As a smart guy like you already knows, all of your remaining Cadet peers, with the exception of four, will be out of here soon on their way to military basic training. We started with 21 Cadets, and now we have four. Before we're done, there will probably be only one or two."

"I am aware of that, Sir."

"Aren't you curious what we are going to do with you four?"

"Yes, Sir, I have been curious since I first asked you, 'why me?' When you didn't answer my question then, I decided it was probably not in my best interest to pursue the issue. So, once again, with all due respect, Sir, 'why me?'

What could you possibly have in store for an egghead polio boy? Especially one that is really only 16 years old."

"You are much wiser, Will, than your years would lead one to believe. Even though we have not spoken in two years, I have been keeping very close tabs on your progress. You are our number one graduate in this class. As a matter of fact, you are the highest academically achieving student to ever graduate from the Academy. Your academic potential far outweighs the minor physical restrictions you have."

"Again, with all respect; potential for what, Sir?"

"Will, I'm not trying to stall. You have earned an answer to your question. It's just that I have to explain a few things to you first.

"The two years you have been here have been a test, a way to select some very special men, for very specialized work. As you can no doubt tell, only four of you passed. Passed everything, that is, except one final test. The other three Cadets will be tested this weekend. The ones who pass will return and join you in advanced training.

"Do you know why you do not have to pass the final test, Will?"

Will looked at the Dean with a very calm face. He earlier guessed he had been chosen for the Academy because of his past violent behavior. "I can only deduce that I have already passed the test."

"And do you know what the test is?"

"During our advanced hand-to-hand combat training, we were taught to respond with lethal force if the situation dictated. We were also taught basic edged weapons' combat.

"The other three Cadets will have to demonstrate the ability to kill without remorse." Will stopped and waited for the Dean's response.

"That's correct. Are you shocked at this?"

"Not really, I figured out early on that my violent past played a major role in my selection for the Academy. It was obvious the military would never have an interest in me."

"So, Will, of the three Cadets trolling the bad side of town in Washington, D.C., how many will make it back with no blood on their hands?"

"I have known the three for two years, Sir; I've watched them train; and I've seen them react to the bullying that took place. In my opinion, none will have the stomach for killing; they will all make it back blood-stain free.

"And, if I may make an observation, Sir, I think you already know that. Of the 20 Cadets with whom I started training, those three are the least violence-inclined in the group. But why do I think you already knew this?"

The Dean laughed. "Still bold and straight forward in your speech, I see. You seem to have an uncanny ability to see things others simply ignore. What else do you think?"

"I'm going to go out on the proverbial limb here and do what you told me to do almost two years ago; I'm going to tell you the truth. It's based on two years of evaluations.

"First of all, the Cadets. Not a single one in my group has a family— no parents, no siblings, and no family at any level. We are all "Lost Boys" as the Academy name translates in English. No Cadet has ever received even one piece of mail.

"I have overheard enough private conversations to know every boy here has had his name changed. Knowing that, I would speculate that we are all *deceased,* at least in any existing records.

"Since we all committed some crime, with at least an

element of violence associated with it, this academy is some sort of screening/training facility for the CIA or some like-minded group.

"This premise is supported by the colorful names of staff: Sergeants Black and White, and Secretary Mrs. Green, to name a few. There's also the whole prison-like atmosphere of the place.

"My last observation is that some group or government Agency has spent a ton of money to harvest only four candidates. That's what I think. Am I close?" Will smiled meekly at the Dean.

The Dean stared at Will. "So, you've got it all figured out, huh?"

"No Sir, I would never be so naïve as to think I've figured out you and this place. I may have scratched the surface, but there are many aspects of the Academy of which I am completely and wholly ignorant.

"For instance, why select a very violence-inclined individual like me for your program and then turn right around and select the three least violent?"

"You think you have been selected, do you?"

"Yes, Sir, I'm pretty sure I've been selected. I just don't know for what."

"Well, I guess it's time I fill in some of the blanks for you, Will. You have intuited a great deal more than I would have thought. It's now time you know the rest.

"Before I do, however, I'm going to give you the same opportunity I gave the other three boys before they went on their little trip. You now have a high school diploma. According to existing records, you are 18 years old.

"At this time, I am offering you an opportunity for advanced career training. If you do not desire such training, you will be given $1,000 and a bus ticket to a city of your choice.

"If you choose the training, you will undergo two more years of very specialized and extremely intensive training. Prior to the training, you will be required to sign a confidentiality agreement with the Central Intelligence Agency. Violation of the agreement will result in your confinement in a Federal military prison for a period of ten years.

"The nature of the training will be solely at the Agency's discretion. At times it will be mentally and physically challenging. Once you accept the advanced training assignment, there is no stopping the process from its completion. This decision is a very serious commitment. So, what do you think?"

"Wow! This is very serious, more so than I had imagined. Will the other three Cadets be receiving the same training as me?"

"No, they won't. They will be trained in a very different fashion. You're right about the Academy; it is a screening organization, albeit a dichotomous one. We screen for Cadets with two completely different mind sets: theirs and yours. As you might suspect, yours is extremely rare; theirs, much more common. With that said, what's your answer?"

"Sir, I have been institutionalized for almost my entire life. I have never known any other type of existence. Even though I look like a man and have records to prove it, I am, in reality, still only a 16-year-old boy.

"I'm smarter than most and more intuitive than many, but I have no experience living on the outside. I suspect smart is not always enough; it must be tempered with judgment born of experience. I feel that guided and controlled experience would be better than what I would get on my own.

"It is my opinion I'm not ready to be on my own. I know I could survive, but I don't think I would thrive. I want more than mere survival; I want some sort of meaningful existence. To have that in the future, I need more training and guided experiences now.

"So, if I go forward with training, will I have more freedom to experience the outside world? Will I be taught meaningful skills? If so, then I accept and thank you for the opportunity."

"You will experience more than you can ever imagine, William Parker. Welcome to the CIA. Please get some rest tonight and pack; you'll be leaving early tomorrow morning.

"May I ask where I am being sent, Sir? Also, will you explain in as broad of terms as possible, what I can expect?"

"Will, I'll explain as much as I can at this point in time. You will be sent to a top-secret training facility closer to the coast of Virginia. The facility will serve as your staging area for the next year. There will be other CIA recruits at the facility. Many will be fresh college graduates. Those recruits will be doing many of the things you completed the past two years.

"You will see the other recruits and even interact occasionally, but you are different. They will never know who you really are or what you are doing. Do not make friends and do not talk unnecessarily to anybody. Just absorb as much training as possible.

"During the next year, you will be taught defensive and offensive driving. You will learn to fly an airplane and ride a motorcycle. Underwater skills will be mastered as well as sky-diving. You'll learn to ski, both water and snow.

"These are just a few of the things you will learn. That's

why I said your next location is just a staging ground. Things not taught there will be taught elsewhere. You are about to have the busiest year of your life. It will require every bit of physical and mental toughness you possess.

"All of the training has a very important place in your future life. Some of it will even save your life. The main reason for it, though, is to prepare you for a very special assignment.

"You will be in a special advanced class for potential agents in a new program we are calling *Read*. *Read* is an acronym for: <u>R</u>edacted <u>E</u>xecutive <u>A</u>ction <u>D</u>irective.

"If you successfully complete the training, you will become a *Reader*. *Readers* will carry out non-sanctioned executive actions. Do you know what an executive action is?"

"If I were to intuit, Sir, I would speculate it is an assassination. One that has not been approved by anybody outside the CIA."

"That's right, Will; do you think you have what it takes to be a *Reader*? I have no doubt you already possess the cognitive and physical skills to complete an executive action.

"In advanced training you will be trained at a higher level than any CIA Agent is currently being trained. My question is whether you have the psychological mindset and mental toughness to complete the action?"

"Well, Sir, you know I have been able to kill before without issue. You are, I'm sure, also aware of what I did my first night at the Academy. So, you are asking if I can do it over and over for an extended period of time.

"I suspect not many can unless they are full-blown sociopaths. You already know I am not. You do know, though, I am a person with sociopathic tendencies who is capable of homicide. Both conditions were, no doubt, a result of polio working its way into my brain and killing off certain aspects therein.

"No two polio victims are the same. Most have significantly more physical problems than I do. Many are even mentally challenged. Very few are like me. Polio seems to have strengthened my intellect and weakened my moral objection to homicide. It did leave my empathy in place, though.

"So, to answer your question; yes, I believe I can. The answer does require some qualifications, however. I can't kill innocent people or children. I will also need to know why? If a person deserves to die, I can live with that. I hope this answers your question."

"It does for now, Will. Now, go get some rest; tomorrow may prove to be a long day. Good luck!"

Chapter 6
Agency Training

Will had survived a year of unbelievable training. It was everything the Dean had said and more. Some of it was a continuation of the conditioning training, something he enjoyed. Weight training was a daily activity as were long runs through the wooded area of the facility.

Weapons training concentrated on long-range rifle work with regular handgun shooting. Additional time was spent on close quarters combat, including edged weapons and hand-to-hand skills.

Considerable time was spent learning surveillance and counter-surveillance skills. This training involved extended periods away from the facility. Will's confidence had grown considerably in urban environments. He was now as confident of his survival skills in the urban jungle as he was in the most challenging wilderness.

Will knew he was quickly approaching some sort of evaluation. The Sergeant in charge, Sergeant Red, wanted to see him first thing tomorrow morning.

The Sergeant was waiting at the motor pool where he had instructed Will to meet him. "Get in, Will. We're going for a little drive."

Twenty or so minutes later, they entered the gate to a small private airport. It was the same place where Will had learned to fly. The other five members of his advanced training group were standing around a small jet. Will was instructed to join them.

"Listen up, guys. Sergeant Blue has a bag into which I want you all to drop your wallets and anything else you have on your person. That means everything. When you're done, you should have nothing left on but your clothing."

Sergeant Blue walked through the group and collected all their possessions. He then frisked each of the men.

Sergeant Red smiled as he did his drill sergeant impression with his hands clasped behind his back. "Here's the drill. In a few minutes, you will all board the plane behind you. You will be flown to Miami where you will deplane and go your separate ways. Absolutely no teamwork is allowed on this exercise. Each of you will be placed in a car and driven to a different part of the city, where you will get out.

"Once, out you have 48 hours to get back to this airfield. Rules for the engagement are: no innocent citizen can be harmed physically; you may not fly back commercially; and if you break the law, you better not get caught.

…several hours later

Will was standing on a street in the Little Havana section of Miami. He had been dropped off an hour's bus ride away.

It had taken 30 minutes panhandling tourists to get bus fare.

Since getting off the bus, he had been observing the bus stop from a close-by alley. When getting off the bus, Will saw a boy just sitting on the bench and not moving to get on the bus.

He thought he would just hang around for a while and see if anything was going on. It didn't take long to figure out the kid, along with a friend, was dealing. Their routine was really pretty good.

One boy would sit on the bus bench as if waiting for the next bus. A buyer would walk up and sit beside him. The boy would take the drug order and payment, then get up and walk away.

Approaching the second boy, he would get the purchased drugs from a grocery bag and drop the money into the bag. Returning to the bus bench, the transaction would be completed with the purchaser walking away.

Will knew from training there would be a third participant in the scheme, a bagman to pick up the cash and replenish the grocery bag of drugs.

That was why he was watching. Will wanted to identify the bag man and possibly borrow his car and cash.

Slowing moving toward the bus stop in the curbside lane was an older Chevy Camaro. The Camaro turned right into an alley just past the stop.

As it slowed, the second boy with the bag jogged over to the car and exchanged his bag for another. The Camaro barely stopped before moving on down the alley.

Will was moving as the car moved. Stopping the car's progress was a delivery van with its side door open and the driver carrying what looked like a slab of beef through a doorway.

Will smiled at his good fortune. Better lucky than good sometimes. He trotted up to the car's driver side window just as the driver stuck his head out to yell at the delivery man.

Just as he uttered "Hey," Will hit the bag man with a hard right to the temple. Falling limply back into the car, he was unconscious.

Will immediately opened the door, pushed the slender and shorter man over the shifter and into the passenger seat. Jumping behind the wheel, he barely had enough time to adjust the seat to his longer legs before the delivery driver came out.

Giving Will a friendly wave, the driver got into the van and drove away. Will put the Camaro into drive and followed the van out of the alley.

Before turning onto the street, Will glanced up at the rearview mirror. No one was chasing; apparently the drug dealers were concentrating on the bus stop and not the alley.

Will slowly pulled out into the street and circled around the block intersecting the bus route two blocks before the bus stop. Will had noticed an interstate sign on his bus ride to Little Havana.

Turning north on I-95, Will and his passenger began to work their way through the busy Miami traffic. Once clearing most of the Miami traffic, he turned west and headed across central Florida in the general direction of Fort Myers.

At a secluded place behind the first rest stop, the drug dealer was transferred to the car's small trunk. Good thing the guy wasn't very big.

Will hoped to get lucky driving the two-lane state highway. He had no intention of driving a thousand miles north to Virginia. There was an easier way.

So far, nothing but scattered farms and a few nothing towns. Will knew he was in the right area. Sure enough, Lady Luck raised her pretty head about 20 miles later in the form of a small sign.

The sign had an arrow pointing north and saying, "Crop Dusting Services seven miles ahead." Will didn't need any crop dusting services, but he did need a lift home. He turned right.

Just as the sun was starting to drop over the horizon, another sign advertising (you guessed it) crop dusting services appeared east of the road.

The dirt and grass runway was visible from the road. One single-seater plane was visible inside a small hangar and another plane with visible spray tanks was in final descent for the short runway.

Will continued north on the road for about a mile until he found an acceptable hiding place for the car. Coming up on the left was a small stand of large cottonwood trees. Probably an old homestead; nothing was left but rotting timber and a collapsed fireplace.

As Will backed the Camaro between two of the cottonwoods, the sun was dropping from the sky. Reclining the car seat, he settled in for a nap.

...a little after midnight

The quarter moon was casting an eerie, yellowish light on the old homestead. Will had been awake for an hour or so and was examining the car for anything of use.

There were four drug drop-bags in addition to the one from the bus stop. The cash in each ranged from $2,000 to

$2,700. Totaling the take resulted in a little over $11,700.

Since there were no additional drugs in the car, the bus stop was obviously the last pick up. There were, however, a folding knife and small 25 caliber pistol in the glove compartment. Exiting the vehicle, Will took the money and weapons.

But now, what to do with the drug dealer/teenager in the trunk of the car. It might take days for someone to discover the car. Maybe, the best bet would be to leave the car at the airfield. That, though, might put the airfield employees in danger.

The kid might imperil the innocent civilians by blaming the whole situation on them. No, that would violate one of the rules of the exercise: no innocent civilians could be harmed.

Will decided on another option. Taking the keys from the ignition, he walked back to the trunk. He knew getting the kid out of the trunk could prove dangerous, but it still seemed to be his best option. He didn't want anybody hurt, not even the drug dealer.

Inserting the key into the lock, Will could hear movement. He knew there were no weapons in the trunk; he had checked before dumping the unconscious kid inside. He had removed a tire iron and set of battery cables.

The kid's best move would be to try and push the trunk lid into Will with enough force to knock him down. That's what Will would have done.

In training, Will had been taught to never underestimate any opponent, even the most docile. That could get you killed. Always assume the other person could kill you with the slightest advantage.

Before turning the key, Will spoke to the dealer in a very

calm and reassuring voice. "I have your gun and I've chambered a round. There is no way you can attack me before I empty the magazine into you. Do you hear me?"

"Yes, I hear you." The voice had a distinctive Cuban accent. The speaker sounded tired. Several hours in a tight trunk space could do that to you.

"I don't want to kill you. Your money is all I want. I will kill you, though, if I have to. I just got out of jail this morning and don't intend to go back." Scary narrative seemed useful at this point.

"Okay, man. What you want me to do? I'll do it; just don't kill me." Genuine fear laced his words.

"When I pop the trunk, count to ten before you move. Anything less than that and I shoot. Then slowly push the trunk lid open. Don't try to look at me or you die. Make a quick movement and you die. Understand?"

"Yeah, I understand."

"Then slowly rise and sit on the back edge of the trunk with your legs stretched out as far as possible into the rear of the trunk. Never look at anything except the inside of the trunk.

"Put your hands down the front of your pants on the inside. Close your eyes and sit there."

The drug dealer was too scared of the calm voice not to follow instructions.

Will then carefully walked up behind the young man and applied a sleeper choke hold. He held it just long enough to render the boy unconscious.

Easing the unconscious body back into the trunk, Will used the battery cables to hogtie him. The trunk lid was left open. The young man should have no trouble getting out of the cables. It might take an hour or two and a few layers of skin, but he would get loose.

…down the road about a mile

It was approaching 1 am; Will had been outside the small airport hangar about 15 minutes. Standing close to the building, he methodically examined the surrounding area as he had been taught to do. Nothing was moving in the quiet, muggy Florida air.

Time to move! The small side door was easily defeated by Will's purloined knife. Moving cautiously toward the interior of the hangar, a small, dimly lit office could be seen in a back corner.

With no windows in the building, it would have been impossible to see without the dim light. Still moving cautiously and with absolute quietness, Will approached the small office enclosure. It was empty.

Inside, Will sat down at the desk and wrote the owner a short note. "Sorry, I need to borrow one of your planes. You'll have it back in a couple days. To defray any financial burden my borrowing creates, I am leaving $10,000 in your top desk drawer. I hope this helps. Thanks."

Taking a flashlight from the desk, Will went back into the hangar. There were two planes to choose from. Both were the Aero Commander model S-2R commonly called the Thrush, arguably the best crop duster plane available.

The first one was fully equipped with spray tanks and appeared ready for morning spraying. The second was the same model but newer. It appeared to be set up for travel as opposed to spraying. There were no spray tanks but instead had extra outboard fuel tanks.

During flight training, Will had been taught to fly

numerous small planes. The trainer had spent extra time, however, talking about crop dusters. The rationale, as explained by the instructor, was simple. It's easier to steal a plane from a rural airfield as opposed to a city location. Crop dusters lock up at night and go home; city airports have guards.

Also, planes like these were on the simpler end of the complexity scale when it came to instruments and such. Will climbed into the second Thrush.

The first thing his light illuminated was a garage door opener. That, no doubt, made life simpler for a small one- or two-person operation.

Shining the light on the instrument panel provided no surprises. There was nothing here he couldn't handle. Will engaged the engine starter switch. As instruments came to life, he was pleasantly surprised to see full fuel tanks, more than enough to get him back to Virginia.

A few minutes later, Will pressed the garage door opener and taxied the plan out onto the runway. Another press of the button and the hangar was once again secure against the night. Well, maybe secured against the untrained criminal.

Increasing the RPM's, Will began to feel the powerful engine. Releasing the brake and starting down the runway, he could barely make out its surface. Increasing power, the Thrush lifted into the murky night sky.

...seven hours later

The Thrush flew a circular pattern over the small CIA-operated airport as Will keyed his radio. Even though there was no tower on the small private field, he knew from previous landings that radio contact had to be made.

Setting the dial to what he had been taught was the correct frequency for the field, he began to speak calmly and softly as he had observed experienced pilots do in the past. "This is the Thrush crop duster currently circling your field. I am low on fuel and declaring an emergency. Please provide landing instructions."

"Thrush, please land on the north-south runway. What is your city of origin?"

"This is Thrush; am proceeding as instructed. Flight origin is south-central Florida."

The Thrush made the necessary flight correction and came in south to north on approach. With no bump, the Thrush made contact with the runway and applied the brakes. It then taxied to the largest of three hangars.

Will shut the engine down and made his way into the open hangar door. He was surprised to see Sergeants Red, Blue, and Green. They were standing in a group with the Dean and two men associated with the airport.

As Will walked toward the group, the Dean stepped forward and extended his hand. "Thank you, Will."

Will shook the Dean's hand. "For what?"

"For making me the winner of our $600 pool for who would be the first cadet back. I figured I'd see you about 8:00; it's 8:30. What kept you?"

Will smiled at the Dean and the rest of the group. "Sorry to keep you busy guys waiting, but I had to work in a nap."

Everyone laughed at his comment. Sergeant Red extended his hand to Will. Congratulations, you're the first one back. I'm not sure if anyone has ever made it in less than 30 hours before."

Will once again smiled. "Any word on the others?"

Sergeant Red spoke again. "Six of you started. Four are

still MIA, so we anticipate seeing them within the next 24 hours. Number five is in jail after losing a race on I-95 with a dozen State Troopers in Georgia. You're the only exercise completer at this time. We'll have to wait and see on the others."

"Sergeant Green, give Will a ride back to his quarters.

Will, I need a post exercise report on my desk by this time tomorrow. Before that, though, get something to eat and some rest."

After turning his report in to Sergeant Red the next morning, Will was given the next two days off. Following the downtime, he was instructed to report to the Dean in the facility's administrative offices.

Will was led to a small conference room in the basement. The Dean was waiting for him. "Good morning, Will, catch up on your sleep?"

"Yes, thank you, Sir. I can't ever remember this much downtime since I left the orphanage"

The Dean motioned for Will to take a seat opposite his at the conference table. "Congratulations are once again in order, Will. You have finished the initial year of training as our top recruit. Of the six of you who started the final exercise, you and two others will move on to year two. The other three will remain with the Agency, but not as *Readers*.

"Starting tomorrow, the three of you will start advanced training in three specialties. After three months training together across the three specialized areas, each of you will complete an advanced rotation of three months in each individual specialty area.

"The initial three months will be more general in nature. The advanced rotation in each area will be one-on-one with the instructor. He will develop an individual training plan for each of you. The plan will be customized to capitalize on your individual strengths and weaknesses.

"The first training will be 'close in' executive actions. These are required to look like accidents; the second will be training in the judicious use of small targeted explosive actions; and the third will be training in executive actions requiring long-range rifle work.

"So, Will, how is your intuition working? I'm curious which of these three you believe I feel will be your strongest specialty?"

Will knew, without a doubt, which advanced training he would be the best suited for.

"Sir, I have a good idea, but nothing is for sure until I hear you say so. Therefore, I'll answer your question by explaining my thought process on the subject.

"Explosives I would rule out because no matter how small and how targeted an explosion is, there is still a high probability of collateral damage. My mind is certainly devious enough to use explosives, but they can get out of control and become messy. That would attract too much attention. I'd list explosives as my third choice.

"As to 'close in work,' I would enjoy the intellectual challenge of conjuring accidents. It might, on occasion, require several simultaneous moving parts. That means teamwork.

"By now, you know I don't play well with others. I can fake it, but I don't like placing my fate in the hands of other agents who are, for all practical purposes, strangers.

"To set up and complete 'accidents' will require the most teamwork of the three areas of training. The best place for me is in a situation I control.

"I believe the Agency would be best served by training

me to be a long-range agent. The challenge of thoroughly planning an executive action that culminates in one clean shot holds a lot of interest for me.

"You no doubt know I am skilled in shooting handguns, but you also know I have excelled in long-range marksmanship at every level of training.

"Even though I feel comfortable in all areas, I'll take a hard-shooting rifle every time."

The Dean sat staring intently at Will. "As usual, you are very close in your thinking. One question, though. Do you think you will ever totally trust another Agency person?"

"Sir, the only person I completely trust in the Agency is you. The only times I have received real answers to important questions have been those times I asked you.

"As a follow-up to my answer, though, I assure you I am not as paranoid as this makes me sound. It's just that everyone else merely tells me what they think I need to know at that moment.

"Up to now, the past three years have been a type of training game. Everyone is playing a role. But now, my intuition is screaming at me that the games are about over. This next level of training is going to be very 'real.'

"I know my future success in the Agency will be guided by a few people whom I can completely trust. I will be actively searching for them."

The Dean had gotten up from his seat opposite Will and walked around the table. Will's eyes followed him. The Dean put his hand on Will's shoulder. "Will, I assure you there are others in the Agency that will earn your trust. If you allow me, I will help you find them.

"Now get your intuitive ass up and go get some more rest. Tomorrow, you start year two training."

Chapter 7
Advanced Training

Will had enjoyed the last nine months of training. He had no idea there were so many ways to make somebody die *accidentally*. Even knowing he would probably be used rarely as a close-in specialist, Will valued the training. One never knew when such training might prove useful.

The same held true for the targeted explosives' training. And Will had to admit, he really enjoyed blowing shit up, even though it was harder to control than a fast-moving bullet.

Before the final three months of advanced specialist training, the three students were given a week off to relax. The other two had left the facility already; however, Will had a somewhat different idea of the relaxation he wanted. He was meeting this morning to discuss it with the Dean.

They met in the same facility conference room as before. Will waited for the Dean to finish pouring himself a cup of coffee. The Dean turned to Will, "Would you like a cup of coffee?"

"No thank you, Sir. I try to avoid caffeine when I can."

"Really, why is that, Will? Haven't developed a taste for it?"

"Well, Sir, even though I love its smell, I never thought it would help in my training. Now that I'm moving into long-range specialty designation, I know it won't. Precision shooting requires a steady hand."

The Dean held Will's gaze, then smiled at the comment. "I'm glad you're taking the job so seriously. Oftentimes, it's the little things that count in the long run. Now, let's talk about this meeting. Is there something you need?"

"Yes, Sir, there is. But a little background first, if you will permit." The Dean nodded and Will continued. "You are aware that I received a considerable amount of long-range rifle training back at the Academy, then the past two years here, I received quite a bit more. That's what I want to talk about."

The Dean gave Will a suspicious glare. "So, do you think you already know everything about long-range shooting you need to know? Are you thinking the next three months of training will be a waste of training?"

Will responded in a somewhat defensive manner. "Sir, I have never thought that even a minute of any training received here or at the Academy was wasted. It's not that."

"Then what is it, Will?"

"Sir, it's the long-range weapon. As I have been training for long-range shooting in both rural and urban settings, the Remington Model 700, sporting a 26-inch 308 target barrel, seems to be the rifle of choice.

"It works just fine in the rural area, but has a couple of major disadvantages in urban areas."

"Really!" The Dean had the kind of condescending smile on his face a father might have when his six-year-old tells him he's not barbequing correctly. "Please, educate me."

Will had anticipated this type of response. "Well, first of all, it's the difficulty concealing such a large weapon as you approach and then exit the shooting location. It's hard to disguise a rifle with a 26-inch barrel as anything other than what it is.

"Secondly, the noise made by said rifle is problematic. The crack of a large caliber rifle is difficult to ignore in an urban area."

The Dean was unconsciously nodding in agreement. "I can't argue with either of those things. Therein lay the biggest dangers for our long-range actions. Each of our three specialty areas possesses its own unique dangers; you have just verbalized those in long-range. They're the major reason we stress one-shot kills, so your location is harder to pinpoint.

"If you are going to suggest silencers, we've been there. They are not used because of their size and lack of effectiveness."

Will had a smirk on his face. "I know, but I think I have solutions for the two problems."

"Of course you do; you're almost 19 years old and, by virtue of your age, you know everything."

Will would not concede his position. "Would you at least hear me out before you make fun of my naivety?"

"Okay, young sage, tell me how you solved a couple of problems the CIA has been wrestling with for years."

Will had been holding a folder since he walked in. The Dean had taken a chair for the lecture, so Will sat down beside him. He removed several sheets of paper from the folder. "Have you heard of a new gun company, Thompson Center?"

"No, I haven't."

"Most people haven't. I became aware of them when I was at the Academy. You might remember I worked in the armory for pretty much the whole time I was there. There was always quite a bit of material on weapons and weapons design laying around. I read every bit I could get my hands on.

"Of great interest to me was a proposed product by Thompson Center called the Contender. In a nutshell, it's a one-shot target pistol with interchangeable barrels of different calibers. It is designed in such a way the barrel can quickly be interchanged for another. The longest barrel they have, however, is 16 inches. The gun is now in production.

"I don't know if it showed up in any of my Academy records, but I am a pretty good gunsmith. The instructors taught me a lot, then through experimentation, I learned a great deal more. I seem to have a natural knack for it."

The Dean scrunched his forehead as he concentrated. "I had forgotten it, but yes it did. I remember now. The armory supervisor said your skills were equal to, maybe even better, than his. So, enough background; cut to the chase."

Will slid a sheet of paper in front of the Dean. "I thought you'd never ask. What you are looking at is a drawing, detailing necessary modifications to the Contender, to convert it to a 26-inch barreled rifle. It has a folding shoulder stock and removable barrel.

"The second sheet shows how to conceal the barrel inside a walking stick. You now have a system that fits in a backpack or attaché case carried by a young, crippled man."

The Dean was dumbfounded. "Are you telling me you can convert this yourself?"

"Yes, I can."

Will had the Dean's interest. "How long to get the gun?"

"The plant is in New Hampshire, so I'd say we could probably get one this weekend if you used the plane."

"If you had a gun on Monday, how long to convert it using our armory and gunsmiths?"

Will was smiling. "We could probably convert it in a few days if we have an appropriate barrel blank in the armory. I believe the gunsmiths could take my drawings and complete the prototype by themselves."

"By themselves, huh?" The Dean had a questioning expression on his face. "And what will you be doing while they do your work?" He thought he already knew Will's answer.

"I was thinking I might work on a sound suppressor."

"You did, did you? And how do you intend to do that?"

"I thought I'd use a 'D' cell flashlight body. I believe I can design it in such a fashion it will still look like a flashlight. Seeing it in a backpack should not arouse suspicion."

"Really, and how would that work?"

"Well, I would use the metal tube type with a screw-off head. The head would not change. I'd use the tube body to house the baffles.

"I'd then build a new design of baffling using metal washers with slots cut into them. By using a special combination of shaved cork and steel wool between the baffles and tube body, a 7mm rifle cartridge should sound about like a 22 short round."

"Do you really think that will work? It does sound like a

different approach, but I don't know."

"Sir, I'll have to experiment with the thickness of the washers and size of slots, but I believe I can reduce the noise of the 7mm significantly."

"You've said 7mm twice now; we typically use a 308. What's the deal?"

"When looking at ranges up to 800 yards, the ballistics are better on the 7mm. Like you said, oftentimes, it's the small things that count in the long run."

"Okay, Will, you have the go ahead for your project. I'll meet you a week from Monday on the range. If I don't like what I see, we go back to standard long-range equipment. Agreed?"

"Agreed, Sir."

…A week from Monday

In addition to the Dean, the long-range instructor was standing behind the shooting benches. Each was staring back at the shooting shed as Will exited.

He began his somewhat awkward walk toward the benches. The two spectators stared at the image of a crippled young man painfully working his way toward them.

The young man had a very halting gait as he moved forward. He was assisted by a black walking stick with a J-shaped handle. In his left hand was a small, tattered leather case, shaped much like a physician's bag. It appeared to be about 18 inches long and maybe ten inches deep.

The cripple's pain was obvious as he grimaced with each step. He smiled shyly at the two men as he stepped up. "Excuse me, gentlemen, can you tell me where the nearest bus stop is?"

The instructor spoke up. "It's about 25 miles east of here." All three men laughed.

The Dean gestured toward the nearest shooting bench. "Let's see what you have, Will."

Will limped to the bench. Setting down his bag, he turned back to the men. He reached down and pulled up the left leg of his pants. Visible was a leather and metal brace attached to his shoe and extending up above the knee.

With two quick motions, he removed the brace and disassembled it into two parts. Then, reaching inside his sock and into his shoe, he removed a small rough stone, his pain inducer for the limp.

Opening the bag from the top, Will removed a large flashlight. Several pair of soiled socks and stained underwear followed. Below in the bag were a spare shirt and pants. The clothing had a rather strong smell.

Under the clothing was a sturdy leather bottom, or so it appeared. Will worked a corner loose and revealed a secret compartment. He removed a Thompson Contender pistol frame (minus barrel) plus a detached metal-framed shoulder stock. He also removed a powerful-looking scope.

All items were placed on the shooting bench close to the flashlight, which had also been laid there. He then removed five rounds of ammunition and a small screwdriver from a compartment in the rifle's stock.

Will then took the walking cane in his left hand. Holding the cane's shaft firmly, he used his right hand to unscrew the J-shaped handle. As he lifted the handle, the attached rifle barrel followed. He then unscrewed the barrel from the handle.

Both the Dean and instructor looked on curiously.

Will finally spoke as he picked up the flashlight. "As you

can see, this looks like a regular flashlight." Will tried to turn on the light. "Damn, my mother told me I needed new batteries." Will looked up and smiled.

Very quickly, Will unscrewed the top of the light and laid it aside. Turning to the instructor, he asked, "Would you please time my rifle assembly?"

In less than 30 seconds, the rifle was assembled and a round loaded.

The finished product was a 7mm rifle with a 26-inch suppressed barrel. It was topped by a 1-12 power scope and sported a pistol grip stock with shoulder padding.

Will held it out for inspection by the Dean and instructor.

The Dean shouldered the weapon. "Very impressive, Will; but how does it shoot?" He handed the weapon to the instructor who inspected it very carefully.

Will pointed downrange. "I have 12-inch, metal-plate targets placed at 200, 400, and 800 yards. Let's see what we can do."

Will turned and placed the rifle on shooting bags. Taking two deep breaths, he positioned himself behind the rifle and cocked the hammer. Taking another breath, he calmed his body to a Zen-like state. Before the spectators realized the shot had broken, they saw the two-hundred yard plate fall. It was quickly followed by the 400 and 800 yard metal plates.

Will turned and looked at the Dean and the instructor. They both said almost in unison, "Good shooting."

Will had satisfaction written all over his face. "What did you think of the noise suppression? You notice I wasn't using ear protection and didn't offer you any."

The Dean spoke up. "About like a 22 short, maybe even less; just like you said. If only one shot is fired, it will be next to impossible to pinpoint its origin.

"Great job, Will. Are you satisfied with the weapon and mode of disguise? Any changes you see?"

"Well, Sir, overall I'm very satisfied. The gunsmiths did great work. I'll probably shorten the stock a little and adjust the trigger, but those are things I will work on as I shoot it more."

…Three months into specialist training

Will's advanced training instructor was named Mr. Bell, no doubt a phony name. It didn't take Will long to determine why the name Bell was used.

Every day of training began at the long-distance shooting range. Mr. Bell arrived early every morning and placed 10 targets at varying distances from 100 to 800 yards.

It was from these early morning shooting sessions that Mr. Bell had received his name. Each of the targets was a cowbell. He felt a regular cowbell was the perfect representation of the kill zone on a human face.

Using the tried and true mil dot method of determining range to target, Will had to engage and shoot each target five times: from a bench-rest, prone, off-hand, improvised rest, and shooter's choice of position.

Even though laser range finders had recently become available, Mr. Bell felt the tried and true was better than the unknown new. He said once the laser range finder had been tested by real soldiers and shooters under real-life conditions, he would work it into the training.

Mr. Bell felt a shooter had to shoot a 99% average over any two consecutive days of practice before he would allow him to go active as a long-range specialist.

Even though Will had met the standard from day one of

advanced training, Mr. Bell still insisted he shoot 50 targets every morning. The shooting was two-pronged. First, it was to insure Will could quickly determine the target's range. Second, it was important that the modified rifles worked 100% of the time.

…A little background

After Will's demonstration to the Dean, two more rifles were worked up to meet Will's needs. After the original was tweaked, Will had three rifles to work with. Each day he shot a different one.

In addition to the three rifles, six additional barrels were made in different calibers. The Thompson Contender (T/C) weapon's system was now declared operational.

…Back to training

Mr. Bell was leaning against a shooting bench as Will arrived for the morning's shooting session. "Good morning, Will. Ready for a little change of pace?"

"You bet, I've shot so many cowbells, I hear them ringing in my sleep."

Mr. Bell assumed a relaxed position as he continued to speak. "You've proven you are very capable of shooting targets. You've also proven a remarkable sense of identifying both rural and urban hides from which the shooter can be concealed.

"At this stage of training, you can outshoot me and any other instructor here at the Agency. I've drilled you over and over until I am confident saying you have mastered all instructional material available and everything else I know about long-range shooting."

"Thank you, Sir; your confidence in my mastery is very much appreciated, although I sincerely doubt I can outshoot you in a real-life environment. I suspect mastery of training is a long way from mastery of the overall skill."

"That's true, Will. I was told you were a quick study and I have seen with my own eyes just how quick you are. I was also told you were intuitive as hell about things. I now see what the Dean meant when he told me that.

"I'm glad you have such a practical approach to your skill level. Such an approach will make the last part of training more useful to you."

Mr. Bell had aroused Will's curiosity.

"Do you understand what I am saying, Will? It's payback time."

"I believe I do, Mr. Bell. The dance is over and now it's time to pay the fiddler. Over the past 4+ years, I have been provided top-notch education and training. I have also been housed and fed. The only thing asked in return was that I give a 100% effort.

"Now, I am being offered a career. All I have to do is use everything I have learned. The years of education and training all come down to this. Will I be able to pull the trigger, with a real life person filling the glass of my scope? And then, can I turn around and do it again?"

"Well, Will, can you? You have mastered everything we have thrown at you. Now it's up to you. Can you take the life of a person who has done nothing to you?"

Will did not answer immediately; he took a minute to stare at the beauty around the shooting range. "I don't know, Mr. Bell. Obviously, I believe I can or I would not be at this stage of training. I suspect, however, everyone says they can.

"The Dean told me to always be honest. So, in all honesty, I won't know for sure until I feel the recoil on my shoulder.

"So, what exactly is the final phase of my training, Sir?"

Chapter 8
Final Exam

Billy Ray Bustine was the object of Will's first redacted executive action directive (*Read*). In other words, Will would stalk him, get to know his habits and current activities, then remove him permanently from the food chain.

Will had been given a very detailed file on Billy Ray, starting with childhood. He had started his career with petty theft and cruelty to animals, then moved on to car theft.

Billy Ray, as everyone called him, was the eldest of five brothers who ran a mid-sized chop shop in the Appalachian Mountains of eastern Tennessee. That was Billy Ray's vocation. The real concern with Billy Ray, however, wasn't his vocational interest; it was his avocational interest.

Most people held little animosity toward a good ole Appalachian boy helping himself and his family to a few cars. Most did, though, draw the line at rape.

Since Billy Ray and his brothers procured most of their cars in the Chattanooga metro area, it was only logical that his avocational activities happened there also.

Three years ago, Billy Ray had been convicted of a string of rapes in a small suburban community in the Chattanooga area. Because of the brutality of his crimes, he had been sentenced to 40 years in prison.

On appeal, his conviction was overturned based on a technicality. Now three years later, he was free to start up where he left off.

The CIA did not usually get involved with this kind of crime. The only reason they did so this time was because of the need for a scumbag their trainee could use as a graduation project. That and Billy Ray was a serious sociopath in need of treatment. Will would deliver the treatment.

In Billy Ray's file was the rural address of his family's business, Bustine Brothers' Retail Auto Parts and Wholesale Distribution Company. As good a place as any to pick up Billy Ray's trail.

Once Will saw the rural address in the file, he knew he'd have to stake out the place. He also knew he'd probably have to follow Billy Ray.

The location of the business was on a backwoods state highway with forest growing right up to the roadway on two sides and across the road in front of the large building.

Because the state highway seemed to go from nowhere to nowhere, Will knew it probably had little traffic. Picking up Billy Ray's trail at the business would be difficult.

First were the woods; they might prove problematic trying to find a suitable place for concealment of his vehicle.

And second, following another vehicle on long stretches of a lonely road was almost impossible without being seen.

After giving the problem considerable thought, Will decided the safest and most expedient approach to the problem was to eliminate the target with a long-range shot from a location in the woods.

He still had the problem of how to penetrate the woods unseen plus conceal his vehicle. Problem one required the Agency accessing aerial photographs of the location and surrounding forest.

As to the vehicle problem, he kept it simple. He chose a Triumph 650 Bonneville motorcycle, widely regarded as one of the fastest bikes money could buy.

Will's plan was to enter the woods by way of a county road about five miles due west of the Bustine brothers' business. Then he would work his way through the woods on a logging road. About a mile west of the business, the logging road turned south and paralleled the state highway for several miles.

Where the logging road turned south, Will intended to hide the bike and work his way the remaining mile on foot. That should put him across the road in front of the brothers' building. He could then move either north or south of the building and construct a sniper hide.

After making out a list of necessary supplies and equipment, Will went to see Sergeant Bell. With some additional discussing of the plan and tweaking it a bit, Sergeant Bell approved it.

The biggest issue with the plan was there was no guarantee Billy Ray would show up at the business. Consensus was, however, he would need money after three years in prison, and the brothers' business was the most likely source.

Sergeant Bell would be Will's backup on the mission. Transporting Will and his loaded motorcycle, he would drive a medium-sized, self-service moving truck to an area a short distance from a small state park located about 30 miles from the target area.

After dropping off Will, the Sergeant would continue to the state park where he would camp for several days waiting for Will's return. They would communicate via military radios with long-range capability.

…two days later, one mile from target

Will rolled the Triumph off the logging road and into a thick stand of brush. After unloading a large pack, he covered the bike with camouflage netting. Will then gathered leaves and small branches and wove them into the netting. When he was done, the Triumph had disappeared into the underbrush next to a very large cottonwood tree.

Using his military compass, Will took a bearing and headed east. He figured it would take at least an hour to cover the mile to the highway running in front of the brothers' business. He should be there between 6:00 and 6:30 pm.

Will moved a couple hundred yards into the forest toward his target location, then stopped and just listened. He stayed still long enough for the birds and insects to continue their indecipherable communications.

Confident he was the only human present in the immediate area, Will moved ahead very, very slowly. Only idiots and large animals moved quickly and noisily through the woods.

Will stayed upright until he could see the edge of the woods 25 or so yards ahead. He eased the pack to the ground. Removing a pair of binoculars from an outside pocket on the pack, he moved forward leaving the heavy pack behind.

Immediately, Will went prone and began a slow crawl forward. The only weapons he had with him were a small 25 caliber pistol he had picked up in Miami and a large folding knife of the same origin.

About 20 minutes later, Will slowly raised his head above a fallen tree trunk about 10 feet inside the tree line. Scanning the state highway, he could see the target area about two hundred yards south of his location. His positioning was perfect for now.

Scanning the building he could see a parking lot in front of the building. Capable of handling maybe a dozen cars, it was occupied by only three.

The building was larger than he had anticipated, maybe 8,000 to 10,000 square feet with two large industrial overhead doors occupying the end closest to his location. Farther down toward the center of the building was an entrance door with a large sign above announcing Bustine Brothers' Retail Auto Parts and Wholesale Distribution Company. Several windows could be seen to the right of the entrance door.

Past the windows at the other end of the building was a wire enclosure. Two large dogs could be seen moving about restlessly. They were obviously expecting something.

Will's attention was pulled back toward the entrance door as he heard faint laughter. All five brothers were exiting the building. Four stood around as the fifth headed for the dog pen.

He soon returned with the two large dogs at his heel. With a single command, the dogs trotted through the still open door. Closing and locking the door, the man turned back to his brothers. They were walking toward the cars in the lot.

The men split off at the cars: two toward one car, two toward another, and one toward the final vehicle. It must be closing time.

Will glanced at his watch: 6 pm, about two hours before dark. Adjusting the focus of his binoculars, he studied the single man now standing by himself at a vehicle. As he turned to say something to one of his brothers, Will could see he weighed approximately 250 and stood at least 6'3".

Will searched for hair on the man's head; there was none. He did, however, have a handlebar mustache. Since none of the other men looked like this, Will knew he had his man.

The three cars pulled out of the lot onto the state highway and headed toward Will's location. He slowly lowered his head out of sight.

With ample hours before dark, it was time to locate a suitable hide location and began settling in. Will figured to be there for at least 48 hours. He had brought supplies for 72, just in case.

…the hide

After retrieving his pack, Will moved another 200 yards farther from the target location. He felt a long-range shot of about 400 yards was optimum for this situation. It was far enough away that a man with average eyesight would have difficulty seeing detail with just the naked eye.

Will moved a few yards inside the tree line and sat on a

fallen tree. His goal was to find a potential hide where he could see the building's parking lot yet still be inside the tree line.

Carefully examining the terrain around him, he got up and moved on away from the target site another 10 yards or so. Will had his eye on a large water spruce tree with its thick foliage hanging all the way to the ground. It sat in such a position that all but about a foot of its dense needles were inside the tree line.

Will placed his pack on the ground then went prone and snaked his way toward the tree trunk. Just as he had suspected, he soon found himself inside the foliage. Perfect!

Dragging his pack into the tree's interior, Will removed a small folding saw and began to remove interior branches. After 20 minutes of sweat- inducing labor, he had created an open-cave type space measuring maybe three feet wide, seven feet long, and four feet high. The space had been created on the back side of the tree so the untouched section of the tree was between Will and the target location.

Will carefully pushed the small severed branches out of sight under the untouched part of the tree. On one end of the space, he dug a hole about a foot deep next to the foliage. The excavated dirt was piled close by.

He then removed a lightweight, 10'x20' camouflaged tarp from his pack. It was laid on the ground and part of it secured with sharpened sticks. Once secured, the other part was attached to the back and top of the opening with para cord tied in quick release knots at three locations.

The shelter would keep rain and dew off him. Will figured he could break the hide down and secure everything in his pack in less than a minute.

He then removed and assembled his rifle. Once the rifle

was assembled, he removed a Browning High Power semi-automatic pistol and shoulder holster. After putting on the shoulder rig, he chambered a round and holstered the pistol. A second magazine rode in a pouch under the arm opposite the pistol.

With the High Power loaded, he had 14 rounds at his disposal, with another 13 in the spare magazine. In his mind, though, Will felt having to use the pistol meant the mission had gone south and he had to escape.

Will had one other thing to do and the hide would be complete. He needed to create a shooting tunnel through the front foliage.

Will had been taught that a rifle barrel should never be visible. What he intended to do was create a tunnel approximately four inches in diameter through the tree foliage between him and the view of the target area. At four hundred plus yards, the four-inch opening should allow him to cover the entire parking lot.

A special tool had been included just for the purpose of tunnel making; it was called pruning shears. The job took just under 30 minutes. It had to be perfect.

At the end of the tunnel closest to the shooter, Will trimmed an additional branch down to a very shallow 'Y' shape. He now had a well-designed shooting tunnel with a barrel rest.

Will tested the rest as he looked through the mil-dot-marked rifle scope at the parking lot. Using the 'Mil Relation Formula' learned in sniper training, he computed the distance as 415 yards. The formula takes the height of the target in inches, multiplies it by a constant and then divides by the number of mils read in the scope.

Voilá, you have the correct distance. The only thing you

really needed to assure accuracy was the height of the target or height of something else close by such as a door. Will knew his target was 6'3".

Will would not leave the hide until the executive action had been carried out. He didn't have to leave; he had C-Rations and water, a crude outhouse hole, a reasonably dry place to sleep, and a view. All he really needed now was something to shoot.

…about 40 hours later

Will had spent the first night in the hide with relative comfort. The weather had cooperated by being dry and not too cold. The brothers arrived at the business about 9 am the next morning, obviously not ones to rush into their day. Four brothers arrived, that is. Billy Ray wasn't with them and never showed. They left at about 6 pm, just like the day before.

The second night was more uncomfortable; the lack of space to move and really stretch was very hard on the body. It would have been one of those tossing and turning nights if room had permitted.

Once again, only four brothers arrived. They opened the business and serviced numerous customers as they had the day before.

Will sighed. It was almost noon when his spirits were lifted. Billy Ray was in the house. He drove a large truck into the parking lot and pulled it up to one of the overhead doors. Then, a couple of minutes after he entered the front door, the overhead door opened.

The four younger brothers minus Billy Ray started unloading the truck. It took Will about 10 seconds to realize the load consisted of auto parts. Some of the heavier parts, such as transmissions and engines, required a forklift to unload and move into the interior of the building.

Will smiled. There was a hell of a profit in auto parts, especially if you didn't have to pay for inventory. Obviously, Billy Ray had been away at their chop shop supervising the disassembly of the stolen cars. Probably way back in the mountains somewhere.

Well, he was here now; it was just a matter of time. Will didn't know it, but longer than he thought.

At about 6:00, the four brothers walked out of the building and drove away in two cars. Will was curious why the dogs were still in their pen. When Billy Ray did not exit, it was obvious. The business was not ready to close for the evening.

To Will, this was an unexpected, but pleasant, surprise. If the scenario had played out as planned, Will would have had to sneak away while avoiding the brothers.

This way, it would probably be easier. He hoped so, anyway. Will kept the rifle on ready. No telling when the target would leave.

Forty-five minutes later, a blue Cadillac pulled up to the building. A well-dressed man strolled confidently into the front door.

Ten minutes later, he strolled out. He shook Billy Ray's hand at the door and briskly walked to his car and left.

Will figured the man was a 'legitimate' businessman who came to check out some parts. A truck from his company would probably show tomorrow and take a load of parts off the brothers' hands.

As the car turned onto the highway, Billy Ray stepped through the front door and headed toward the dog pen. Just before opening the gate to the pen, something made him turn and look in Will's direction.

Will had the big man's head centered in his scope. As Billy Ray had turned, the trigger broke releasing the bullet.

The low report of the round leaving the rifle could barely be heard. Billy Ray never knew he was about to die. He just did. Falling very close to the dog pen, he was out of sight from the state highway.

The serial rapist had reaped his just reward. He would lie on the cold ground until his brothers found him tomorrow morning.

Will had just graduated.

Chapter 9
Training Over

Will's exfiltration from his hide and subsequent reconnection with Sergeant Bell had been uneventful. Agency sources would later report Billy Ray had been discovered the morning following his death. News reports would imply the murder was a revenge killing related to the deceased's past criminal activities (i.e., rape).

Once again, Will found himself with the Dean in the conference room at the training facility. The Dean had poured himself a cup of coffee and was gesturing for Will to take a seat across the table.

"Will, all reports of the executive action point to a job well planned and executed. Your after-action report was well written in exacting detail. I appreciate the time you took in explaining what you did and why. I do have a few questions, however.

"First of all, what was the first thing you felt after pulling the trigger?"

Will had, what many would describe as, a shit-eating grin on his face.

The Dean held up his right hand to stop Will's answer. "I know, I know, you felt the recoil, but I'm interested in a more psychologically rooted and less glib answer."

Will's demeanor turned to a more serious venue. "To be perfectly honest, Sir, I felt satisfaction with a bullet hitting its intended target. It wasn't different from ringing one of Sergeant Bell's cowbell targets.

"My next thought was to break down the hide and move out as quietly and with as much stealth as possible.

"I know you're more interested in whether or not I hesitated to pull the trigger and whether or not I experienced any remorse at taking another's life. Both answers are, 'No.' He was a bad man doing bad things. I was instructed to stop him, and I did.

"It was probably less challenging for me than others because I've been there before in a much more personalized fashion and with people I had known for years. After my first involvement with taking lives, I had a lot of time to think—some of it in the isolation of a hospital bed.

"After hashing things over and over, I came to the conclusion that many people in the world are just plain evil. When one sets off on a path of evil behavior, violent death is a very likely destination.

"Therefore, I didn't have a problem with the first three killings, and I don't have a problem with the most recent. For whatever reason, my brain seems to have been modified, through polio's destructive force, and now ignores certain feelings.

"I don't know if you believe in predestination or not, but if you do, you have to see that I have been predestined for this type of work. As long as the person in my scope is evil, I'll probably never have a problem with it."

The Dean was perplexed and his face revealed it. "Do you really feel polio somehow predisposed you to killing? How is that possible?"

"Yes, Dean, I do. Polio works its way through your body on a direct path to the brain. Once there, the virus proceeds to destroy nerve neurons and who knows what else.

"In my case, it destroyed a part of the brain dealing with guilt and somewhat, but less so, with empathy. Subsequently, those traits are not as ingrained in me as others. Whether this is a curse or blessing remains to be determined."

The Dean wasn't sure he bought into Will's premise or not. Having no empirical data supporting one view or another, he chose neutrality. "Well said, Will; you have obviously given the subject much thought.

"I can't support nor dispute your thinking on the subject. Whatever gives you this level of distraction, however, is good for us. So, let's not overthink it; let's just accept it as an asset in our line of work.

"Any problems with equipment, intelligence provided, logistics, etc.?"

"No, Sir, intelligence was spot on, equipment was exemplary, and logistics were excellent. If I'm not careful, I'll start to believe this is easy, even though I know it's not.

"What now, Sir?"

The Dean slid a large manila envelope across the table. There were several smaller packets contained within the larger envelope.

Will removed all the contents and created an array of packets on the table. He picked up a packet labeled "ID" and emptied contents on the table. He picked up a driver's license and read the name aloud. "Wilber Rodríguez Villa?" Will looked across the table quizzingly.

The Dean had his version of a shit-eating grin plastered across his face. "Since you have a darkly pigmented skin, I decided you were Hispanic. We don't really know, do we, so you might be. As a matter of fact, from this day forward, you are Hispanic of Cuban descent. Your file says you are quite proficient in Spanish.

"I chose your ethnicity so you can blend into your hometown, Miami. If need be, you can disappear into the Cuban section of town with minimal difficulty. You see, the license is from Florida and your address is in Miami. The address will hold up if checked.

"There's also a passport, a social security card, a wallet, and various items often kept in a wallet.

"One of the other packets contains a complete background built for you. You are 21 years old; a birth certificate is included. You graduated from a very large high school in Washington D.C. Friends call you Will.

"You attended college and have degrees in English and Spanish from George Washington University in D.C. Included is a list of courses taken along with a list of your professors. Grades are also included.

"A draft card included shows your draft status as 4F, meaning you are not eligible for military service.

"You were orphaned at a young age and raised by your grandmother. You no longer have any living relatives. Please memorize your full biography and support material.

"Your new identity will survive scrutiny by all local, state and Federal agencies. Information has been entered in all pertinent records to support the aforementioned.

"Initially, you will live in Florida. You may live anywhere in the state of Florida, although Miami is suggested because of its population density. With your proven ability and intuition, though, I am allowing you more flexibility. I usually specify the hometown.

"Your executive actions will not be in Miami and if in Florida, they will be cities where you have not had contact. Most of your actions will be in other parts of the southeastern U.S. and possibly in Spanish-speaking countries.

"There's a phone number in the material; memorize it, then destroy. You will need to call the number every Friday and inquire about your investment account. Your contact code name is "Florida 1." The line will be monitored 24/7. You will be given instruction if necessary and/or connected to me. It is imperative I be able to contact you within any seven-day period.

"So far, everything should be straight forward. I'll explain a few more things, then you can ask any questions you have.

"I am your immediate supervisor and you are employed by the Central Intelligence Agency as a contract employee. Your *Reader* designation is for internal classification only. I am the only person privy to your identification. This gives the Agency total deniability of you and your actions.

"That means your current nom de guerre will never show up anywhere in Agency files after today. As of today, you were tragically killed in a training accident. Your life as Will Parker is over. Since that was never your name anyway, I suspect you don't care.

"No one, and I emphasize no one other than me, knows your new name. I had a dozen identities developed by our technical department and then personally destroyed all their records. By now the technicians have created dozens more.

"Your identity is safe until compromised operationally. Let's talk about compensation as a Contractor.

"In another of the smaller envelopes is $30,000. That's your compensation for the executive action successfully completed. There's another $30,000 for you to get established. Spend it wisely.

"You should find a small, secure location for storage of operational supplies. It should be in an obscure location and be a minimum of 2,000 square feet with vehicle access to its interior. I'll have a load of supplies delivered in three weeks.

"It is important that the executive action compensation not show up in regular bank accounts. To help with that concern, an offshore bank account has been opened for you in the Caymans. All future contract payments, including a $2,000 per month retainer, will be deposited in the account. Directions for accessing the account are included.

"Okay, Will, do you have any questions about what I have gone over?"

Will, now a different Will, had a look of concern on his face, but it was tinged with the excitement of a small child at Christmas. "I have several, Sir, if you don't mind indulging my curiosity and obvious naivety."

"Ask anything you want, Will. I've thrown a lot at you. I'll clarify anything you need."

"In the course of day-to-day life, I am sure to meet many people and even develop casual relationships. When I do, the first question of a new acquaintance is usually, 'What do you do for a living?' What should I tell them; do I just make something up?"

"You're right, Will, people always have a need to pigeonhole new friends. It increases their comfort zone. You are free to develop your own story, but I would suggest something like a 'writer.' It's innocuous enough based on your education and wimpy enough to hide what you really do."

"What kind of writer should I be? Novelist, technical, what do you suggest?"

The Dean assumed the demeanor of one talking to a third party about Will's ability. "Will was so talented in college, one of his professors got him a job 'ghost writing' a book for a local celebrity athlete. In other words, the athlete told Will his story; Will secretly wrote the book for him; the athlete published it under his name; said athlete wrote Will a check; and like a ghost, Will disappeared and no one ever knew he existed."

The Dean dropped the third-party charade and addressed Will. "An advantage of this profession is it requires frequent absences from home and absolute secrecy about where you were or what you were doing. What do you think?"

Will had been absorbing in great detail what the Dean was communicating. "I understand why you're the boss. It's a perfect cover. No one will ever think anything about my absence. When they ask who I was writing for, I grin and say 'Sorry, if I say who, I'll never get another job.'

"That takes care of my profession; now where do I live? Do you need or want to know? Are there any protocols for living arrangements?"

The Dean was shaking his head no; "I don't need nor do I want to know where you live. That is probably the most dangerous part of this life.

"This job is 24/7; you will have to always be alert. You

cannot let down your guard. Practice paranoia in all you do; don't trust any person outside the Agency. And trust very few in the Agency.

"There's always an enemy waving around enough money to buy a person's loyalty. Even those you trust should be verified if possible. Do your own homework; question all Agency intelligence until you have investigated the intelligence yourself.

"The work you do as a *Reader* is important to our country. Hopefully you realize the importance, and that's why you do it.

"Thus ends my formal Agency speech before throwing you out into the operational arena.

"The next part is one old grizzled contractor giving a young agent he is fond of the benefit of three decades of surviving in this world.

"First, as a personal piece of advice, open another offshore account the Agency knows nothing about. As soon as possible, contact the bank we set up for you and, using the enclosed account and password information, change the password.

"Then move most of the money to the new account. Always leave a balance of about ten grand in the original account to use as basic living expenses.

"Depending on your Contractor skill, you'll get maybe five to seven contracts a year. That may seem like a lot of money, but it's not. If you ever get sideways with the Agency and have to run, a few hundred thousand dollars won't get you far. The Agency's assets are just too many.

"It takes a great deal of money to stay off its radar. You are not allowed to take contracts outside the Agency; I assume you know that. You'll be tempted, but don't. Every contractor has a certain way of working that is tantamount to fingerprints. If you take an outside contract, we'll know.

"The minute we know you took outside work, we start hunting you. You will truly become the lone wolf of 'easy prey' fame. Don't go there.

"Also, find a place to live and keep it to yourself. Never check in from the same phone twice. You can completely trust me but no one else in the Agency. Again, I say be paranoid in everything you do; it'll keep you alive.

"When you call in every week, assume others are listening. Never ask me a question or say anything you want kept between just the two of us.

"If you need to talk to me privately, call this number exactly three hours after a regular check-in. During the check-in, mention you are recovering from a cold." The Dean handed Will a piece of paper.

"It's a number I have never given to another agent; memorize and destroy it.

"Create another three or four identities and keep them to yourself. I'll help with that over the next couple of years. As you are prowling around Miami, though, keep your eyes open. Look for the contacts you will need. Get to know the Cuban community; you'll find everything you need there.

"The last piece of advice may be the most important. Oftentimes during the course of an assignment, the agent comes into possession of cash. I will never ask you, in an official capacity, if you did. If you do, keep the money; find a way to deposit the money in your secret offshore account.

"Access to a large amount of money is your insurance in this business. Every contract agent of any longevity has one.

"Now, for operational protocol; back to the Agency speech...

"Agent Villa, when the Agency has an Executive Action, you will receive basic information during a weekly check-in. If further written or other physical information is required, a drop will be arranged.

"Typically, an agent is given a minimum of four weeks to observe the Executive Action target and develop a plan. No one will second guess your plan. As a matter of fact, only you will know it. Once you decide what your approach will be, you request necessary equipment and any other support required.

"Evaluation of your work and subsequent value to the Agency will be determined by one thing and one thing only: successful implementation of the Executive Action.

"No excuses are accepted. If you miss for any reason, you have 24 hours to correct the situation. Nothing can lead back to the Agency. Whatever or whomever it is must be eliminated. If you cannot do the job, your name will be added to the elimination action.

"Will, you are unique in my experience of 30+ years in the business. Life dumped a load of shit on you and named it polio. Nevertheless, you survived and, in my opinion, even thrived.

"The polio seems to have taken an unusual turn in you and created a rare intellect plus other positives we discussed earlier. You have skills I have never seen. Your intuitive powers are unheard of. You are going to become a legend in this business.

"But, to get off script again, I believe there will come a time when you want out of this life. If I am still alive when that happens, contact me and I will help you. If it doesn't happen, then one of these days you're going to be one hell of a trainer.

"Now, back on script. It's about time for you to leave. You will not return to this or any other facility where you either lived or trained. "Remember, you're dead. At least you will be in a few hours. If you need emergency medical attention in the future, call the check-in number; they will provide the necessary assistance.

"A car is waiting for you at our airport. It's clean and should be safe to use for quite some time unless it's involved in criminal activity. It was purchased legally in Baltimore and registered in your name. It's in good shape mechanically but has some body damage. It should fit right into the Miami culture.

"In the glove compartment are a Browning High Power pistol and a box of ammo. There are also keys and address to an apartment in Miami. The apartment is available to you for one month, but my personal advice is to stay no more than a week. Find your own place as soon as possible.

"Don't use the weapon unless you absolutely have to. Once used, it needs to be disposed of, preferably in the ocean or everglades.

"I will try to hold off at least a month before your next executive action. Use the time wisely. Get everything in place we talked about. You may need it sooner than later. You never know.

"Stay low and stay safe. Goodbye, Will, and happy hunting."

"Thank you, Sir. I appreciate what you have done for me; I won't forget it."

Chapter 10
The Legend Begins

The "car" waiting for Will at the airport actually turned out to be a white Ford 250 pickup truck. It was two years old with body damage on the right rear panel. The damage had been repaired and covered with a coat of brownish red primer.

Will walked around the truck checking the tires and general condition. He liked what he saw; there were probably a thousand just like it in Miami.

Opening the driver's side door, Will looked inside. It was neat and clean but not too much so. It had the appearance of a working man's vehicle. Checking the glove compartment, he found everything the Dean told him would be there.

Using his knife, he was able to break the seal holding in the center console. It was something that had started showing up, as an accessory, in trucks a few years ago. It was basically just a simple box fitted into a shallow tray between the seats. Will figured its main purpose was to hold the eight-track tapes for the new tape players. The original owner must have been into music.

Working carefully, Will managed to lift the box part of the console out of the tray. The design was really pretty simple. The tray was secured to the floor between the seats by four screws. The box was then held in place by friction and a very light seam of glue.

Will had learned this during training. He had been told there was just enough room between the bottom of the box and the tray to hide a pistol and ammo. To his delight, it worked perfectly. He'd throw some receipts and other near trash items in the box on his way down to Miami.

Will spent the next four days leisurely driving the back roads south. For all intents and purposes, this was the first time in his life where he was absolutely on his own. At least he was supposed to have been.

He looked in the truck's rearview mirror and smiled as he had the thought. *On my own except for the vehicle which had shown up several times.* It revealed itself when he decided on some unexpected detours during his trip.

Because they no longer knew his route, the surveillance team had to keep him in sight. He saw them almost immediately.

Will didn't believe for a minute the Agency had invested four years training him at probably a high cost, and then just merrily send him on his way with a slap on the back and a hearty "good hunting."

No, they were back there watching and reporting. He also figured they were protecting him at some level. But as the Dean had pointed out, on more than one occasion, you never know.

He also took some other Deanly advice. *Be paranoid; don't trust without verifying. Be safe.*

Miami coming up…

Will had thoroughly enjoyed the trip south. He had timed his arrival in Miami so he would have all day to accomplish a few chores including finding a place to stay.

Chore one: lose the tail. Will knew the tail so far had been extremely loose; after all, they thought they knew his ultimate destination. Wrong! Because of the heavy morning commuters, though, the followers would need to close the distance to a hundred yards or so.

If they had lost him on the way south, no problem. One phone call would have another team pick him up in North Miami. If that didn't work, they could always go to his apartment.

Wrong again. Will drove on thinking about his last conversation with the Dean. The Dean had warned him not to use the apartment more than a week. He decided not to use it at all.

Besides, he was not running; he was simply relocating. No muss, no fuss. The followers would later have their casual attitude called into question.

Will slowed down; an area ahead had exits on both sides of the interstate. He remembered it from his earlier experience with the city. As Will slowed, he moved from the right lane to the middle.

His maneuver caused a lot of horn honking and, no doubt, undecipherable profanity. The purposefully awkward traffic move caused traffic to close ranks creating a moving blockade between Will and his tail.

The tail was not worried; they also moved to the center lane. They, no doubt, figured Will was going to stay on the interstate for a while.

Imagine their surprise when, at the last moment, he accelerated and moved quickly to the left exit lane. A chorus of horns, fist shaking and middle-fingered salutes encouraged him on his way.

His friends behind were caught in the sluggish menagerie of vehicles created by Will's maneuver. All they could do was swear at the white truck as it exited. They, however, were pulled by traffic congestion past the exits with no egress possible for them.

They would have sworn even more if they had heard Will's laughter as he quickly hit an east/west boulevard and made his way east toward the ocean. Several directional changes and 45 minutes later, airport exit signs could be seen.

Will drove into one of several enclosed structures designed for short-term parking. Choosing a parking spot toward the top of the structure, he backed into the space and locked the truck.

A brief walk took him into a terminal; another one took him back outside to a waiting queue of taxis. He jumped into the lead taxi and asked to be taken downtown to the Hilton Hotel.

Several taxis and hotels later, he asked the taxi driver to take him to a downtown location where there were banks in the area. Twenty minutes and another taxi fare brought him to Dade National Bank.

Will looked up the front side of the bank's facade; it was 20 stories or more. *Might as well try here*, he thought to himself.

He entered the massive double doors and stepped over to a building directory on the wall. The bank seemed to occupy the first five floors of the building. The rest of the floors were occupied with a myriad of service-oriented businesses, enough so they were categorized on the directory.

There was a large category for lawyers; what a surprise. He decided to start there. He was looking for a specialist in international law. He found only one such lawyer, a Conrad Jenkins, III.

Opposite the directory were two courtesy telephones. Will stepped to the one farthest from the door. After a couple minutes looking through the phone book next to the phone, he punched in a number.

"Conrad Jenkins, Attorney-at-Law, how may we be of assistance?"

Will found the young-sounding voice on the line to be courteous and friendly. "Hello, my name is Wilber Rodríguez Villa. I would like to arrange an appointment with Mr. Jenkins as soon as possible. Does he have an opening in the next few days?"

"Let me check, Mr. Villa. He has an opening day after tomorrow at 4 pm. Would that be soon enough?"

"Yes, I think that works into my schedule just fine."

"May I ask the general nature of your visit with Mr. Jenkins? He likes to be prepared for all his appointments. It saves both of you time and avoids unnecessary fees."

"Yes, of course. I am interested in purchasing a small international corporation and also the establishment of an offshore bank account. Additionally, I already have an offshore bank account I'd like to discuss. Does Mr. Jenkins deal with these types of work?"

"I don't think any of those requests are outside his legal

expertise. Shall I make the appointment?"

"Yes, please. I'll see you day after tomorrow at four in the afternoon. Thank you."

Will walked back across the entry lobby and again looked at the bank building's directory. He soon found what he was looking for. Once again, Will took advantage of the lobby's courtesy phones.

"Good morning, Dependable Answering Service, how may I direct your call?"

"Good morning; I'd like to sign up for your services. I'm in the lobby of your building; may I come up?"

"Yes, of course."

"I'll be right up."

Will wasted no time in getting upstairs to the answering service. They proved easy to find, located to the right and directly across from the elevator. Opening the glass doors, he walked to the receptionist. "Hi, I'm Wilber Rodríguez Villa; I just called from the lobby."

"Yes, Mr. Villa; Mary in accounts management will help you. Her office is the third door on the left side of the hall."

Fifteen minutes later, Will had the service set up and paid for a year in advance. By paying extra, he could simply call his number, enter a four-digit code, and receive his messages electronically.

The answering service provided a way for his future lawyer to contact him. He would need to stay in touch and be reachable at all times.

On the way out of the bank building, Will once again stopped in the lobby. He needed a couple more addresses.

He walked outside and flagged down a taxi. The taxi headed off for the waterfront area. He eventually dropped Will in front of a large, fenced-in storage facility on the waterfront. Will chose the business because it advertised long-term storage for business and personal use.

Security at the facility was such that visitors had to ring a bell and be buzzed in. After meeting with the manager and looking at a two-car sized unit, Will once again paid for a year of service in advance. The answering service number was given for emergencies.

He liked the security set-up of the place. The outer perimeter was a 12-foot fence with razor wire on top. Clients could enter 24/7 by using a code to open the gates. The second layer of security consisted of a heavy-duty overhead door on each unit accessed by a coded key pad. Only the owner had the code. If the unit were entered forcibly without the code, an alarm sounded in the office. It was monitored at all times.

The next thing on the shopping list was about a 15-minute walk along the waterway. After a leisurely walk in the salt air, Will could see his destination ahead, Quality Camper Sales. The last thing on the list was a place to live.

Will had a lot of time on his hands as he had driven south from Virginia. He decided no one would know where he was nor what he was doing at any given time. His plan had started to materialize as soon as he left the meeting with the Dean.

The offshore account had been the catalyst for what he was doing. During the years of training at the Academy and the Agency, Will had a lot of unused time in the evenings and often on the weekends. He spent those times reading any and all books he could find. At the Agency, there had even been a rather large library on almost any topic one desired.

Will had been interested in almost everything. One of the

less interesting areas of literature had been in finance. Will knew he would eventually get paid, but because of the way he had been raised, he had no real concept of what to do with money.

He obviously understood about buying basic necessities, but how is money handled if you happen to accumulate a great deal of it? What did wealthy people do with their money? In particular, how could it be hidden and moved about?

Will had spent the last several months at the Agency reading and digesting the ins and outs of money management. At this point, because of his exceptional intellectual skills, Will was extremely well-versed on the theories of the subject. What he lacked, however, were any practical experiences. These he would start to accumulate day after tomorrow with his attorney.

Will walked into the office of Quality Camper Sales. He was greeted by an artificially blonde young lady probably in her late twenties. She gave him the kind of smile he would come to recognize as heavily flirtatious.

She rose from her seat behind a desk and walked around the counter separating them. "I'm Suzy, and you are …?"

"My friends call me Will, as in Wilber Rodríguez Villa."

"What may I help you with, Will?" She was now standing close enough to him for the lack of space to cause a bit of nervousness.

"I'm interested in purchasing a used camper, particularly something that has full-time living capabilities. Are you a salesperson here?"

"I do a little bit of everything around here. Right now, I'm a salesperson. Why don't you sit down and I'll ask you a few questions. That'll help me determine if we have any inventory that meets your needs.

"Please spell your entire name and give me your date of birth."

He did.

Her grin was still going strong. "What kind of camper is your preference?"

"I believe a small 25- to 30-foot length would work.

"How about budget?"

"About $15,000 is what I have to spend."

Suzie looked up as some people do when they are trying to concentrate. "I've got an idea. This morning I got a call from a woman who just lost her husband to an industrial accident. She said she had a 26-foot Airstream Overlander she wants to sell.

"I tell you what. I'll send one of my guys over and bring it back. We'll check it out and I'll tell you what it's worth. If you like it, I'll sell it to you for whatever I pay her plus 10%. Okay?"

A couple hours later, Will had a home on wheels. He left a thousand-dollar deposit and agreed to pick it up in three days. Suzie promised to have the Airstream completely serviced and cleaned by then.

Since it was mid-afternoon, Will continued to walk along the waterfront. Even though training had brought him to waterfronts before, he had never had a chance to just walk without a schedule or objective.

By early evening, Will could see a number of hotels and small motels starting to dot the landscape. Losing track of time, he had just kept walking. Obviously, he had left the industrial waterfront and was approaching the beach area.

His stomach had been shouting at him for the last hour that he had not eaten since early morning.

About a half block ahead was a small diner. Will figured it was as good a place as any. As he reached the diner, he was about to open the door when it was violently shoved open as two rough-looking young men made their way out.

One of the men was about 6'6" tall and easily weighed 250 pounds. The other was just as tall and maybe a little heavier. Will stepped to the side as they made their way by. They both looked at Will with angry stares obviously fueled by abundant amounts of alcohol. "Look, Buck, a spic that knows his place."

Buck, the fatter of the two, must have felt the need to comment. "He's kinda cute, too; maybe he'd like to ship out with us tomorrow."

Since Will had no desire to tangle with two huge drunks, he just smiled at them and entered the diner.

Will took a booth in the back where he could see the door. As he had been taught, he also identified a rear emergency exit. He could still hear the Sergeant's command, *Don't ever go anywhere you haven't identified at least two ways to get out; three would be better.*

The waitress walked up to his booth. "I saw the two idiot twins hassling you outside. You were smart not to mess with them. They come in every couple of weeks; I think they own some kind of boat that goes down to the islands or something. They're always bragging about all the money they make.

"They are usually drinking and pushing people around. I'm afraid one of these days they're going to really hurt somebody.

"What can I get for you?"

Will did not respond to her comments; he simply smiled and ordered a medium-rare steak, salad, and water to drink.

The waitress thanked him and walked back to the counter to place the order.

Will had also been trained to speak only when necessary. People were a lot less likely to remember you that way.

His food arrived shortly. It was good, but not great. What could he expect? It was, after all, a diner; not a five-star restaurant. He finished his meal, left a generous tip, and resumed his walk along the waterfront.

A couple of blocks past the diner, an alley intersected the street. By now it was dark with few lights around. Will knew he should amp up his caution level; he was still a couple of blocks from the string of hotels and motels he had spotted.

As he was passing the alley, he heard a scream that was quickly muffled. If it had been a male, he would probably have kept going. But it wasn't; it was a female.

Will stepped into the alley and put his back against a wall. He was able to make out a whimpering voice saying, "Please don't hurt me. I don't have any money."

A male voice responded, "We don't want any money; we just want to have some fun."

A second male voice joined the first, "Yeah, we just want a little fun."

When the second male voice chimed in, Will knew exactly who was in the alley. There was no way he could just keep walking and leave a woman with those two.

He had been told over and over to mind his own business. Concentrate on anonymity and the mission; don't get involved in other people's business. There was no upside to it.

Will sighed. Just a couple days out of training and breaking rules already. It probably wouldn't be the last time.

He eased farther into the alley. Not far from his mind was the fact he was about to go up against over 500 pounds of mean drunks. Will had been very well trained; he knew he could easily deal with the drunks if he killed them. That, however, would draw unwanted attention. In one of his front pockets, he had the small 25 automatic pistol he had taken from the drug dealer. In the other pocket, he had the knife.

He decided on the knife. It would not be the first time he had used one. This time, though, he would not be relying on luck; at the facility, he had received extensive training on armed and unarmed close combat.

Moving on into the darkness of the alley, Will could make out two hulking shapes hovering over a much smaller shape on the ground. Moving closer to almost touching range, Will almost laughed. The two drunks were both unbuckling their belts in preparation for their "fun."

The not so fat one knelt down on his knees and grabbed the girl's shirt. Before he could rip it off, Will stepped to within a foot of the other. He had consciously made a noise with his feet. Both drunks turned toward the sound.

"Hi, boys. The last time I saw you two, you were wanting me as your shipmate. What's the matter? Couldn't you find a little boy to rape?"

"What the hell? Hey Buck, it's that spic fag from the diner."

Apparently, Buck never spoke first. He did, however, make a movement toward Will. Using the knife in his right hand, Will swung it in a cross-hand cut.

Suddenly, blood blinded Buck. He didn't know it yet, but he was going to need about 20 stitches to close the gash extending the entire width of his forehead.

Before the blood even registered with Buck, a stiff fingered jab landed just below his Adam's apple. The blow was not hard enough to kill; it was just hard enough to make him think he was dying.

As all this began to register with the drunk on his knees, Will's foot connected with his nose-shattering bone and causing blood to fly. He landed on his back with both hands covering his nose.

Over 500 pounds of drunks had been put out of the fight in less than three seconds. Will helped what he discovered was a young teenaged girl to her feet. "Are you okay, Miss?"

She was crying but otherwise seemed unhurt. "Thank you, thank you so much. I was just walking down the street and they grabbed me. I couldn't get away no matter how much I fought."

"Well, I'm glad you're not hurt. I suggest you get away from here as far as possible. These two guys will probably think before they do something like this again; they just paid a big price for their stupidity."

The girl, having regained some composure, smiled up at Will, then ran toward the street. She was soon out of sight.

He looked down at the two drunks; each was lying on the ground writhing in pain with their legs splayed apart. The temptation was just too great. Before leaving, Will delivered two very powerful stomps to each of the drunk's fun-making equipment.

...a few hours later

The pay phone was about a half mile from the motel Will had selected for the night. He didn't need anyone trying to determine his location by tracing a phone call. Will called the number given to him by the Dean and inquired about his investments. Will was instructed to hold for a minute, his investment advisor wanted to speak to him.

"Hello, Will. Have you encountered any difficulties or unusual circumstances?"

"Well, Sir, I discovered that I was being followed after I left the Agency facility. I didn't know if they were Agency babysitters or somebody else. For a time, I considered eliminating them; they were really sloppy."

"What changed your mind, Will?"

"I was afraid they might be on the same team as me. That's why I chose to simply lose them in early morning Miami traffic."

"As you probably deduced from my question, they were Agency. Even though protocol, I advised against it in your situation. Our surveillance unit laughed at my caution. A new agent had never discovered the teams following them.

"They were very embarrassed when you lost them on the interstate and then never went to the apartment. They were sure their second team would reacquire you there."

"Sir, I came within a heartbeat of eliminating the team. What should I do in the future if I am being followed?"

"Kill them, Will. I'll communicate our conversation to the surveillance unit. They have been warned.

"Are there specific items you wish to include with the basic supplies being gathered for your safe house?"

"Yes, Sir, there are. Once I move into full operational mode, I feel that my most dangerous exposure will be when making physical contact with Agency personnel. To minimize that exposure, I would like a year's worth of supplies. Also, I would like two additional vehicles: a long wheelbase cargo van and a small but fast motorcycle.

"As to supplies, I am requesting: ten pounds of C4 with an assortment of timers and detonators; two silenced High Standard 22 pistols plus several boxes of subsonic ammo; two T/C sniper units with a half dozen barrels (two in 22 mag, the rest in 7mm mag); ten boxes of ammo for each caliber and 9mm for the Browning; a box of 7mm tracers; a supply of detcord and a dozen grenades; high-powered binoculars; and enough military rations for two months."

"Anything else?" the Dean asked sarcastically.

"I know I am asking for a lot of supplies, but I don't want to be delayed waiting for some specific item. I know it will happen sometime, but I don't want it to be a common thing."

"Okay, Will, I'll grant your request. Everything should be ready in about three weeks; make sure you have a secure safe house by then."

"I will, Sir. Thank you."

…Little Havana

The next day Will retrieved his truck from the airport and headed for the section of Miami referred to as little Havana. His next task was to begin creating a Cuban persona.

His Spanish was flawless and would be interpreted by a native speaker as the dialect of a first generation American-born Cuban whose first language was English.

The first step in creating the persona was to find a small apartment suitable for a college graduate making his living as a ghost writer. That meant one nice enough for a writer, but not too nice. He was, after all, still young and still building his reputation.

The apartment would be more of a "beard" or

misdirection. Most nights he would be mobile using the Airstream camper as his home base.

After spending the morning getting familiar with the area, he rented a small, one-bedroom apartment in what used to be a Woolworth's Five and Dime. Woolworth's had followed its Anglo customers to the suburbs and left its old store vacant.

The store had been subdivided into eight apartments designed for middle-classed Cubans who wanted a home close to other Cubans and the culture therein. Will picked a furnished, first-floor unit with a small storage area in back which had been converted to a one-car garage.

In addition to the apartment, Will also found two nearby parking garages where he rented a space in each, one for his truck and another for the van. His apartment's small garage would be used for his motorcycle.

That evening, Will ate in a small, family-owned Cuban restaurant not far from his apartment. Walking several blocks, he located a phone and checked in with the Agency. He finished the evening at a bar frequented by other Cubans his age. A new persona was under development.

…the financial expert lawyer

Will showed up at the lawyer's office at 4 pm sharp. He was immediately escorted back to the office of Mr. Conrad Jenkins, III. The lawyer rose and walked around his desk to shake the hand of possibly his newest client. He extended his hand while displaying his warmest smile. "Hello, Mr. Villa. Please have a seat." He extended his arm to indicate a very expensive-looking, wingback chair upholstered in distressed leather finished with brass accents.

"My assistant informed me you are interested in purchasing a small international corporation and also the establishment of a foreign bank account. Also, there's an offshore bank account you'd like to discuss. Is this information still correct?"

"Thank you for seeing me on such short notice. I have a new international account and need some knowledgeable advice."

Mr. Jenkins was having some difficulty hiding his surprise that this potential client was so young. "Mr. Villa."

"Please, call me Will. It's a lot easier to remember."

"Okay, Will, maybe we can start with you giving me a brief bio and telling me the nature of your business. And please call me Conny."

"Thanks, Conny, I appreciate that. First of all, I'm 21 years old and, as you might suspect, of Cuban origin. I was born here in Miami and raised, since I was an infant, in the Washington D.C. area. My parents died when I was young and I was raised by my paternal grandmother.

"I graduated from George Washington with double majors in English and Spanish. I recently relocated to Miami with the hope of reconnecting with relatives and my Cuban heritage. My parents did not want me growing up to be anything other than a good, old-fashioned American.

"After they were killed in a boating accident, my grandmother took the opposite approach. Before she died, she encouraged me to move here and immerse myself in my Cuban culture. I took her advice.

"During senior year at GW, my English advisor recommended me to a Central American professional baseball player who wanted to write his autobiography for publication back home. He needed a native speaker for the project.

"Long story short, I spent the summer after my senior year in Central America writing. Since the player was a national hero in his country, the book made a ton of money, as in millions.

"Because my advisor had suggested I take expenses plus a percent of sales instead of a flat writing fee, I consequently made a lot of money.

"Now, I need help managing the money without sending most of it to the IRS. I do need to make something very clear, though. I came to you because I want to be legal in all of my actions."

Conny was by now leaning back in his office chair. He seemed satisfied with Will's explanations and also with his young age. "So, Will, you are a 'ghost writer' who has been paid several hundred thousand dollars for writing a book about a professional baseball player. Are there any other sources of income?"

"Not yet, but I am in negotiations with another international Hispanic player to write his book. Since the first book sold so well, I think I will be able to work with several other players.

"My problem is, how do I deal with the money? I'm sitting on over $500,000 and don't really know how to bring it home. That brings me to this visit."

Conny was obviously thinking as he sat staring off into space with his ten fingers forming a tent shape. "So, if I could help you buy a small, family-owned foreign corporation, the corporation could then become your employer for purposes of the writing fees. Said corporation could then pay you as an employee. As long as you don't work in the U.S. or receive payment here, you would have a foreign exemption for most of your income.

"The corporation should be one that has been defunct for several years and has no real value. I have a European associate who maintains a list of such corporations.

"I could then open a numbered account for you in … say, Brussels, and you could move the money as desired. A corporate-numbered account would also need to be opened for the corporation.

"Now about the numbered account you already have. What do you need to know?"

"What I need, Conny, is some serious tutoring on international banking with concentration on setting up and closing accounts plus how to move the money between accounts. I also want to buy some local property through the foreign corporation."

"That's easy enough; my assistant has graduate training in international banking and can handle the tutoring."

"That's great, Conny, but can I afford your services? This sounds like a lot of work."

"It is quite a bit of work, but it is what I do and I've been doing it for a long time. My best guess is that the corporation and other expenses on that end will run about $20,000-$25,000. My piece will be $5,000.

"Do you want me to proceed?"

Will had been studying Conny's demeanor throughout the meeting. He seemed very sincere and not at all anxious for the work. From the looks of his office, he was doing quite well without Will's business. "Yes, do you accept cash?"

With a huge grin on his face, Conny stood and once again extended his hand to Will. "As a matter of fact, I do."

…businessman

Two weeks later Will was the sole shareholder in Brussels General Services, Inc. He also had two numbered accounts in Brussels, the original numbered account in the Caymans, and a second Cayman numbered account. He also had been tutored on the various aspects of international banking he needed.

Now all he needed was a safe house where he could store his supplies and himself, if necessary.

…the safe house

Will found his safe house about 100 miles northwest of Miami. He had discovered it in a real estate brochure for rural properties. It proved perfect.

The structure was small in size, only 12'x12' and 6' high. It was in an isolated section of central Florida on an old farm. It had been built during WWII to store military munitions and other explosive ordinance.

The old widow to whom Will talked was no longer able to live on the farm and was moving to a nursing home. She had already sold most of the farmland and house. The only remaining piece was a three-acre parcel located in a very undesirable area with old growth trees and scrub brush.

There was neither road nor driveway to the parcel. The widow told Will the story of how, during the war, the military had taken possession of the three acres and built a small concrete building on it. It wasn't until the war was over and the property reverted back to the widow and her husband that they learned its use.

The building had been one of about a dozen such

structures built in the interior of Florida. The network of buildings was designed to store munitions as an emergency cache in case the enemy tried to invade somewhere along the vast shoreline of the state.

When the war ended, the land and structures then reverted to the original owners. The widow's husband was always leery of the building. He knew the military had a history of just locking the doors and walking away from such locations while leaving everything inside for the owners to clean up.

Since the building was on an isolated and non-farmable section of the property, he fenced and posted "No Trespassing-Danger" signs every few feet. He never reentered the area and just let nature reclaim the property. He had never even tried to enter the building for fear of being blown up. All his neighbors were equally wary of the area.

Because the military had taken the land and then given it back, it was on a separate deed. Realizing the land was pretty much useless and had a building of questionable safety, the widow offered the three acres to Will for $500 per acre. He bought it on the spot without even looking inside the building, explaining to the widow that he needed an isolated area to park his camper and write.

Within the week, all due diligence had been performed and the building's ownership registered to Will's newly acquired Brussels General Services, Inc.

...the building of questionable safety

Will moved his Airstream camper to the isolated property. The camper provided a comfortable escape if needed and the concrete structure a safe supply storage area.

It took a great amount of very slow maneuvering to position the Airstream out of sight from the road. He had to cut a rudimentary gate in the heavy wire fence. He positioned the camper about twenty yards in front of the building.

He did not want to disturb the vegetation to a point it looked like a road or even a trail. The isolated and almost inaccessible location was among the property's most desirable features. Once the Airstream was positioned, it was impossible to see from the road.

Parked in such a location, Will could use the camper as home base without moving it every few days. All in all, a great location.

It took Will about an hour to open the small door to the building. He first applied a copious amount of penetrating lubricant to the lock and along the left side hoping to reach the hinges just inside.

While he waited for the lubricant to work, he walked around the building. It wasn't a long trip. Because of the heavy growth of vegetation, the building was practically invisible. There were no more doors.

Will then began to circle the small building in ever increasing distances. At about 20 feet on the side of the building opposite the camper, he found what appeared to be an air vent. About 20 feet farther in the same direction, he found another one. His suspicion was confirmed; the building lay mostly underground.

Taking the key the widow had given him, Will approached the building. Inserting the key, he held his breath as he turned it in the lock. To his amazement, the key easily unlocked the door.

Turning the door's oversized handle, Will put his shoulder against the door and pushed. Again, to his surprise, the door swung inward. Either the penetrating lubricant had been very effective or the door and lock were of unusually high quality.

The building was made totally of concrete; the door was set into a very thick steel facing. The fitting was such that no dust or foreign matter was able to enter and freeze the mechanism, even after almost two decades.

Swinging inward, the door allowed sunlight into the structure. The first thing Will saw was a staircase leading down. Using a flashlight, he examined the walls of the small landing upon which he was standing.

There was a light switch on the right; not much of a surprise there. The real surprise would be if it worked. He reached across and flipped the switch; to his amazement, an overhead fixture flooded the staircase.

As he thought about the fact that the building still had electricity, it really made sense. The military had simply dug a trench and tied into the local power. Since they didn't put in a meter, there was no need to disconnect when they left. The local rural electric power company probably never knew. He figured there was probably a backup generator somewhere.

Will closed the outside door and began descending the stairs. His trip was at least two stories down. The main part of the structure was at least 20 feet underground.

He encountered a second locked door and repeated the process above. He had no idea what he would encounter. He hoped the old farmer had been wrong; if explosive ordinance had been abandoned, it could be very unstable after all these years.

Lights and empty space were the first things he saw. The light switch above had also turned the lights on down inside the structure, at least the front section. Looking around, Will quickly discovered an electrical box. There were several switches clearly labeling their area of the structure.

He then turned on all the remaining switches prior to turning off the light in the staircase. He didn't think it could be seen from the outside, but taking chances was not high on his list.

Will actually gasped at what he saw. The space was huge; he was probably looking at 5,000 square feet of open warehouse space, and that didn't include the spaces off several doors he could see.

The ceiling was at least ten feet high and the space was lit up like the outdoors. Support beams were placed throughout at what seemed exact distances apart. Wow!

And thank goodness; not a bomb in sight. Will took his time examining the space. Through one of the doors, he found a fully furnished office; through another, he found a type of small barracks complete with beds and footlockers. Adjacent to the barracks was a latrine. Where the waste went, he had no clue.

Will also found a mess hall, of sorts. There was a sink and several dining tables and chairs. No stove or refrigeration was evident. The stove he understood. Fire with munitions was probably not a good idea, but what harm could a fridge do?

There was, however, a water tank capable of holding 500 gallons. It was probably for drinking and maybe even fire suppression. It had to be filled by some type of underground well because it still had water in it.

There were also a great many cabinets, most still

containing K-Rations. Yum, yum! Soldiers probably didn't look forward to chow.

There were other interesting aspects of the structure that Will also discovered. The walls in the large open space told the history of inventory which had been stored there.

They were all labeled: Garand rifles, Thompson submachine guns, antitank weapons, grenades, flamethrowers, sidearms, ammunition (bunches and bunches of ammunition), radios, batteries, explosives, and everything else needed to fight a guerrilla war campaign. Of course, they were empty now.

Will also found the vents, six to be exact. They were obviously designed to be invisible under the scrub brush. Each was enclosed in its own small room, which was capable of being sealed off in case of discovery. One of the vents was especially interesting. It did not appear to be open to the outside. Instead, there was a downward opening door at the top. No doubt an escape tunnel.

A second vent room contained the back-up generator and fuel storage. The vent doubled to vent exhaust fumes.

The last thing, which was of major interest to Will, was in the office he had discovered. It was no doubt the CO's office. Within the office was a door leading to a walk-in sized closet. Within the closet was a fairly large-sized cabinet. In the cabinet was a safe, the type you used to see in small town banks.

Will returned to the office and approached the safe, which was locked. He had checked earlier. The Agency had taught all agents basic safe cracking; Will was about to see how much he remembered.

The safe proved uncomplicated. Inside, Will found two Browning 45 handguns, 10 boxes of 45 ammo, and a

Thompson submachine gun. To most, this would have been a very interesting find, but not to Will; not today, anyway.

In addition to some code keys for sending radio messages, there were 100 packages of American currency, each wrapped in a type of cellophane material. Each package contained 3,000 dollars.

Obviously, the money was destined to small bands of citizens fighting for their country. What was equally obvious was the Commanding Officer had not been around when the place was vacated at the end of the war. In the confusion of clearing the place out, the closet was overlooked. The CO was probably transferred and the secret safe forgotten.

Will's biggest problem now… how to get the money into his new offshore corporate account.

…money

Will spent two more days exploring his new property. He needed to know every inch of his three acres by heart. You never knew when such information would come in handy. He also spent time thinking about the money and how he could transfer it to his new Cayman account. Once there, it could be easily transferred to a Brussels account. He figured the task needed completing prior to the arrival of his supplies.

After walking the property over and over and over, he decided the simplest way was probably the best. He'd just charter a plane and fly to the Caymans.

…

The next day Will called the Cayman bank and inquired about the procedure for making a large cash deposit. It proved simple enough: bring the cash in, pay a percentage handling fee, and it was deposited.

A couple days later, he chartered a small plane and flew to the Caymans, deposited the money, and immediately moved 90% of it to Brussels.

Maybe, international banking wasn't that hard, after all. Not hard, that is, if you didn't mind double-digit handling fees.

...

After returning from the Caymans, Will spent the next two weeks at his property. To him, it had become his bunker. He brought in more food and a comfortable sleeping cot.

Time was spent making sure the ventilation escape hatch was well lubricated and easy to open. By moving all the trash and assorted junk found on the property, the escape vent was made to look like a pile of discarded metal and trash. To the casual observer, it would appear as the property's garbage dump, an area most people avoided like the plague.

The metal and trash were available in great quantities. There were construction concrete fragments, a couple of four-foot diameter drain culverts, numerous downed trees, assorted construction wood, and miscellaneous items gathered and piled in such a way that the hatch could be opened without disturbing the material covering it.

Will had also crafted a tunnel of sorts through the rubbish providing an escape route if needed. After his escape "structure" was built, he moved some assorted vegetation to the area and threw dirt and leaves over everything. In a few weeks and a couple of good rains, the whole thing would look like it had been there for years.

His instructor's advice was never far from his mind. *If you go in, make sure you have an alternate way out.* He now had a well-conceived alternate way out. Probably some of the best advice he had received.

Will also moved some vegetation to the other vents. By transplanting several thick bushes to each location, he made each almost invisible to the average observer.

Since the bunker proved to be so useful and large enough to occupy for extended periods of time, he no longer needed the Airstream camper at the site. He'd figure another use for it later. For now, it could stay where it was.

Since there were still several days before the supplies were due to arrive, Will decided to spend them at his new apartment in Little Havana.

By the time he arrived, the sun was down and his stomach was shouting "dinner." He had stopped on the northern end of Miami and checked in with his "financial advisor." No messages.

Once again, Will ate at the family-owned restaurant close to his apartment. If he were to become a believable Cuban, he had to familiarize himself with the food and acclimate his stomach to said same. Most of his life, he had been fed a bland diet of inexpensive institutional food. A culinary expert he wasn't.

His meal was followed by a trip to the bar he had visited before. He really needed to become enough of a regular there so people would begin to develop a degree of comfort with his presence. The bar was called Rum Grande and was also within walking distance from his apartment

When, during his training, he had been taught how to drink, he thought the subject matter somewhat unusual. His instructor, however, had stressed the importance of controlling alcohol intake.

His advice had been to never order mixed drinks. Mixed drinks had the unknown variable of how much alcohol was actually being consumed. Instead, agents were encouraged to order straight liquor, thereby ensuring knowledge of alcohol consumed.

The name of the bar, "Rum Grande," meant some derivation of Big Rum. As Will pushed through the double front doors, he took a moment to look around. It was a very nice bar, not too fancy and not too grungy. The bar was a long, semicurved affair taking up most of a side wall. It appeared to be a native cypress wood heavily varnished against the wet nature of a bar.

Opposite the bar and separated by an open corridor about six feet wide was an area filled with small bar tables. Some were tall and encouraged patrons to stand; others, regular dining height and held from two to six people. All useful for consuming bar grub.

If one were to pass through the bar toward the rear, a medium-sized, glassed-in area became visible. Probably used as overflow on the weekends and maybe private gatherings. Restrooms were just past the glassed-in area. Just past that was a kitchen entrance and a bit farther, a back entrance/exit.

Will had checked all this out on his first visit to the bar. He had also discovered a window in the men's john big enough for emergency egress if needed.

The clientele during his first visit had been primarily an

under-40 crowd consisting of young management types. It was the type of place where people dropped in after work or on weekends to meet friends and other young professionals.

The music was Cuban and the atmosphere upbeat. Just the kind of place for Will to establish his presence in the Cuban community.

Walking up to the bar, Will saw a trio of two women and a man he had seen on his first trip. He decided it was time to start contacting the local natives and procure a position in the community.

As Will walked up, a bartender put a napkin on the counter while smiling. "Hi, there. Same as the last time?"

Will's jaw would have dropped, if he didn't have such good control of his emotions. "You remember what I ordered the last time I was here?"

The trio on Will's right had obviously heard the exchange. As they turned toward Will, one of the women smiled. "We call him Einstein; he never seems to forget anything. If you leave and come back six months from now, he'll remember. That's his upside.

"The downside is he also remembers every conversation, who was with whom, did they bicker, were they lovey, lovey? You get the idea."

Will returned the bartender's smile. "Thank you, Einstein. My name is Will; and yes, I'll have the same. And for future reference, it will never change. Dark rum on the rocks and a water back is the only thing I drink other than a little wine or beer with dinner."

"You got it, Will. Anything else?"

"Yes, please give my bar mates here a round of whatever they're drinking."

As Einstein turned to prepare his order, Will turned to the

group. He extended his name to the young women who had spoken. "Hi, I'm Will; I appreciate the bio on our bartender."

"Thanks for the drinks, Will; I'm Maria. Tony is the good-looking hunk, and this is Juan, short for Juanita." She had pointed to Tony and placed her hand on Juan's shoulder.

They all smiled, and each said "Hi" and offered a hand as introduced. Maria seemed to be the small group's leader. "Well, Will, what brings you to our little watering hole?"

Will noticed none of the three spoke with anything other than a south Florida accent. "I just relocated from D.C. and rented a small apartment not far from here. I'm just trying to get the lay of the land."

Tony had been studying Will closely. "What brought you here? Miami is, I imagine, very different from D.C., especially little Havana?"

Juan spoke up quickly as she slapped Tony on the chest. "Don't be so nosey; we just met Will."

Maria was laughing at her two friends. "You two might as well already be married the way you bicker. Please excuse my friends, Will; it's just that we don't meet a lot of people from out-of-state who move to Little Havana. Most young people are trying to do the opposite—escape."

Will could see the trio had, no doubt, been friends a long time. Their interactions were a dead giveaway. "It's okay; I don't mind telling you.

"I was born here in Miami and raised, since I was an infant, in the Washington, D.C., area. My parents died when I was young and I was raised by my paternal grandmother.

"I graduated from George Washington with double majors in English and Spanish. I recently relocated to Miami with the hope of reconnecting with relatives and my

Cuban heritage.

"My parents did not want me growing up to be anything other than a good, old-fashioned American. My grandmother, however, felt the opposite. Shortly before she died, she made me promise to 'go back home' as she phrased it.

"Since Grandma devoted the last part of her life to me, I figured I'd devote part of mine to her. Besides, the weather's a lot better down here."

All three seemed intrigued with Will's story. Maria more so than the other two. "You must love your grandmother and her memory very much to so drastically change your life. So, what do you do now?

"Are you looking for a job? If so, maybe we can help; we know a ton of people."

"Yes, I loved my grandma very much and no, I don't need a job. I just want to meet Cuban people my own age and try to reconnect with my heritage. I don't really know if that's possible or not, but I promised I would try."

The trio didn't make any jokes or snide remarks; they could tell this was a serious endeavor for Will. Maria spoke for the three of them. "You're making a good start; we're all Miami-born and Cuban-bred, just like you. And we all still live in little Havana. If we introduce you to our cousins, you'll know about a hundred people."

All four of them laughed, with Juan and Tony adding, "Yeah, possibly more."

"So, what kind of place did you find to live?" Tony asked.

"Well, like I said, it's not far. It's in an old Woolworth's Five and Dime."

Juan jumped in excitedly. "Maria lives in the same

building. What a small world."

Maria jumped in. "There was only one left empty, so I know exactly where you live. I live in exactly the same floor plan on the opposite end of the building. I really like my place; how about you?"

"Mine is really nice and has all new furniture. First time in my life I ever lived in anything new."

"So, Will," Marie asked. "If you don't need a job, how do you pay the bills; you rich or something?"

Will let out a huge laugh. "Rich? I wish it were true; I'm afraid I have to work just like all the other ghetto kids I grew up with."

"I know what you mean," said Tony. "As a matter of fact, we all know. The three of us grew up in the same neighborhood. Just getting to school every day required tactical training. We all made it out, though.

"I'm an engineer, Juan is an accountant, and Maria is a corporate lawyer. If it were not for maternally induced guilt, we'd probably all be on South Beach. Mamas, however, usually win the arguments about us moving."

"Then you can understand why I'm here. Saying no to a grandmother was really hard to do. Since I know what you guys do, I'll explain how I pay the bills.

"My senior year at GW, my English advisor recommended me to a Central American professional baseball player who wanted to write his autobiography for publication back home. He needed a native speaker for the project.

"Long story short, I spent the summer after my senior year in Central America writing. Since the player was a national hero in his country, the book made a ton of money, as in millions.

"Because my advisor had suggested I take expenses plus a percent of sales instead of a flat writing fee, I consequently made a lot of money.

"Currently, I'm in negotiations with another international Hispanic player to write his book. Since the first book sold so well, I think I will be able to work with several other players.

"As luck would have it, Miami is a good geographic location for me. I can hop a plane on a minute's notice and be meeting with a client the same day."

All three new friends looked at Will in amazement. Maria asked the questions all three probably had in their minds. "So, as I remember, you majored in English and Spanish. You must be a really good writer to get that kind of recommendation from your advisor. As I remember, my advisor asked me if I had considered another major."

They all laughed.

"I studied hard at GW because I was on scholarship. Writing always came easily for me. The verbal Spanish I learned at home, but I needed to get better at reading and writing it, thus the Spanish major.

"I guess I'm also lucky. Right guy at the right place and all that."

Tony had a quizzical look on his face. "That all sounds too good to be true. There has to be a downside. What is it?"

"You're right, Tony; on the surface it sounds real easy. But at the end of each project, I need about 90,000 words structured into a format that not only the client likes, but also, the reading public will buy. Screw up one project and you'll need to find another way to pay the rent."

Juan, like the other two, was fascinated. "Any other

downsides?"

"Yeah, a couple. You may get a call in the middle of the night requiring you to get on a plane and be in a meeting the next day. If you get the contract, you may be away from home for several weeks or even months.

"The life of a writer can be very lonely. You have big blocks of time where you hole up and just write and rewrite. Then you have the editing.

"Some of these I haven't experienced yet. My advisor went into great detail explaining these things to me. He has been doing it for 20+ years. People like us are called 'ghost writers.' We write the books, however, our names never appear anywhere."

"Wow" was all any of the three could say.

The three new friends got up to leave. Tony shook Will's hand. "We're here three or four times a week. I look forward to seeing you again."

As Maria got up, she asked, "Going my way, Sailor?"

Will smiled, "Yes, I just happen to be."

Once outside, Tony and Juan walked one direction, Maria and Will the other.

"So, Will, how's your Cuban immersion program going so far?"

"Well, so far, I've met three really nice young Cuban professionals. There is an initial immersion problem, though."

"Really, what?"

"The problem is we are all pretty much the same. Don't get me wrong; I really enjoyed you guys tonight. I look forward to developing our friendship. But to understand where my father and mother came from, I probably need to experience less refined people than you three."

"No, I completely understand what you are saying. Those of us at a bar like Rum Grande have been where you want to go. We, however, see ourselves casting off what we consider the yoke of our heritage. You, on the other hand, are seeking to understand your heritage. If I may, I have a couple of suggestions."

"Please, as you can no doubt tell, I have no real direction here. I'm just floundering around."

"First, I suggest you develop friendships with young Cubans like myself and my friends. I know I would enjoy introducing you to my family. Most of my older family members were born in Cuba and experienced much of what your parents did.

"Second, I suggest you pick a secondary watering hole in addition to the Rum Grande. Say the Casa Bonita which is located in a less prosperous area of Little Havana. As friendly as you are, you would no doubt make friends with young Cubans there.

"If you do those two things, your immersion into your Cuban heritage would be well rounded. I have to caution you, though, the Casa Bonita has a pretty rowdy reputation. You'd have to be very careful."

"Thank you, Maria, you are a very kind person. I am so glad I met you tonight."

"Thank you, Will."

"One other thing, Maria, do you know the big guy that has been following us since we left the bar? He's about a half block behind us and closing quickly."

As Maria quickly turned around, her demeanor immediately tensed. "Will, that's my ex-boyfriend. He didn't handle our break-up well. We'd better run, he's really a mean guy when he's drinking. That's the reason I dumped him; he slapped me a couple weeks ago."

"Too late, Maria; he's here."

The ex was right on them as Will stepped between Maria and the very obviously intoxicated ex. He was a big guy, heavily muscled and probably a gym rat.

Will knew by looking the muscle was show muscle; his arms were so heavily muscled, he'd have trouble throwing a decent punch. That was his upper body. But like a lot of his ilk, he paid little attention to his lower body. His legs bore more of a resemblance to a chicken.

The ex spoke directly to Will. "Get out of the way, pretty boy, before I rearrange your face. I need to talk to my girlfriend." His speech was slurred to a point of misunderstanding. Spittle hit Will in his chest as the man spoke.

"Not going to happen, big boy. You're drunk and will probably just insult my friend."

"Insult, hell! That's the least of her concerns. After I break your face, she's coming with me. She needs to be reminded of what she's missing."

Will knew the ex was about to go ballistic. No amount of talking could stop a mean drunk, but he decided to try one more time anyway. "How about the three of us go our own way and then meet tomorrow evening for a cup of coffee. We could talk then."

Will could feel Maria trembling with fear directly behind him. He used his left hand to reach back and gently move her farther back.

"A cup of coffee? What kind of pussy are you? I'm going to fix you up so your next cup of coffee will be through a straw." He started prepping his swing before the words were out of his mouth.

Given Will's level of hand-to-hand training, the guy might as well have mailed his intentions.

Before the ex could start the forward motion of his swing, Will stepped inside its possible arc. Having turned his right hand into a claw shape, he raked it across both of the man's eyes. Will's fingernails sliced both eyes much like a knife, just shallower.

The claw hand was joined by the left in grabbing the man's meaty right wrist. The movement caused the ex to shift most of his weight to his right leg, just as Will had planned. As he stepped slightly behind the man, Will raised his right foot and delivered a devastating kick to his opponent's knee, breaking it very badly. The man fell awkwardly to the ground and began moaning loudly.

Intoxication was the only thing between the man and a horrific level of pain.

Will turned quickly to Maria and hugged her to his body. Hopefully, his body heat would stave off the shock that was building. He held her for a couple of minutes, then helped her the few blocks to his apartment.

Inside, he immediately gave her a carbonated beverage to fight shock and help her settle down. Very few people had ever been around the level of violence she had just witnessed.

It was several minutes before Maria had the composure to speak. When the first words out was a joke, Will knew she would be okay. "Well, I guess you didn't need the warning about the Casa Bonita."

"Like I said, I grew up in a ghetto. You learned to fight or you got pounded on a regular basis. My father knew what I would face so he started training me early. He told me he had been in a special part of the military in Cuba.

"He never told me exactly what he did and never shared any of his experiences. He just taught me to fight." Will was surprised at how easily lying came to him. Of course, he had a complete section of training on the subject.

"How badly did you hurt him? He's pretty tough; he'll probably come after you and me again."

"It doesn't matter how tough you are or how big your muscles are, your eyes and knees are very weak points of your body. To answer your question, his eyes will heal in a couple of months.

"His knee is a different story, though. It will require reconstructive surgery and about six months in a cast. Even after all that, he'll have a significant limp for the rest of his life. He may even have to depend on a cane for walking."

"Did you do those things to him intentionally?"

"Maria, I've been around bullies like your ex all my life. The only 100%, for sure way to stop him is death. Since I don't kill people, I had to pick the second option, take some of his physical weapons away, which I did.

"A gym rat like him who can't work out will become just a big fat guy over the next six months. I doubt very seriously if he will bother you again."

"Was all that going through your mind in the few seconds before he tried to hit you?"

"Not really. I considered all this years ago when my father told me about the philosophy of fighting. He said there were playground fights and there were back alley fights. The first hardly ever left you injured or the two participants wanting to do it again.

"The second type was usually very serious. It could often be life or death. Playground fights are done so people can watch. Back alley fights are so no one can watch. You have to be willing to kill or maim. If you aren't, you may have to go through it again. Back alley fights are mostly personal and will continue until one of the combatants is no longer physically able.

"My father obviously had personal experience; I could tell by his demeanor when we talked.

"Our encounter tonight was back alley and imminently personal. If I had not seriously hurt him, you and I would forever be looking over our shoulders. I didn't come to Little Havana to be paranoid all the time.

"I hope you understand."

"Yes, I think I do, Will. I'm glad you were with me tonight. If you hadn't, he probably would have seriously hurt me, maybe even killed me. Thank you."

"You're welcome. I'm glad I was there. May I ask you for a favor?"

"Of course, what can I do for you?"

"Please don't tell anybody about what I did tonight. I don't want some sort of reputation as a tough guy. I know from experience what comes with that. After a couple of drinks, every other tough guy in Little Havana will come calling.

"I didn't move down here for that, just the opposite; part of my moving here was to escape it. I'd rather be known as the nerdy writing guy who hangs out in the Rum Grande Bar."

"You have my word, Will. I won't tell a soul."

Chapter 11
Fully Operational

Will chose a shopping center in northwestern Miami for the delivery of his supplies. He had talked to the Dean two days earlier about the logistics of transfer.

"Please don't send more than two people with the supplies, and please don't have me followed. Once I'm in possession of the van, I will assume any surveillance to be hostile."

The Dean chuckled on the other end of the line. "I see you are taking my advice on being paranoid to heart. That's good; it will add years to your life.

"Don't worry about being followed. I will instruct the delivering agents to park on the far side of the lot next to the street. One person will exit the vehicle and be immediately picked up by a trail car.

"Everything you requested will be in the van. May I ask again why you requested so many supplies?"

"Of course, Sir. My reasoning is very simple. In my

opinion, I am most vulnerable when meeting somebody at a designated place at a designated time.

"Also, from this day forward, I will never expose my face to any Agency personnel again. Within a couple of years, there won't be anyone capable of identifying me.

"Anonymity will be my first line of defense. If I can't be identified, I can't have my Agency contract cancelled.

"My new mantra of life is 'paranoid lives; trust dies.' I suspect there aren't too many old agents in my line of work. I plan on being an anomaly.

"Don't get me wrong. I am looking forward to this next stage of my life. It is not my intention to escape the Agency; it is because of my loyalty I am doing this. Hopefully, I'll be around for a long time helping you eliminate people who need to be eliminated."

"I agree with your actions completely, Will. I can see you have given your new life a lot of thought. To add to your peace of mind, I will be your sole contact with the Agency. If that needs to be changed, I will tell you.

"The Agency is just as interested as you in minimizing contact. The reason is obvious; if you make a mistake and get caught, we will deny any connection. There is no file on you anywhere. All records of your past with us have been destroyed by me personally.

"Your compensation comes from an offshore shell company completely untraceable to us. We cannot be connected to you. It's in both our interests not to be associated in any official capacity."

"Thank you, Sir; I'm glad we agree on this.

"Everything you asked me to do has been accomplished and is in place. Once I secure the supplies, I'll be fully operational."

"That's good, Will, because details of your first executive action are included with the supplies. Look in the container with your rifles.

"The assignment will require a small motor yacht; instructions for its procurement are included. Its ownership will be another offshore corporation.

"Using you current cover, you will be the boat's new owner. You're taking a break and cruising to Key West to complete a writing assignment. A boat slip at your destination has been rented for one month.

"After the assignment has been completed and you have checked in, please dispose of the boat as you see fit. Then disappear for a month before you check in again.

"All assignment details are included with your delivery plus a few assignment specific supplies that might prove useful.

"Good luck, Will. If you hit a snag on the assignment, just remember your training. You'll be okay."

The Dean hung up.

…three days later

Will was in the motor yacht headed south to Key West. He was a little nervous handling the motor yacht. Even though he had received extensive training in small boats and their operations, he had only motored solo in open water once.

The great thing about being on the open water was the solitude. He thought back to the past couple of days.

The supply pickup had gone well. Will had parked his truck in the storage facility he had rented. A taxi was then taken to the shopping center.

The van driver dropped it off and was picked up by the trail car, just as expected. No one followed him as he drove to his bunker. After unloading the supplies, Will drove back to Miami and replaced the van, with the motorcycle inside, for the truck.

Before leaving, however, he had studied the details of his first solo executive action. After reading and memorizing the pertinent details, the file was burned and its ashes flushed down the toilet in his storage unit's small bathroom.

Will's mind returned to the task at hand. He was no longer nervous. He was on his own, it was a beautiful day, and he was heading to, arguably, one of the most beautiful cities in the United States.

The executive action involved a naturalized American citizen of Cuban heritage who had been identified as an independent travel agent of sorts. His specialty was getting people in and out of the U.S. without the need for all those pesky immigration rules.

The majority of his clients, it seems, were agents of countries not on friendly relations with the U.S. The "travel agent's" cover was a small charter service offering dive adventures to ancient wrecks just outside the territorial waters of Cuba.

The diving spot, incidentally, was also a popular diving spot for wealthy Cubans. Cubans wanting to dive there had to have special permission and were always accompanied by a Cuban patrol boat.

According to the file provided by the Dean, it was a pretty cool setup. The charter would leave Key West before dawn and head for the wrecks. Most of the charters were solos with one person renting the entire boat.

The Captain and one deckhand would handle the boat and

the deckhand would dive with the client. Two divers would go down and two would come up.

At the same time, a Cuban boat would also be over the wrecks. Two divers would go down from that boat as well and two would come up.

What could not be seen were two of the divers exchanging facemasks and tanks. After an appropriate amount of time had passed, the four divers surfaced and swam to their boats and went back to their appropriate boats.

The Key West diver would immediately drive to Miami. The process could then be reversed at the client's wish.

No muss, no fuss.

…Key West

The object of Will's executive action was 45-year-old Ricardo Ruiz, "Ric" to his American friends. Ric lived in a two-bedroom, middle-of-the-road condo. His charter service was run out of a somewhat decrepit boathouse. Its neighbors looked much the same.

He ate most of his meals and did his drinking at a local's bar called El Cactus.

Contrary to the Chamber of Commerce's literature, Key West was not all sun, sand, and trendy bars. If you looked hard enough, you'd find a seedy side to the place.

Will's moorage was at a slightly rundown marina catering to the less than affluent boat owners. Not too nice, but better than crappy. He had taken the time to stop at the fueling dock and refill his tanks prior to docking. You never knew when you might need to leave in a hurry.

Will's marina was only a short walk to the row of dilapidated boathouses where Ruiz kept his boat. Its location was obviously well scouted in advance by the Agency's reconnaissance team.

The marina had slips for probably 50 boats and most were occupied. Amenities included on-shore showers and restrooms, a laundromat, and a small convenience store, all amenities required for the convenience of boaters living full-time aboard their vessels and the steady flow of travelers.

A young teenaged boy materialized to help Will dock the 34-foot Marinette Houseboat he was on. Although technically a houseboat, it had a strong V-shaped hull capable of handling open water. With an 11'6" beam, the boat was plenty big for Will to live aboard. It could sleep six people comfortably and included a nice-sized galley, head, and lounging area. There were also nice decks aft, forward, and on top.

With a draft of only three feet, the boat would be excellent in shallow water. No doubt an important consideration in its acquisition.

The young boy caught the rope as Will threw it. "Hey, Mister, nice boat. You don't see many Marinettes. Had it long?"

"No, just picked it up in Miami. Thought I'd run it down here and check it out. So far, it's been purring like a kitten and with great gas mileage. The inside is better than I thought it would be. Plenty of room for me to live aboard."

"Yeah, I saw where you're booked for a month. Vacation or work?"

As Will studied the young dockhand, he related his cover story. "… So, I've got the book written in initial draft form; now, it's time to edit the work. By far the most boring part of writing.

"I'm not sure how long it will take, but I usually get it

done in two to three weeks. I tacked on an extra week just in case. If I finish early, I'll head back to Miami. My client is anxious for the book."

The boy was finishing tying up the boat and making the shore connections. He shook his head slowly back and forth as Will talked. "Don't know much about writin'. I do know about boats, though. If you have any questions about your new girl here, just holler."

"Thanks, I will. I'll probably wear your ears out before I leave. A good boatman like you is a lucky find."

The boy grinned with satisfaction at Will's comment. Will had flattered the young man on purpose; never know when he might come in handy.

The boy pointed to the office as he walked away. "Take care of the paperwork up there. They can also tell you where to eat and other town stuff."

...El Cactus

By the time Will checked in with the marina's office, it was getting on toward happy hour. He thought, *What better place to get a drink and supper than El Cactus.* Time to go to work.

Included in the written brief he had received was a map with pertinent locations and directions from the marina to each. It seemed to him it would have been easier for the recon team to just hit the guy.

In his heart, he knew why it was not easier, though. A lot of people could be trained to follow and report, but only a very small number could be taught to kill.

The bar was not far; neither was the boathouse or Ruiz's condo. As far as that went, nothing was really far in Key

West. The city measured about two miles by four miles.

In Will's mind, the size was both a blessing and a curse. Small enough to where Ruiz would have trouble hiding, and small enough that Will could easily get caught if not careful. Well, if the job were easy, anyone could do it.

El Cactus, as you no doubt guessed, wasn't that far away from the marina. It was located across the street from the row of shabby boathouses and down a one-way street with very poor lighting. Will found the bar and stood for a minute studying its facade.

If they were going for the Key West, shabby-chic look, they forgot the chic part. The appearance practically screamed, "Tourists not welcome." If the weathered wood siding and weeds growing through the sidewalk weren't enough, the sign over the door sealed the deal. "Not an English-speaking business."

It made Will smile to himself as he pushed through the heavy door and entered the bar. Standing just inside the doorway to let his eyes adjust, he surveyed the room.

The room contained numerous cigarette- and liquor-stained tables scattered about without any conceivable scheme. Most were occupied by hard-looking men and a few women. Peppered throughout the bar, however, were men and even some couples who were no doubt higher up on the social scale.

The bar looked rougher on the outside than it really was. Catering to fishermen and blue-collar workers, it also appeared to serve as a local's bar. The noise level was loud but not obnoxiously so. The lighting was low but still allowed you to recognize faces across the room.

As a matter of fact, Will saw a face across the room that he recognized. Holding court in the back at a large table was

Ricardo (Ric) Ruiz.   Laughing and motioning other people to the table, he was simultaneously signaling the barmaid for another round by making a circular motion over the table with his hand.

Ruiz was, no doubt, a popular guy within the local Hispanic community. That one quick glance gave Will a very valuable piece of information.

If he wanted a clean kill and quick getaway, the hit would need to be very private or otherwise appear as a tragic accident. If not, a lot of angry people would be looking for him.

As Will walked up to the ancient-looking bar, he knew numerous sets of eyes were following his every step. Everyone in the bar recognized him as a newbie. They would continue their glances his way until the bartender communicated to them, by his demeanor, if the new guy was a problem.

Will was not dressed like a tourist. As a matter of fact and by design on his part, he closely resembled the fisherman in his manner of dress. He had not showered in two days and his fingernails held the grime of a boat.

The bartender, as advertised out front, spoke to Will in Spanish. "Cuban?"

"Si." Will responded.

The bartender then reverted to English. "I thought you looked Cuban, but you can't tell these days. I always start the conversation with any new customer in Spanish. We're a neighborhood bar and don't want the Bermuda shorts, loud-shirt-wearing bunch in here.

"You don't look much like a tourist; what brings you in?"

The bartender was now smiling and just making bar talk. Will could almost feel the tension in the room recede. "Me, a tourist; not likely. I just brought my boat down from Miami. Heard about your bar from a guy at the marina in Miami.

"He said if I wanted to avoid the obnoxious tourist crowd, El Cactus was the place to eat and drink. So, here I am."

The bartender wiped the bar in front of Will and put a napkin down. "What can I get you?"

"Do you have anything that is close to Cerveza Cristal?"

"I might have some, but if I did, it would be reserved for special customers. Tell me why you want a Cristal beer."

The bartender seemed genuinely interested, so Will decided to tell him the back story he had developed. He hoped the story would make a friend. "My father and mother were both native-born Cubans. I was born in Miami and raised in Washington, D.C.

"My father didn't talk much about Cuba because he wanted me to be an American, not a Cuban refugee. The only thing I ever heard him say he missed from Cuba was the beer, especially Cristal.

"The main reason I moved to Florida was to reconnect with my Cuban culture. I'm the only member of my family left. After my parents were killed, my grandmother began to talk to me about reconnecting with my 'people' as she called them. She died not long ago leaving me alone. So, here I am.

"I have a small boat that I came down on. I also live on it. This is as close to Cuba as I can get physically. So again, here I am. In a Cuban bar surrounded by Cuban people, 90 miles or so from my parents' home.

"My work allows me the freedom to live where I choose. For now, I choose the marina not far from here."

Without a word, the bartender turned to a beer cooler behind him. "Here you go, one Cerveza Cristal. It's on the house in honor of your deceased family. I'm also going to get the cook to serve up some real Cuban food for your supper.

"As soon as I get the drinks prepared for the table in the back, I want to know your name and more about your work."

...a few days later

After the first night at El Cactus, Will was accepted as a Cuban who belonged at the bar. He was sure the bartender shared his story with most of the bar's patrons.

The bartender, Ray, greeted Will as he approached the bar. Will had taken all his meals seated in one of the bar's high chairs which were crowded from one end of the bar to the other. "Hi, Will; getting any work done on your book? I'll give you free beer for a week if you'll tell me which Chicano player you're writing about."

"Sorry, Ray; if I told you his name, you'd have to adopt me 'cause I'd never get another job. I tell you what. When the book is published, you'll get a copy in the mail with no return address or note; it'll be our little secret."

Ray wiped the bar and placed a napkin down in front of Will as was his habit. "Cristal or rum tonight?"

"How about rum and a big glass of cold water; heat's a bitch tonight."

As Ray was putting Will's drinks on the bar, Will head-gestured toward the back of the bar. "So, who's the life of the party back there? Is he an important man in the community?"

"That's Ric Ruiz; he owns a small charter boat business

out of one of the old boathouses. I don't know how important he is, but he buys a lot of drinks for people. He likes to gather a crowd and talk about the old days in Cuba.

"He also likes to brag about his family's old plantation in Cuba back before the revolution. Another favorite topic is how well-connected he is with important people in Cuba.

"He must have some connections, though; he takes his charter clients closer to the island than any other boat can get. My guess is he's paying off some third-rate officer in the Cuban Navy.

"Ric spends a lot of money in here, so I don't want to piss him off. I figure he has a little smuggling going on in addition to his charters.

"Hell, the other boat captains have told me he hardly ever has more than one person booked on most of his Cuban diving trips. Since he settles up his tabs in cash every night, I don't care what he does. If he's not hauling in a little grass here and there, he's probably one of the few Captains who isn't."

Will could tell from Ray's comments he didn't really like Ruiz very much. He filed that piece of information away in the ole mental bank. Never know when it might come in handy.

As Will took a sip of his very dark and somewhat sweet rum, someone walked up to the chair beside him. Turning to see who the person was, he was somewhat surprised to see who was there.

"Hi, may I introduce myself? I am Ricardo Ruiz, Ric for short. And you are the writer, correct?"

"Hello, Ric, it's my pleasure to meet you. I'm Wilber Rodríguez Villa, Will for short. I've been wondering who you are. You're obviously an important and well-respected community leader. Your table seems to always be full of well-wishers."

"Thanks, Will, but I'm not a community leader; just a man with many friends who like to talk of the old times in Cuba. Is it true you are trying to reconnect with your Cuban roots?"

"I'm not sure I'm trying to connect with my Cuban roots so much as to understand Cuba and its culture. You know what they say, 'You'll never know where you're going if you don't know where you're coming from.'

"I don't have any family left so I figured the next best thing would be to connect with other Cubans who are more enlightened to the culture than me. I would very much like to know where my family comes from."

"Why don't you join us, Will. I cannot attest to the veracity of the stories you will hear, but the Cuban culture and spirit will be honest."

"I'll join you under one condition, Ric."

"And what condition is that, Will?"

"You let me buy the next round of drinks for the table."

"You've got a deal."

By the evening's end, Ric had invited Will to visit him at the boathouse. He even suggested Will join a group of tourists who had booked a charter for Saturday.

Will thought both invitations were a good idea. Somewhere in the boathouse or on the roundtrip to Cuba, there had to be a serviceable idea of how Mr. Ric Ruiz could accidently blow himself up.

...a boat ride

The boathouse was not really a house, it was more like a

large shed built on pilings extending from the seabed and supporting the shed structure at a dozen points around its exterior. A quick glance told Will the boathouse provided only minimal security provided by a lockable entry door and a garage door-type opening in the rear. The boat was now secured to the dock immediately adjacent to the boathouse.

Will had been invited to show up an hour before the charter's departure time. Ric wanted to give him the grand tour. The boat was a newer 40-foot job with what looked like a custom paint job. Anyone walking up to the boat along the dock would, no doubt, be impressed.

The name of the boat, *EASY MONEY,* caused Will to chuckle to himself. The name was obviously Ric's inside joke.

One would think a smuggler of high risk human cargo would want something a bit more subtle. Ric's philosophy was obviously go big or go home. Not a bad strategy, really. Conduct all your business right out in the open. How much more honest could a guy get?

No one would suspect that such an ostentatious vessel would be involved in such treasonous activities. Ric's larger than life personality also helped enhance the smokescreen.

As Will walked up to the boat, Ric was busy polishing a brass rail. "Hey, Will, come aboard." Ric did not bother to introduce the deckhand who was manhandling a large pop/beer cooler.

"Thanks for having me. It's a beautiful day for some blue water time."

Ric's smile was so large, Will thought it might escape his face and continue wrapping itself around his head. "This is an absolutely gorgeous vessel; it's obvious you spend a lot of time keeping it shipshape. It makes my boat look like something from the wrong side of the tracks."

"I've seen your Marinette and know that's not true, Will. My boat's custom paint job and shiny rails are all about impressing my paying clients. It's what pays the bills.

"Come on; let's go below deck and I'll show you around. I'm particularly proud of the engine room."

As they entered the boat, Will paid careful, but not overly obvious, attention to the door's lock. He was truly impressed as Ric talked him through the salon, into and through the galley, and on to the two sleeping berths. Both were large with adjoining heads.

Last on the short tour was the engine room. Ric definitely had reason to be proud. The area was full-standing-room height with two very large engines.

"Wow! This is a lot of power for your typical charter boat. You must have to add a fuel surcharge to your fees."

Ric was smiling much like a proud father would after watching his son hit a homerun. "Yeah, it's a lot of horsepower; but without it, the Cuban diving charters would take too long. A 180-mile round trip can get very tiring without the extra get up and go. So far, I've never had a client complain about my fees."

"I can understand after seeing the quality of your boat with its first class amenities and now the power capability. I can't wait to feel the power on an open ocean in full plane."

Ric patted one of the engines as if were a favored child. "You will not be disappointed, I promise."

The charter, Ric soon discovered, was a three-hour tour taking in many of the individual keys and some time on the open ocean. The charterees, if that's a word, were two middle-aged couples from a small town in Western Colorado.

After a while, Ric asked if Will wanted to take over the helm while he and his deckhand attended to the paying customers. It gave him a great opportunity to get a feel for the boat and also give some thought to possible ways to cause a fatal accident.

Right offhand, Will began to ponder the possibilities of using the pride and joy engine compartment to his advantage. As with any large engine compartment, numerous crooks and crannies existed for hiding any number of treacherous goodies.

…later that day

Will had been back on his own boat for several hours. It was time to complete his job and move on. As he prepared a little something to help redesign Ric's boat, his mind wandered back to his target.

At first blush, Ric appeared to be a larger-than-life charter boat captain. It was a common pretension for pseudo seamen who found themselves owning some sort of seagoing craft. Will knew he himself probably also fell into that category.

Ric wanted all those around to covet his lifestyle. Holding court at the bar every night was his stage; his bravado, the swagger of a terrorist trying desperately to hide the reality of his bottom-feeding profession.

Will could not understand the psychology of a man whose actions pointed toward a deep hatred of America, while his lifestyle took advantage of all the low-hanging fruit on the American tree. What an asshole.

If a person truly hated America, why not go back to Cuba or whatever third-world hole they crawled out of. Why pretend to hate a country they fought to get to and one they would probably never leave.

What psychology would allow the destruction of a lifestyle one immersed himself in and drew so much pleasure from? Maybe Will was just overthinking the whole thing. It was probably just the money.

It no longer really mattered, though. Will had been around Ric enough to know he was not a very nice guy, not down deep in his soul where it really mattered. He was a sicko narcissist who needed a fatal form of shock treatment.

Will put Ric's psychology out of his mind as he prepared a new accessory for the gaudy charter boat. It involved two pounds of a very special explosive much like C4 only enhanced somewhat by his employers.

During the early morning charter, Ric bragged about the single person charter he had scheduled for tomorrow morning. Apparently, the client was a very wealthy client willing to pay triple the daily rate for an opportunity to dive in Cuban waters.

As the early morning charter progressed, Will got Ric to reveal the route used to get to Cuba. He also learned departure time and the time of return from the trip.

By seven that evening, Will had his work done and was having his usual beer and meal at El Cactus. During the meal, he told the bartender thanks for everything and that he would not be in after tonight.

The book was complete and he was leaving at first light tomorrow morning. The two men discussed the book and also Will's desire to see Cuba. The bartender suggested it would be a shame to be so close and not at least get a glimpse of the island. One more beer and Will had been convinced; he should make a side trip to Cuba and spend a few hours cruising around. It was, after all, his ancestral home.

The bartender had even been kind enough to suggest a small island just north of Cuba's territorial waters. It was a good spot where Will could tie up and spend the night if he didn't want to make the run to Miami the same day.

...2 am the following morning.

It took Will less than an hour to make the swim from his dock to the boathouse. Swimming a couple feet beneath the surface, he had no trouble navigating. Will surfaced just outside the old boathouse. He saw nothing of danger to him.

Diving under the shed's external walls proved no harder than falling off the proverbial rock. The shed's walls extended no more than a few inches under the water.

Covered head to toe in a black scuba suit, Will was an invisible apparition moving unseen through the water. He surfaced with the utmost stealth, mimicking what he was taught during training. Initially, only his eyes broke the surface. Scanning the water and the boat's hull, Will detected no signs of life. He knew there was the possibility a deckhand could be aboard.

Part of Ric's modes operandi (M.O.) was a deckhand being the diving partner with the "client." That fact had caused Will to redesign his explosive device. He could not risk going aboard *EASY MONEY* and secreting a device in the engine room. The risk of getting caught was just too high.

Will went to work. Immediately upon returning from the cruise, he had gone to a store stocking boat repair supplies.

He purchased numerous supplies used for patching holes and cracks in fiberglass.

He then fashioned a cup-shaped bladder from the fiberglass supplies. It was designed to use a quick drying strong marine epoxy glue to secure it to the boat's bottom.

It was large enough to hold the explosives and a 12-hour-delay model fuse to ignite the explosive. The fuse had been developed during WWII and operated much like a windup alarm clock.

Will had learned during training how to modify the fuse for shorter time frames. Since the charter was due to leave at 6 am this morning and it was a little after 2 am now, the fuse had been modified to ignite at 8 am.

The fuse and extra explosive material had been included with Will's earlier shipment of supplies. Apparently, a boat explosion was an expected option considering the target's occupation.

The fuse would ignite once *EASY MONEY* was well into international waters. No muss, no fuss.

…RIP Ricardo Ruiz

By 5 am, Will was motoring slowly through the no-wake zone of his marina. His destination was Ballast Key, an island nine miles to the south of Key West. From conversations with Ric, he knew *EASY MONEY* would pass within sight of the private island.

Sometime a little after 6:30, Will maneuvered his boat into a small cove where he would be able to watch Ric pass by yet be shielded from view himself. He relaxed and waited.

Ric arrived at the boathouse as his watch displayed 5:30

on the dot. His deckhand and charter client had spent the night onboard the boat. The client currently occupying one of the berths had arrived via Cuba about two months ago.

Today, as per Ric's carefully choreographed system, the three of them would head for the Cuban dive site. Stepping onto *EASY MONEY*, he greeted his deckhand and client. "Mario, let's get the engines warmed up. Make sure you check the engine room carefully and pay attention to the gauges. We'll be shoving off at 6:00 sharp."

"I'll take care of everything, Ric. I did a walk around of the boat and everything looks normal."

"Mr. Johnson, good to see you again; I trust your business went well. We'll get underway shortly. Please make yourself comfortable. Feel free to help yourself to anything in the galley. Let me know if you need anything."

"Thanks, Ric, my business trip was very successful. I've got all the information I came for." He patted the diving dry bag he had slung over a shoulder.

At 6:00 sharp, Ric assumed his position at the ship's helm. Since his habit was always to back the boat into the boathouse, he eased the throttle forward and pulled out into the no-wake zone of the surrounding water.

It seemed a shame to keep such a beast of a boat below 5 mph. With his power plant, he could have been almost to international waters by the time they finally broke free of the no-wake zone.

Ric gradually moved the throttle forward so as not to surprise his client and possibly dump him overboard. He steadily added power until the boat was flying through the water at full plane.

A little before 7:00, *EASY MONEY* was passing Ballast Key. Mr. Johnson had stepped up to the helm so Ric could hear him. "Well, Captain, isn't this about where we enter international waters? I always feel better when American waters are behind me."

"Yes, Mr. Johnson, Ballast Key is the last part of America you will see for a while. Now you can settle in and enjoy your trip to Cuba."

Because of Will's concealed position, he could not see *EASY MONEY* until she cleared the island. *Wow, now that's one fast mother,* he thought to himself. *Good thing he didn't have to catch her; it would take all his boat's power just to keep her in sight for the next hour.*

Will throttled up and moved from his point of seclusion. By the time he was at full power, *EASY MONEY* was about half a mile in front. Checking his radar, Will could see the little dot quickly eating up the ocean.

It was a beautiful day with little wind. With so little chop in the water, Will sat back to enjoy the ride. The sun was up and the day presented a clear blue sky with visibility for miles. As the Indians would say, "It was a good day to die."

Ric was left alone to his thoughts as *EASY MONEY* ate the ocean miles with ease. *Not a bad life,* he thought to himself. His job had very little danger other than that presented by a sometimes temperamental ocean.

He spent most days on the ocean enjoying the luxury of his boat and the ever-changing sea scape. A job like today's was worth 20 grand. How many other charters working out of Key West made even a tenth of what he did?

He could afford to relax every evening in El Cactus and buy his friends a few drinks. Then he'd go home to his condo. Even though run of the mill on the outside, he had furnished it with the best money could buy.

Although Ric enjoyed the company of women, he did not

keep one around on a regular basis. That way he could "rent" one whenever he wanted, and she always left before morning coffee. No muss, no fuss.

Yes, Ric had it made. Other than his clients, no one knew what he really did. Even Mario was not privy to the real story. He thought the clients were simply illegals who had a lot of money and whose criminal records kept them from entering the country legally. Ric paid him well to keep his mouth shut—and he did.

Ric had never given much thought to the dichotomous nature of his chosen life. The fact that he took money from and transported people hostile to the very lifestyle he embraced never crossed his mind.

He was crafty and shady in his dealings but not really very smart. It had only taken a mistake by one client to trace said client back to Ric and his transportation service. He was sure no one was aware of what he really did. His time of full awareness was very near, though; it would last for only an instant.

Will was studying his boat's radar very intently as the clock struck 8:00. One minute the *EASY MONEY* radar dot was there—and the next, it was gone. A smile nudged its way onto his face. Maybe explosives weren't such a bad tool after all.

It took about 15 minutes for Will to reach the explosion site. The water was littered for a hundred yards in all directions with debris. None of the pieces were large enough to identify the vessel of origin.

It was as if *EASY MONEY* had gone through a large salvage yard shredder; nothing of significance was left. Within another quarter hour, the ocean would have consumed all evidence of Ric and his evil little enterprise.

Returning to his radar, Will saw nothing within its five-mile range. By the time another vessel came this way, nothing would be left to see. Years from now, the people at El Cactus would still be wondering what happened to good ole Ric.

Will set a course well outside the waters of Key West. Later in the day, he docked at a Key many miles north. After refueling and calling in to report, he set another course heading to Mobile, Alabama. He had an idea how to dispose of the boat he had been provided.

Chapter 12
Mobile, Alabama

Will didn't have to report back in for a month. Over the years, institutional life had not provided opportunity for travel. He had seen very little of the United States. Will had never had so much unencumbered time in his life. It was time to see a little bit more of America.

The day was overcast with low cloud cover. It wasn't the bright blue sunshine he loved, but it had its own kind of beauty. Will had decided to make a run up the west side of Florida and around the coast to Mobile.

One thing about travel by boat; you had a lot of time to think. It wasn't like an airplane ride measured in a few hours; a boat ride of any distance would usually be measured in days.

By the time he reached Clearwater Beach, Will had decided to sell the boat to Brussels General Services, Inc. After a paint job and renaming, the boat would simply disappear into the great international world of commerce.

At a refueling stop, Will called his attorney, Conny, and gave him the details of what he wanted to do. Conny instructed him to bring in the ownership documents when he returned to Miami and he would take care of the transfer.

…Mobile

As Will headed north on Mobile Bay, he felt as lost as a long-neck goose in a new barnyard. There had been no advance surveillance team to provide maps and make docking arrangements. Consequently, he spent several hours motoring around and getting a feel for the geography of the place.

As the sun was going down, he headed into a marina consisting primarily of live-aboard boats. Most of the craft appeared to be well-maintained, and the area was clean and free of the boat trash that often accumulated around some locations.

Will had radioed the marina when he passed it a couple of hours ago. He inquired as to the availability of long-term, covered dockage. The gentleman on the radio advised him they were full with the exception of one slip.

The slip was permanently leased to a couple who were on a year-long cruise to the Caribbean and points beyond. The leaseholders had advised the marina owner he could sublet the slip for up to ten months.

Will told the owner he would be in within a couple of hours and was interested in a six-month sublet. The owner was waiting by the dock as Will pulled in. He waved for Will to follow him as he walked around to the extreme north end of the marina.

Will tossed a rope to the owner, and the two of them

docked and secured the boat. "You're Will, I assume. Welcome to the Panther Run Marina. Where you out of?"

Will gave the owner his best good ole boy smile. "Picked the boat up in Miami a few days ago. The owner wanted me to bring her directly to Mobile and find long-term dockage. I'll be here for about a week and then be back and forth."

The owner extended his hand to Will. "I'm Bob Brian. My wife and I own and manage Panther Run."

"Hi, Bob, I'm Will Villa. I'm the U.S. rep for Brussels General Services, Inc. We're a Belgium-owned company just moving into the American Market."

"Nice to meet you, Will. What does your company do?"

"Well, Bob, I'm real new to the company, so I don't know what all we do. Me, personally; I work out of their publication division. Basically I'm what you call a 'ghost writer.' I write books for people who can't write their own. They put their name on the finished product and we cash a big check."

Will continued to relate what he had told his Cuban and Key West friends. "I may leave in the middle of the night and not show up again for months. It's not for everybody, but it suits me. I love to travel and can't tolerate routine."

"Why Mobile, Will? What is the boat going to be used for?"

"Oh, I forgot to tell you that part of the deal. Because I brought a couple of contracts to the table, I negotiated my living expenses.

"My deal with them included free use of the boat. I've always wanted to live on one. They bought the boat, let me live on it for as long as I am employed with them, and when I'm gone, sell it.

"Considering the tax write-off for the boat and slip rental, they'll make out like bandits in the end. It works out well for me, also.

"As soon as I have time, I'll find a small, enclosed boathouse for the company to buy. I'll then move the boat there and the company will be able to write off even more expenses. What a deal, huh?

"First things first, though. The company wants to change the name of the boat. It will help with the tax break. They want to call it BGS America."

"I think I can help you with the boathouse and the name, Will, if you're interested. Why don't I give you some time to get settled in and tomorrow we can talk more about what you need. We can take care of the rental paperwork then, too."

Will double-checked that all shore connections and moorings were secure. After a run through the marina's shower facility, he made himself a meal and took a glass of dark rum on deck.

The stars were out in their full glory and life was good. Will had successfully completed his first solo executive action. He had officially joined the very exclusive *Reader*'s club. At least he assumed it was very exclusive; to his personal knowledge, he was maybe the only member.

Thanks to a piece of absolutely unbelievable luck, he had over $300,000 safely hidden away in offshore accounts and the ownership of a Belgium corporation to smokescreen the whole thing.

People who knew him, which were few in number, might ask, why Mobile? Will, alone, knew the answer. As an orphan, Will had often wondered about his family. There were many questions that had repeatedly flooded his young mind.

Did he even have a family? If so, why had they abandoned him? Did they know he was alive? Did he have brothers? Sisters? Grandparents? Big family? Small family? As to his past and his family, there was only one thing he knew for sure. He had been born in Mobile, Alabama.

His file at the orphanage had not contained much information, almost none about him before the orphanage. It listed William as his only name and Mobile as the location where the orphanage picked him up.

Another question Will had frequently asked himself was, *why should he care? His parents got rid of him. But why? There were plenty of parents who kept, loved, and raised their polio babies. What was different about his situation? There had to be an answer.*

Will knew he was on a fool's errand and would never have any of his questions answered. How could he? He didn't have a clue to his last name. He wouldn't know his family if he sat down with them. No, his was truly a fool's folly.

But then again, why not Mobile. He had to be somewhere. Finding his family was, no doubt, impossible, but at least he had come back home.

...noon the following day

Will was sunning on the deck when Bob walked up. Seeing him, Will stood and stepped down to the dock. "Hey, Bob, ready to get that paperwork done?"

"If you're up for it, let's take a ride first. There's something about a mile from here I'd like to show you."

"Sure, Bob. I'd like to see a little more of Mobile than

the bay."

The two men walked off the dock and up a hill to what was, no doubt, the marina's parking lot. It was well maintained with lights evenly spaced around the asphalt lot. Bob led them to a nice, late model GMC pickup truck.

Bob eased the truck out into the light morning traffic. The street seemed to follow the topography of the bay as it snaked its way farther north.

True to his word, Bob turned about a mile down the street and entered a small gravel parking lot. It was adjacent to a medium-sized commercial building on the water.

"Will, you mentioned your company's desire to buy a boathouse on the bay. This building belongs to my wife and me. Before we bought the marina five years ago, we ran a shrimping operation out of this building.

"As we got older, we knew we'd not be able to keep up the physical requirements of shrimping. The marina was owned by my uncle who kept telling us we couldn't shrimp forever. He was in his 80's and wanted to just sit in the sunshine on his boat and fish.

"We finally decided he was right and bought the marina from him. Even though he gave us a very attractive financial deal, we didn't know anything about running a place like Panther Run and dealing with the boating crowd.

"Because we were so unsure about the whole marina thing, we hung on to our boathouse just in case. Well, here we are a little over five years later, and the marina is doing great. The wife and I have better health than we've had in years, and we love the laid-back marina lifestyle.

"Bottom line, we no longer need this building. When my wife and I were having a beer on our deck last night, I told her about you and your company. I guess you got me off dead center about putting the boathouse on the market when you said you were interested in one.

"My wife agreed we should sell the property and that I should show it to you. So, here we are. I hope you don't think I'm too pushy."

"Pushy, absolutely not. I consider this a personal favor that you show the boathouse to me before you list it with a real estate agent. Let's go inside."

"Thanks, Will, I told my wife you seemed like a very nice young man. I appreciate you making this easy for me."

The boathouse proved to be a good-sized building, quite a bit bigger than it looked from the parking lot. There was a large overhead door which looked extremely sturdy. Bob opened it with a garage door opener. To the left of the overhead door was an entrance door.

Bob pointed at the smaller door as they entered the building. "That door is solid metal in a metal door facing. Won't be any kicking in going on there.

"The overhead door is extra heavy-duty as is the back overhead door, and both are secured in metal frames securely attached to the building's frame. Both can be opened with garage door openers plus each can be locked down from the inside with metal rods and padlocks."

"Very secure, Bob. Why so much security."

"A dock is always an attractive target for thieves. But about four years ago all the owners in this area hired a security company to patrol the area and check our buildings. Haven't had a break-in since. Service costs you $50 a month."

The two men walked farther into the building. As Will examined the open area at the front of the building, he immediately knew his Airstream camper would fit there with room to spare.

Bob pointed back to the front of the building. "There's a large office and bathroom in the bottom space there." He then pointed to a set of stairs leading up to another space above the office. "We built the upstairs several years ago. Sometimes during shrimping season, we didn't have time to go home.

"My wife decided we needed a bedroom and bath that we could use when we needed them. It's really a nice space. My wife insisted it be more like a home bedroom than just a bunk in a warehouse.

"It's one big room about 400 square feet and a large bath with a big shower and the kind of sinks and stuff that a woman wants. Hell, I don't even want to think about what that space cost. And, it's still furnished. Come on, I'll show it and the office to you."

The office space was large with only the necessary business furniture plus a couple of chairs and vinyl-covered sofa. Will figured in the shrimping business, the place would need hosed out occasionally. The office john was pretty much what you would expect in a warehouse/boathouse.

"Opening the door upstairs, Bob waved Will in. "Pretty nice, huh? My wife is a good decorator. Thank goodness most of this was a tax write-off."

To say Will was surprised would be a colossal understatement. Even though furnished in what most would call a minimalist style, the furnishings were all topnotch. The floor was cypress and the walls were painted an off-white shade.

At the end of the room nearest the door and facing a large window overlooking the boathouse interior was a seating arrangement. It was furnished in a masculine style with distressed leather sofa and two matching chairs. No vinyl allowed in here.

A wool area rug and two walnut end tables completed the area. The furniture was arranged to look out into the boathouse.

On the opposite wall was a very efficient-looking kitchen with a small dining table and four chairs. The bed and nightstands were at the far end of the room and separated by a sheer off-white curtain on a rod extending across the room.

Bob had not understated the bathroom adjacent to the bedroom section. It included a double sink enclosed in a cypress vanity. The mirror was beveled around the outside and large enough to service both sinks.

The shower looked big enough for two and had a built-in marble seat. Bob had not lied; this place was nice.

Back downstairs, the rest of the space was devoted to a large boat bay more than large enough to accommodate Will's boat. To Will's surprise, there was also a boatlift incorporated into the bay.

Bob kept up a continuing narrative of the building as they looked around. "The boathouse is constructed on sturdy concrete support walls extending from the bay's bottom and out of the water about three feet with the cypress wood boathouse built on top."

Cypress was a wood native to the area and actually grew in the water. Consequently, it was water and insect resistant. Most of the boathouses on the bay were built using cypress wood. The concrete was an added feature that extended the life of the boathouse for decades.

"I am impressed, Bob. This is exactly what my company is interested in. The mini apartment is really nice; your wife did a great job. I'm afraid it wouldn't be of much interest to my company, though. Our executives won't stay in anything less than a four-star hotel when they come stateside.

"The location on the bay is really a concession to me and my desire to live aboard my boat. Other than that, it shows a physical investment in the area and an address where some of our products can be drop-shipped."

"Yeah, I know Will. When I had the place appraised last year, I was told the room upstairs did not add any value to the boathouse. Even though nice, most buyers would probably not be interested in a premium price because of it.

"So, are you interested in the boathouse itself? It's close to a bunch of restaurants and bars, and downtown isn't really that far.

"Real estate prices in this area dropped 10% last year and will probably keep going down for a couple of years. Boathouses aren't moving well according to the appraiser I hired."

"Damn, Bob, you are way too honest to be selling. Maybe you need a hot-looking blonde in a tight dress doing this for you."

Both men laughed. "I know, Will. I should probably just keep my mouth shut, but whoever buys this place is going to be my neighbor on the bay. I'd feel real bad seeing them all the time if I had pulled some kind of fast deal. Hell, man, life's just too short."

"I can appreciate that, Bob. Neighbors can be around a lifetime. So, how much are you asking? I'm not into haggling like the place is a used car; give me your best price and I'll give you an honest response."

"I like your style, Will. The appraiser said last year that, given its location, the boathouse was worth $103,000. Since

I know there's a lot more of these on the market and the market is soft and getting softer, I'll take $80,000."

"I have to say that sounds fair. With the 10% devaluation of property this year, the current value is about $93,000. You're figuring in another $13,000 continuing devaluation to get to the $80,000 number.

"So, here's what I think my company is willing to pay. I'll tell them I negotiated the price from $103,000 down to $85,000. Let me move my boat immediately with no marina fees and I'll make the phone call."

"Will, you're as bad a buyer as I am a seller. I think you and I are going to be really good neighbors."

The two men shook hands on the deal and headed back to the marina. As with most marinas, there was a payphone on the walkway between the marina's parking lot and docks. Will stopped and made a phone call.

Two weeks later the money had been wired from Brussels General Services, Inc. to Bob's account.

…later

Will knew he would be lucky to get 12 to 15 years out of his "career." It was definitely a young man's game. When the time came to retire, he wanted to live in Mobile, not Miami. His retirement home should be in a place where he had developed a plausible existence spanning many years.

To protect his retirement plans, Will decided he would close down his Miami life and protect his current name at the same time. From now on, he would only use his current name in Mobile.

All future executive actions would be undertaken with another identity. He also would do as many of the assignments as possible without unnecessary people contact. He was, after all, the *Reader*'s long-range man.

There were a lot less moving parts in a job using one shot from a high-powered rifle. Will determined that in any location other than Mobile, he would remain invisible. In Mobile, he would develop a low-key lifestyle.

He would become known to a few people and make a few select friends. He would live a public but private life. To do that, he needed to do a few things.

First, he needed to break the lease on his Miami apartment. He'd fabricate some sort of story for his friends and landlord. Perhaps he was spending so much time in central America he was taking an apartment there. When in Miami on business, he would stay in a hotel.

Second problem: where would he live in Miami under the radar? An obvious answer was to not stay in Miami. In south Florida, there were hundreds of small parks designed to accommodate tourists and their campers.

He would either live in the Airstream and move about once a month to a new location or commute to his farm location.

Problem number three involved the amount of travel time between south Florida and Mobile. The obvious answer was a small Cessna or similar airplane. Of course, a small, extremely fast and agile plane might prove useful for several parts of his life. He'd keep his eyes open.

Chapter 13
Memphis

Will, now Robert Branson, for at least the next couple of weeks, was flying a leased airplane out of Miami headed to Memphis, Tennessee. Any job not within driving distance of Miami was handled these days with rented aircraft.

The plane arrangements were made through an agency front company. As the Agency grew, it became apparent that a large number of personnel and equipment had to be moved around the country and oftentimes now, around the world.

Logistically, it was just easier to start their own aircraft rental and freight shipping company with conveniently located subsidiaries. It had certainly made Will's life easier.

The latest choice for an executive action was a local hood heading an international airfreight company based in Memphis. The company was used as a front for the largest weapons smuggling operation in the southeastern United States.

Mr. Joseph Hadad was a naturalized citizen with family ties in Lebanon and Egypt. He had moved to Memphis as a young teenager to live with his uncle and family. Fifteen years later, he had climbed the criminal ladder from petty street crimes, to strong armed robbery, to helping his uncle run his small-time, drug-smuggling operation.

Joseph enjoyed the profits in the drug-smuggling operation but detested the street level thugs it took to keep the drugs flowing to the junkies in Memphis. There were just too many people who knew what was going on in the business. There had to be a better way to make money.

After his uncle died five years ago, Joseph took over the small criminal empire and started a metamorphosis from drugs to weapons. Using relatives in the Middle East, he began to make contacts around the world.

The transformation of his uncle's business was now complete. He had contacts in Russia, Cuba, China, and Afghanistan where he could secure every conventional weapon desired by his customers. The wars in Africa were especially profitable for his growing criminal empire.

Oftentimes, he made money from both sides in a conflict. By 1971, Hadad was dealing with the Japanese Red Army, the Red Army Faction, the Red Brigade, the IRA, the KKK, the Weathermen, the Democratic Front for the Liberation of Palestine and numerous small countries in Africa, especially the on-going wars in the Congo.

Joseph Hadad lived the good life in Memphis. From his mansion down the road from Elvis' place, he ruled his empire with merciless fervor. No one person in the organization knew all the critical components except Joseph. It was his form of life insurance. The company would dissolve without his constant communications instructing the various components' operations.

Joseph's closely guarded control of the criminal enterprise was also his Achilles Heel. The day he died, so would his business. Sure, all the components would still be in place; but without their grand puppet master, each would eventually wither and die.

Will's assignment was to eliminate the puppet master and thus kill the organization. The show would not go on much longer.

Will banked his small plane to the west and then back to the east as he settled into a landing pattern crossing over West Memphis, Arkansas, and then Old Muddy itself—the mighty Mississippi River. Time to initiate the latest executive action.

This action would be number three for the year. All totaled, it would be number 37, including his first, the car thief/rapist. Most of the actions had been long-range rifle work, with a bomb here and there, with one close-in.

Hopefully, the current action would also be a good, flat-shooting rifle. Surveillance had been mixed in relation to taking out the target. Hadad might require a more creative approach.

Glancing through the plane's windshield, Will could see the light drizzle of rain falling and slightly obscuring his view of the river below. Very quickly, the view of the Mississippi River was replaced with a landscape of high-rise buildings dotting the landscape of downtown Memphis.

Queuing up behind a large passenger jet, Will's plane soon touched down. He taxied to a private hangar where the plane would be refueled and stored until it was needed again.

Waiting for Will in the hangar was a nondescript, white commercial van, his preferred operational vehicle. It was a long wheelbased van with back and side windows darkened to preclude passersby seeing in.

As per his request, the van had an army cot secured to one side behind the driver's seat. Opposite the cot on the opposing van wall was a black, stainless steel chest welded to the floor and secured with a cut-proof, pick-proof lock made by the Snap-It tool company.

Into the chest went a large duffle bag Will had unloaded from the plane. It was his tool kit individually packed with anticipated supplies for the current assignment. He had a Thompson Center rifle with two suppressed barrels, one in 22 Magnum and the other in 7mm Magnum.

Included was a High Standard suppressed 22 LR pistol and shoulder holster. He also had his Browning Hi Power pistol and the Baby Browning 25 pistol. Extra ammo was also included for all firearms.

Explosives included C4 and detonators plus a new type of grenade. The grenade was a type secretly obtained from Holland. It was the size of a golf ball. Designated the V-40 mini grenade, it weighed only 3.5 ounces.

Numerous other items were also included for possible use. The bag and contents, with the exception of the Baby Browning 25 auto pistol, were locked in the chest. The small 25 joined his pocket knife in his front pants pocket.

When in Miami or Mobile not on assignment, Will carried only the knife he had procured from the Miami drug dealer. He did not want to draw any unwanted attention with a full-sized 9mm printing its shape under a shirt.

Will harbored little concern for the type of trouble encountered in a tourist camper park or his ability to deal with it.

An assignment, however, was a different story. He was

on full alert every minute of every day until it was completed. Don't get the wrong idea, though; even in the camper parks, his level of vigilance was very high.

A contractor like Will had to live life on high alert. He never knew when the political winds could shift in D.C. and make his kind of work an embarrassment to the Agency. Such embarrassments were, no doubt, dealt with in a most finite manner.

Will had stuck to his initial plan, though. Since he completed training 5+ years ago, he had not come face-to-face with a fellow employee. Mission supplies and instructions had passed to him according to his plan, not the Agency's.

Will let his hair grow as was the local fashion. He also vacillated back and forth between facial hair and clean shaven. Another characteristic he incorporated into his persona was that of a Cuban refugee with minimal English skills.

If a fellow camper where he was staying started asking questions, Will morphed into his minimalistic English. That had not been much of a problem, though; he had been pretty busy since going operational. Between being on assignment and time in Mobile or trips to his bunker, he probably hadn't spent 30 days in a campground.

As a matter of fact, he was currently negotiating with an older gentleman who had interest in swapping a small airplane for the Airstream trailer. The man's eyesight was rapidly deteriorating and he wouldn't be able to use the plane much longer.

...back to the matter at hand!

Since the Memphis International Airport was located only a few miles from Hadad's mansion, Will decided to do a drive-by and see the place firsthand. The surveillance team had done a good job observing the target's home, business and daily habits.

The mansion was located on a five-acre lot dotted with mature pecan trees and the occasional blooming Magnolia. It was still located in a somewhat nice section of Memphis; but in a few years, it might not be. The location was on HWY 51 as it meandered north through town.

As Will slowly drove by, he studied Hadad's security setup, what he could see of it anyway. The entire property appeared to be surrounded by an eight-foot, black iron fence. The front had thick shrubs on the inside preventing line of sight to the property. The entrance had enough room for a car to turn off the highway and stop in front of the fence.

A speaker was attached to a metal post allowing access without exiting the vehicle. The driver would then request admittance. No doubt, a guardhouse of some sort was out of sight just inside the fence.

Everything Will saw validated the report he had received from the surveillance team. He decided to drive on downtown and check out Hadad's place of business.

Once you got downtown, everything seemed to head down one hill or another toward the river. Hadad's warehouse was on Riverside Drive in a shabby commercial area of rundown businesses.

His warehouse had no identifying signage to guide potential business his direction. If you belonged there, you obviously didn't need a sign. Nothing about the place encouraged drop-in business.

The first thing you saw was a warehouse occupying

maybe 10,000 square feet on each of three stories. The structure was surrounded on three sides by a 12-foot cyclone fence topped with razor wire. The back of the building was bordered by a dock area on the river.

According to Will's information, Hadad didn't store any weapons in the place, so why all the space? Maybe, it was needed in the previous incarnation. Or, maybe there was a part of Hadad's business that was flying under the Agency's radar. Might be worth a look.

Will left the riverfront in search of a downtown parking garage, one with a top deck in proximity to the warehouse, if possible.

The closest he could find was about a mile away on the edge of the downtown retail area. *Well,* he thought, *finding one within rifle range was too much to hope for. He'd just have to find something else.*

Parking the van on a lower level out of the sunlight, Will decided to get a few hours' sleep while he could. He needed to get eyes on the warehouse tonight and observe after hours' activity.

...Four nights later

Will had observed the warehouse for three nights. The routine had varied little. About seven each evening, Hadad could be seen through the fence getting into a dark Lincoln Continental with tinted windows. He was joined by a driver plus one additional bodyguard. Accompanied by a support vehicle of three men in a dark sedan, Hadad left his business.

Getting close to Hadad would be problematic. He took his security very seriously. You could tell a lot about a man's paranoia by how he gunned up just for the ride home.

Will had followed him the first two nights to determine if he went straight home. He had. Again, just as the surveillance team had reported.

It wasn't that Will didn't trust the advance team, but it was his life on the line, not theirs. Check, double-check, and then check again just to make sure. After all, the Dean had pounded into his head that he should trust noone. Will didn't.

Before Hadad left the warehouse each night, a crew of three men arrived for the night shift. Their routine was just that, a routine. Every 90 minutes, one of the men would do a physical walk around the grounds. He would exit the front door and circle the entire warehouse. Time required: about ten minutes. Just like clockwork.

Lights moving through the warehouse at the same time indicated an interior search of the first two floors. Why not floor three, Will wondered?

When not on patrol, lights in a first-floor room indicated where the three men spent the rest of their time. Night after night, the same routine.

On night four, Will decided to breach Hadad's warehouse. The most expedient method appeared to be entrance at the back of the building from the river dock.

Following the shadows along the north side of the building, he soon came to the river. Paying careful attention to the fence as it approached and continued into the water, Will could detect no security alarm devices.

He didn't really expect any external security measures; the river moving by would constantly be forcing all manner of debris against the fence. Security would be used on the exterior of the actual structure concentrating on doors and windows.

Will was dressed all in black as he eased his body around the end of the fence. He effortlessly made the transition to the dock without getting wet. Lying on his stomach, he did a slow crawl to the back of the building.

It contained several entrance points. There was an overhead door on each end of the back wall plus a single-wide entrance door spaced evenly between the two. Adjacent to the smaller door were two sets of double-hung windows.

By using a small, red-lensed flashlight, Will was able to determine the windows were wired to alert any entry attempt. The condition of the wiring indicated the system had probably been in for several years. It had been painted over at least once.

The doors were, no doubt, wired in a similar fashion. No surprise here; Will had expected nothing less. He knew he could attempt to find a method of climbing to a second floor window, but maybe there was an easier way.

Will decided to follow the fence back around to the main entrance door; this time, however, he was on the inside of the fence. The easiest way in seemed the simplest; just walk in through the front door.

Having watched the outside guard over the past several nights, Will knew his routine. It never varied; neither did that of the inside patrol. Both started their patrols by moving from the street side of the warehouse, then working their way to the river side of the building. How convenient for any assassin seeking covert entry. Will smiled at the predictability of the two men.

The nightshift's car was parked adjacent to the front door. Will was barely able to squeeze his body beneath the vehicle. He made it, though, and began to wait. The next patrol wouldn't be for about 80 minutes.

As Will waited, he reviewed what he had witnessed the three previous nights. Each outside patrol had begun with the front door opening and the guard walking straight out and turning toward the river.

This type of guard duty is the most boring work in the world. Every 90 minutes you get up out of your chair, walk out of the room you are in and initiate patrol. If patrol is outside, you must stop each time and turn the alarm off before you exit the building. It must then be reactivated before you go outside, with say a 60-second delay built into the system for just that reason.

Guess what? Most of your run-of-the-mill guards are a tad bit lazy, especially when they are in their third or fourth patrol. They're tired, sleepy, and generally in a "no one has ever tried to break into this place" kind of mood. By then, they disable the alarm and leave it disabled until they reenter the building.

Will was counting on the guards being tired and lazy. Truly a bad combination. He'd find out, that was for sure. Tired and lazy, he'd walk right in; not so tired or lazy, and he'd have to shoot his way out of the compound.

Eighty or so minutes later, Will walked right in and immediately went prone on the floor. It didn't take him long to find the stairs. A minute later and Will was on the third floor.

In about eight minutes, the guards would be back in their break room watching TV, playing cards, shooting craps, or whatever. Will would then have 90 minutes to wander around and see what he could see.

While he waited, Will found a secluded spot behind a pile of discarded wooden shipping pallets. He put his pack down and removed a Starlight Scope. Using ambient light, it allowed the user to see in the dark. Looking through the scope caused everything to take on a ghostly green appearance. It wasn't as good as a light, but it was surely better than darkness.

Thanks to several windows on the third floor, ambient lighting was in bountiful supply. Will would only need the scope when he moved into the darker recesses of the warehouse.

The third floor appeared to be just a storage space for discarded furniture and assorted shipping supplies such as the wooden pallets he was currently concealed behind.

Consulting his watch, Will gave the guards five extra minutes to finish their rounds, then he started his exploration of the third floor. The more he moved through the space, the more he began to think the third floor held nothing of interest.

As he made his way through an unusually large pile of what looked like worthless junk, Will had to ask himself why anyone would keep such a pile of junk. The part of his brain that usually provided him with possible answers to such questions spurred another thought instead.

Maybe the almost unnavigable mountain of refuse was just a "beard" used to disguise something of great value but very undesirable for the police to find. Could it be weapons for the southern U.S. homegrown terrorists? The horde of militia groups operating in south Florida alone was a big enough market of potential customers to keep Hadad in Kibbe and cabbage rolls for a lifetime.

Or maybe it was a large cache of money. When the Dean had explained the action early, he had said to be careful. An arms business required storage and availability to large amounts of cash.

The weapons business, after all, was a cash business. It took cash to secure weapons and also to make payoffs to local officials. The large amount of cash coming in had to be securely stored until it could be moved offshore or domestically laundered.

It was almost as if the Dean were pointing Will toward a large stash of money. Telling Will to be careful was not something he usually did prior to a mission. Will was trained to be careful.

An early conversation with the Dean popped back into his mind. The Dean had informed him that if he came into contact with cash in the course of an assignment, he should take it. He told Will to build as large a cache of cash as possible. The day would, no doubt, come when he would need to disappear. An effective disappearance took money and a lot of it.

Entering and searching the warehouse was not a necessary part of this assignment. Will had no intention of eliminating Hadad close up; he was more interested in the cleanliness of a one-shot, one-kill type scenario.

Will brought his attention back to the present; he'd have time later to psychoanalyze the Dean's parting comment.

As Will examined the mountain of trash seemingly piled against a back wall with no windows, his wilderness training came back to him in a flash.

The instructor taught him that there were always trails through what might appear to be an impenetrable tangle of thorns, vines, brush and trees. Always look for the small indications of animal travel. Where they passed, possibly you could too.

Will backed away a short distance and carefully studied

the biggest pile of trash in the area. Looking through the Starlight Scope, he examined it in great detail.

He discovered that by moving a couple of larger pieces of construction refuse, he could navigate the trash behind them and move rather easily toward the wall.

The cleverly hidden trail led Will to a corner where it abruptly ended. The entrance to the hidden room was just as cleverly disguised as the urban game/criminal trail had been.

As Will stood looking at the wall, he could find no indications of a hidden door; no scratch marks from opening such a door were visible on the floor. The only thing that seemed somewhat out-of-place was a large, upright Coca-Cola machine.

The machine was very old and rusted with little paint left. It obviously had no value, so why go to the trouble of hauling the thing up to the third floor? Will tried opening the door of the machine; it was locked.

Now, Will's curiosity was really peaked. Taking his red-lensed flashlight, he began to examine the machine and the wall behind it. There were no obvious wires or booby-traps.

Will carefully tried to ease the Coca-Cola machine away from the wall; it would not budge. He smiled to himself. It was very securely attached to the wall behind it.

Using the small light again, Will examined the machine's door lock. It appeared to be newer than the machine itself. Removing one of his latex gloves, he wiped the lock with his finger. He brought the finger to his nose where he caught a faint scent of lubricant.

It took less than a minute to defeat the rudimentary lock. The room's security was more about stealth than locks.

Will eased the well-lubricated door open about 1/32 of an inch. Once again, a careful examination revealed no alarm wires or booby-traps. Opening the door enough to squeeze through, he stepped into a space extending the full length of the outer wall and about 10 feet in width.

The small flashlight revealed floor to ceiling shelves on both walls extending almost the full length of the space. Occupying the wall directly opposite the secret entrance was a heavy-duty workbench built against the wall. It was probably 10-12 feet long.

Beside the workbench was an old, heavy-duty metal safe reminiscent of those stand-alone vaults still found in some older banks. Will knew he would be able to open it in less than five minutes. He had done it before.

Working his way down the cavernous length of the secret room, Will felt he was in a military armory. There was crate after crate of M-16 assault rifles such as those used in Vietnam. He also found 45 caliber handguns, shotguns, grenades, LAW rockets, and copious amounts of C4 and assorted detonators. On the very back end wall, he found two crates of Claymore mines.

Will was glad he had decided to breach the warehouse. The weaponry he discovered would put a lot of innocent people in peril. After seeing it, there was no way he was going to just put a bullet in Hadad's head and walk away. This place had to be destroyed.

Leaving everything untouched, Will reversed his steps and carefully closed and locked the Coca-Cola machine door. A short time later, he had retreated from the warehouse and was once again parked in the downtown parking garage.

Since arriving in Memphis, he had parked each night in the garage and slept on his cot in the van. He decided to get a few hours' sleep then give the situation more thought when he was rested.

Early the next day, Will left the garage and drove to a nearby Wafflehouse Restaurant. After ordering a large breakfast, he examined his current situation. First and foremost, he needed to kill Hadad. Secondly, he needed to destroy the weapons cache.

If Will didn't destroy the weapons, he knew there were enough armaments in the warehouse to turn the Southeastern United States into a war zone. He needed a plan which would achieve both needs.

Will spent the rest of the day working out his plan as he shadowed Hadad to make sure he wasn't leaving town and would be home tonight.

By seven o'clock in the evening, Hadad had been safely delivered home and Will was on his way to the parking garage. He had picked up some food and would catch a few hours of sleep before heading back to the warehouse.

...a few hours later

Will observed the security routine until 2 am to insure there had been no changes. Once again, as the outside guard exited the building, he entered and made his way to the third floor. He was carrying a large military rucksack filled with necessary supplies.

At the top of the stairs, Will rigged a trip wire attached to one of the small grenades he carried. On his first trip into the warehouse, he had located the freight elevator. It had not appeared operational, but he attached another booby-trap just in case. He didn't want anyone slipping up on him in the secret room.

The safe, as expected, was not hard to open. Will never

ceased to be amazed by people like Hadad who trusted a 30-year-old safe, because *they don't make them like that anymore.*

In Hadad's defense, though, he did have three armed guards in the building at all times. And the safe was very well hidden. The average person, such as a burglar, would never find it.

Will expected to find a large amount of cash, but not what he found. There were stacks and stacks of bound 100 dollar bills. With each bundle containing $10,000, he estimated the cache of money to be in the neighborhood of four million dollars.

Based on the Dean's advice and the fact he had pointed Will toward the cash, Will had brought the large rucksack with the intention of replacing the used supplies with cash. He hadn't counted on so much cash, though.

A million dollars in hundred dollar bills weighs about 22 pounds. Humping almost 90 pounds of money out of the warehouse was not on his agenda.

Will quickly replaced the supplies in his rucksack with 44 pounds of cash. Greed could kill a man; Will had no intention of dying trying to lug all the cash out of the building.

Will searched the safe thoroughly. There was an inventory of available armaments stored in the safe room. Also stored in the safe were some personal items belonging to Hadad. There were deeds for several properties including the warehouse. Will checked everything he could see. Before preparing the safe for Hadad, though, he made one last check.

Everything in view had been checked. The only area of the safe not visible was the facing of the safe around the door. Using his hand, Will felt carefully around the space. In the right corner, pushed into the safe's lining, he found a small red notebook about 3 by 5 inches in size.

Will opened the small notebook and used his small flashlight to read its contents. Inside was a list of all Hadad's clients, contact information, plus dates and amounts of all sales. It also contained locations for three other weapons' storage sites in the U.S.

Will added the notebook to his rucksack. Knowing the location of three weapon caches might be useful information at some time in the future.

After the last conversation with the Dean, Will's gut had been sending him subliminal messages. There had been something about the Dean's conversation; it was slower and he paused more than usual, as if he wanted Will to really concentrate on what was going on.

The Dean had been trying to convey something to Will without really saying it. The Agency was led by politicians, not career agents. When politics were involved, the winds of change could alter direction overnight.

Will's gut was telling him change was afoot, and it probably wasn't going to be favorable. He needed to be more cautious than he ever had before. And he had better be prepared to disappear.

As Will had been thinking, he had also been rigging the safe for Hadad's next visit, a visit Will intended to orchestrate in about an hour.

First, Will "borrowed" some C4 from the safe room's supply. He replaced the money he had taken with ten pounds of the explosive. Next, he placed a Claymore mine directly in front of the safe's door and rigged the trip wire to trigger the explosion directly into Hadad's face as he opened the door.

Will then dropped several blocks of the explosive into the space behind the safe. He wanted the entire room to explode when the safe was opened.

Given the amount of ordinance in the room, the entire floor would be destroyed. The ensuing fire should be hot enough to take out the rest of the building. The whole warehouse would be fully engulfed before the fire department could get there.

Destruction and injuries would be confined to the warehouse and fenced property. No innocents would be out and about this time of the morning.

With the building wired to explode, Will had to get out of the building safely yet somehow trigger the intruder alarms. He decided he had tempted fate enough with his "follow the guard in and out routine." He needed a fresh way of vacating the place.

Will worked his way out of the safe room after leaving the place in a state of chaos. He had dumped ordinance on the floor and even drug some out the secret door, which he left ajar. These, he left haphazardly on the floor as if the intruder had dropped them on the way out.

Even though he had created quite a mess, he had done it very quietly. Will then made his way to the river-facing wall. He had been correct in his assumption that the upper floor windows were not protected by the alarm.

Using a small pry-bar he had brought along for the purpose, he went to work on the window. It had not been opened in years and thus resisted his effort with great vigor. Will finally prevailed and worked it fully open.

Looking around, he found a ten-foot length of iron piping. To that he attached 40 feet of climbing rope he had brought along. Bracing the long pipe against the much smaller window opening gave Will the necessary anchor to repel down to the ground.

Once on the ground, he dropped two grenades and a block of C4 from the safe room. He was creating the impression of a hurried getaway by the intruder. Will also left the rope hanging from the third floor opening. The guard would walk right into it.

Will made his way around the outside of the warehouse's fence and quickly moved toward his van a short distance away. He'd been in the warehouse for 50 minutes. Things should get interesting in about 40 minutes.

…inside the warehouse

The three guards were well into a serious poker game. The pot was growing, with numerous dollar bills showing. They used a one dollar limit on raises to keep everything friendly. A large pot hardly had more than ten dollars in it.

Charlie, Joe, and Mike liked their jobs. They always made their patrols on the exact schedule set up by Mr. Hadad. The money was great and most nights were spent playing cards or watching ballgames.

The three men had been with the boss for over a decade and were very loyal. He trusted them to do their jobs and keep their mouths shut about the business. All had been criminals since they were old enough to see over the steering wheel of a car as they stole it.

They knew the real business of the company but didn't care. People died everyday with or without the weapons. Who cared if a few more were added to the list? The money and lifestyle were great.

As the time rolled around for the next patrol, Mike and Joe pushed back from the table. Joe pointed his finger at Charlie. "Don't steal any of my money, asshole; I know exactly how much I have."

Charlie responded with a middle finger salute. "Why should I steal it? You practically give it to me anyway."

All the men laughed as Joe and Mike left the room. Joe turned and started his two floor patrol. Mike disabled the door alarm and stepped into the parking lot and turned toward the river for his patrol.

Each of the men carried a walkie-talkie to provide communication. Charlie served as a back-up and also manned a walkie-talkie. Usually, there was little communication required.

Charlie was stealing two dollars from Joe's stack of ones when his walkie-talkie abruptly came to life. "Charlie! Charlie, come in! I found something on the river side! Come in! Come in!"

Charlie almost dropped his walkie-talkie as he jumped to respond. "Charlie here; go, Mike, what did you find?"

"There's a rope hanging out of the third floor window. And I found some stuff on the ground. Better get out here!"

Charlie quickly contacted Joe and told him to get back to the front door and keep watch. Joe had heard the earlier communication and was already on the move. "I'm on my way, Charlie."

Charlie was on the move as he listened to Joe's response. It didn't take him long to reach Mike's location.

Mike had his flashlight trained on the ground with one hand and his gun in the other. Charlie yelled at Mike when a few yards away. "Mike, I'm coming around." He also had a gun in one hand and a flashlight in the other.

"Charlie, look what I found on the ground." Mike flashed his light on the grenades and C4. He then pointed to the rope and up to the third floor window.

Charlie glanced down at the stuff on the ground, then glanced up the rope. "I'll be damned."

Mike was as surprised as Charlie. "I wonder how he got up there?"

As Charlie was bringing the walkie-talkie to his mouth, he glanced over at Mike. "We can discuss that later; right now, we need to call Mr. Hadad.

"Joe, get on the phone and call the boss; tell him we've had a break-in on the third floor and he might want to get over here."

Joe was more than a little nervous as one of the house guards woke Mr. Hadad and handed him the phone. "It's Joe at the warehouse; there's some kind of trouble."

Hadad sleepily took the phone and yawning, placed it to his ear. "What's wrong? One of you jerkoffs set off the alarm again?"

Joe's voice revealed his level of anxiety as he spoke. "Mr. Hadad, we've had a break-in on the third floor."

"We've had a what?"

"We've had a break-in on the third floor. Mike found a rope hanging out a third floor window just a few minutes ago. There was some of our third floor stuff lying on the ground, too. Looks like the guy dropped it when he hit the ground."

"What kind of stuff we talking about, Joe?"

"It was some grenades and C4, Mr. Hadad. We just now found it. Whoever did it is gone. We know we don't go to the third floor without you so Charlie told me to call. It ain't even been five minutes since Mike found the rope."

"I'll be there in 20 minutes. In the meantime, one of you numbnuts check everything inside the fence. One of you stay by the rope, and the third one by the front door. Kill anything that moves! Understand!"

"Yes, Sir!"

Hadad threw the phone to his guard. "Wake up the guys sleeping and bring the car around. We're heading to the warehouse. There's been a break-in.

"Tell all the guys we're going in heavy; no telling what we'll find. I want every man with an M16.

"Now, get going. I'll be downstairs in five minutes. I want everybody gunned up and ready to go."

…back at the warehouse

Mike was on the front door, Joe at the rope, and Charlie was making a careful and thorough search of all grounds inside the fence. So far, nothing unusual to find.

Will was secluded behind a bin of garbage about 75 feet across the street and south of the front gate. What few outside lights present at the warehouse were on, and he could see one of the men guarding the front door and another sweeping the open ground around the building. He figured the third man was around by the open window and rope.

Since there was no effort to reenter the building, Will figured the three guards were waiting for Hadad and reinforcements to arrive prior to clearing the building in search of intruders.

With his knapsack on his back, Will headed for his van parked a block south of the warehouse and secreted behind a small auto repair shop. He needed to put the knapsack and its contents in the van and return with his rifle.

The rifle was a backup to his primary plan. If Hadad somehow escaped the explosion, Will would take him exiting the warehouse. A Browning High Power 9mm pistol would be his backup.

The backup to his backup guns was an M72 LAW Rocket he had brought out of the warehouse. Will intended for Hadad, most of his crew, and all the armaments to vanish into the inferno he had planned for them. Within the hour, he planned on being back at the private hangar and within two hours, leaving Memphis International Airport on his flight back to Miami.

Will returned to the garbage bin across from the warehouse. He assembled the T/C Rifle and leaned it against the back of the garbage bin. It was joined by the LAW.

The M72 LAW (*Light Anti-Tank Weapon*) is a portable, one-shot 66mm unguided anti-tank weapon. The LAW rocket is very easy to prep for action. It is constructed containing a tube within a tube. When the inner tube is telescoped outward toward the rear of the outer tube, the trigger is exposed and pretty much ready for firing.

Will hoped he wouldn't have to go so far as to arm the rocket. If so, his plan had failed.

He intended for the warehouse explosion to take care of Hadad and crew. If for some reason Hadad escaped the explosion and made it back to the warehouse gate, the LAW would seriously interfere with any further progress.

Will knew over preparation was preferred to under preparation. Hope for the best; plan for the worst; and live to see another day.

Will much preferred a one-shot kill to explosives because a bullet eliminated the chance for disastrous collateral damage. Sometimes, however, like this assignment, sniping was not the most expedient choice.

And, collateral damage was not a big issue with the planned demise of Hadad. The warehouse had no close neighbors, and this time of the morning pretty much insured no innocent citizens would be in the blast zone.

…Welcome to work, Mr. Hadad

Because of almost nonexistent traffic this time of the morning, Hadad and his five minions came rolling up to the gate in record time.

Mike hustled across the parking lot as he saw the two vehicles approaching. He was able to unlock and swing the gate open, allowing the small caravan to roll through at a fast speed.

Heavy dust was released from the lot's gravel surface as the two cars both came to screeching halts adjacent to the warehouse's front entrance. Car doors immediately sprung open and five gunners exited and formed a half-circle in front of Hadad's car door.

The irate crime boss was out the door immediately and moving rapidly to the front door as Charlie ran up. "Mr. Hadad, I've searched all the grounds inside the fence; nothing looks out of place. Joe's around by the rope hanging from the window. No movement since we called."

Even under the faint lights of the warehouse, the redness of the boss' face was clear as day, as was his expression. It was a dangerous mixture of anger and unadulterated fear. "Charlie, you come with us; leave Mike and Joe where they are."

Nodding to his driver, Hadad pointed at the front door.

"Once we enter, you clear the first floor."

Pointing to one of his gunners he held out his hand. "Let me have your handgun. And when we get inside, you go to the second floor and clear it. The rest of us will go immediately to the third floor.

"You other two join us as soon as you clear your floors. Joe, make sure nobody gets out the front door. Now, let's move."

With Joe holding the door open, Charlie led the men inside. With one peeling off, the group quickly gained the second floor where another man separated. Still led by Charlie, the remaining four gunners and Hadad made their way to the top floor.

Since Will had removed the two booby-traps on the stairway and elevator before exiting, the group made their way safely beyond the stairs and stopped.

Hadad sent two of the gunners to clear the top floor as Charlie led the remainder of the group toward the hidden room. Hadad remained just behind them.

Charlie held up his hand signaling the group to stop. Moving carefully through the trash and toward the secret door, he stopped and bent down. Straightening up, he motioned for the group to advance.

Hadad had moved up to join Charlie. "What you got?"

Charlie pointed to the floor. "A rifle and a block of C4 on the floor. The door to the armory is open. I'll move inside and check it out. Wait for me here."

He moved carefully through the armory/secret room door. In less than a minute he was back at the door motioning the group inside. By then the four men clearing the floors had joined them.

Hadad instructed two of them to stand guard outside the

room. Led by Hadad, the remaining men made their way into the room.

"It's hard to see in here, Charlie. Flip on the lights so we can get a better look." Charlie had been using his flashlight to check out the room.

Charlie stepped to the door and hit a switch. The room was flooded with light. "Everything's a mess, Boss, but it don't look like all that much is missing. Something must have spooked the guy. It don't look like he messed with the safe. Kinda weird, if you ask me."

Hadad had moved to the center of the room where he could see down its length. His expression was much more relaxed now that he could see the untouched safe. "How is it possible someone knew exactly where to come and find the secret space? It's almost like they knew precisely where the room was and what was in it.

"Smells fishy to me; got to be an inside job. How else could the guy know where stuff was? Exactly nine of us know about this room. No one other than us is allowed on the third floor.

"We're going to have to have a little discussion about this. Until we do, nobody leaves this warehouse.

"Now, all of you— outside the room! Wait for me right outside. When I'm through in here, we're heading downstairs and get the other two guys. Then we're going to get to the bottom of this.

"Now get out and close the door." Without exception, all the men had fear etched on their faces. Eyeing each other, they followed their boss' instructions.

Once the door was closed, Hadad stepped over to the safe. He was sure the safe had not been tampered with. No marks or any sign reassured him. Plus, this whole thing seemed to be the work of some nervous wannabe who didn't know the combination. He'd sort that out in a little while, though.

Right now, as was his habit, he'd double-check the safe. Spinning the dial back and forth between the three-number combination, Hadad reached for the door's handle.

…back at the garbage bin

Will had been watching the warehouse since the group of men had entered. The guy guarding the front door was nervously pacing back and forth. He was clutching the gun in his right hand and had quickly raised it to a firing position three different times. He had, no doubt, reacted to unknown noises.

According to his internal clock, Will figured the men had been inside a little less than ten minutes. It was about time for the excitement to begin.

Taking out a pair of earplugs, Will ducked down behind the garbage bin and inserted the plugs. He had no sooner gotten the second plug in his ear, then he sensed more than saw a brightness appear in the early morning darkness.

Almost immediately, Will felt the ground quake and heard the deafening sound of the explosion. He raised his head to a view of hell on earth.

The initial detonation had vaporized the warehouse roof directly above the armory. The rest of the roof quickly came apart and fell inward and downward destroying the second floor.

Secondary explosions of ordinance threw flames into the air as the second floor crashed to the first. Additional explosions occurred as chemicals and gases stored on the first floor added their synergistic effect to the blistering destruction.

The initial destruction took out the guard by the door and set ablaze the three vehicles occupying the close-in section of the parking lot. The guy around by the rope might have survived, but it was unlikely.

While standing out of sight behind the garbage bin, Will broke down the T/C rifle. Walking away with his rifle and LAW Rocket, he never looked back.

He knew he was safe and it would take days, if not weeks, if ever, to determine what had caused such a destructive fire.

…back at Memphis International

Will pulled the van into the private hangar where he had left the plane. All remaining supplies were loaded into the large duffle bag with which he had arrived. The LAW Rocket was included and, with the knapsack of money, was loaded into the plane.

The next 30 minutes were spent sanitizing the van and any area of the hangar where he had been. Satisfied he had left nothing behind to connect him to Memphis or the fiery explosion, Will proceeded to a designated runway and departed. He had filed a flight plan for a small commercial airport outside Denton, Texas.

By mid-morning, Will was setting down in Texas. While the plane was being refueled, he called the Dean.

"Hello, Will, I got word earlier this morning of a horrible explosion and fire in Memphis. It seems the owner, a Mr. Hadad, and several of his employees were presumed lost in the tragedy.

"You seem to be developing a liking for things that go boom. I'm not questioning your plan; I'm just curious why you chose that method on this assignment."

"Bad intelligence, Sir. While surveilling the warehouse in anticipation of an ambush site, I discovered a hidden armory capable of supplying weapons and explosives to most of the southeastern U.S.

"I thought it a good idea to insure said supply never happened; thus, the explosive plan. Don't be too hard on the advance team, though; the hidden room containing the armory would have been very difficult to find."

The Dean was frowning into the phone. "Difficult or not, it is very disappointing the intelligence was incomplete. An agent less skilled than you would probably not have discovered the armory.

"Well done, Will. Now, I want you to fly the plane to Corpus Christi, Texas. At the airport, you'll be directed to a private aviation service company owned by Wade Johnson.

"Wade is not associated with the Agency. He'll service your plane and give it a new paint job. He'll also change its identification numbers and give you the ownership papers in your Will Villa cover name.

"Keep the plane and use it as you see fit. Consider it a bonus for a job well done. Your current Will Villa identification is still secure. Other than me, no one else knows it exists.

"Lately, I have been under considerable pressure to identify you by cover name and location. Will, you are the only *Reader* left.

"Leadership at the Agency has changed and I am sensing a desire to eliminate and cover up projects such as ours. If certain people knew what we really do, a number of important people would have serious problems.

"I want you to leave Miami and find a secure location elsewhere. Any future business you need to conduct in Miami must be extremely covert and invisible to anyone searching. Also, change your appearance as much as possible.

"It has been several years since anyone from the Agency has seen you, so I may be somewhat paranoid. Especially since you have, no doubt, changed quite a bit because of simple maturing.

"The only people who would have even a remote chance of identifying you are your last set of trainers. If you happen to encounter one of them, do not, and I repeat, do not initiate contact. Leave the area immediately and contact me as soon as you can thereafter.

"I know this is a lot to digest. Just trust me and disappear. Contact me again in one month. Use the alternate number I gave you. Good bye, Will; stay safe."

The line went dead.

Flying out of Denton, Will flew southeast toward Corpus Christi on the Gulf of Mexico. Flying the Cessna 414 he had been using, the trip was less than two hours.

Will loved the Cessna 414: it had twin engines and could be handled by one person. With a maximum speed of 270 mph and a range of about 1,500 miles, the plane could transport up to eight passengers comfortably. Quite a bonus for the Memphis job!

The private aviation service company owned by Wade Johnson proved easy to find. It was the biggest such company at the airport and occupied two large hangar areas.

After taxiing to one of the hangars bearing the larger than life name of the company, Will secured the plane and went into the office. A man in the neighborhood of 60 years old approached him as he entered. "Hi, Will, I'm Wade Johnson; I told the girls out front to keep an eye out for a Cessna 414. They buzzed me when you were taxiing up to the hangar. Come on back to my office."

Will had shaken Wade Johnson's hand upon entering the office but had only smiled as the older man had talked. He followed him back to a very large and luxurious office.

Looking around the office, Will redirected his attention to Mr. Johnson. "Aviation services must be a very good business, Mr. Johnson. You have some very beautiful furnishings in here, not to mention those half-dozen very beautiful women hanging around outside the hangar. Since they all have your company name on their tee shirts and the back of their shorts, I figured they must work for you."

Mr. Johnson let out a belly laugh and slapped his knee in amusement. "First of all, Will, call me Wade. Second, those six lovely ladies do work for me, but it's not what you think. Ninety percent of all the customers coming through my business are men.

"Men like to see pretty girls, especially after being cooped up in a small plane for hours. The girls clean the plane's windshield, deliver food and anything else ordered for the plane, and in a pinch, even refuel. They earn their money, that's for sure.

"You're a pilot, Will; would you rather land and see those pretty faces or a bunch of ugly guys in greasy coveralls?"

"I get your point, Wade; the girls are a part of your promotional plan. And in answer to your query, yes, I'd rather see the pretty girls. Greasy guys in coveralls have never been my thing."

Both men laughed as the small talk continued. Wade was trying to get a feel for Will just as Will was of him. To conduct their particular form of business, they had to have a basic level of trust.

Will was, at one level, trusting his life to Wade; Wade, at another level, was trusting his business reputation and future to Will. A few minutes spent in small talk getting to know each other were obviously a good investment for both men.

"You're a lot younger than I thought you'd be, Will. When our mutual friend said you were a young colleague of his, I had you pictured as fortyish or so. You haven't seen thirty yet; have you?"

"No, Sir, I haven't; I'm still a few years short. I hope that isn't a problem."

"No, Will, it isn't at all. Our friend said I could trust you, and I've not often heard him give that kind of absolute endorsement over the years. He's very fond of you, and your safety is very important to him."

"Thank you, Wade; he also trusts you. May I ask if you know our friend professionally or in some other capacity?"

"You want to know if I work for the same agency the two of you do. That's a fair question. The answer is no, I don't work for the Agency and never have.

"Many years ago, I shared a foxhole with our friend. A friendship forged within the horrors of war is like no other; we're closer than brothers. After the war, we kept in touch and from time to time have done each other favors.

"I don't know what is going on in the Agency, but it's big. Big enough to cause our friend to cover his ass and yours. He told me he needed for you to disappear and in a fashion where you'd never be found."

"But, what about him, Wade? Is he going to disappear

also?"

"I doubt he'll run, Will. He's in his 60's, just like me. It takes a lot of energy to run and survive. He is sure you'll make it; you're young and according to our friend, extremely bright with unparalleled skills in your profession.

"They may take him down, Will, but he won't go meekly; he'll take a lot of those SOB's with him. With that said, I know he would never ask for help and probably wouldn't appreciate any interference, but there is something you can do.

"Maybe you could keep an eye on him from a distance and make sure none of those bastards sneak up on him when he's not looking. A good, flat-shooting rifle, with a set of young eyes, might just make all the difference in whatever he has planned."

"I can do that, Wade, and I will do it. If you give me his home address and any private contact information you have, I'll leave as soon as you make the changes to my plane. How long will it take?"

"Depends on what you want beyond what our friend requested."

"There are a couple of things I'd like. First, I would like to have half the seats removed and replaced with a bench type sofa big enough to sleep on. Second, I'd like a false wall installed in the cargo area so I can hide certain tools of my trade. Are these two things possible?"

"Yes, neither is a big problem. As a matter of fact, you'd be surprised at the number of planes flying around with secret compartments in them. The most time-consuming part of the job will be prepping the plane for new paint. And I also thought I'd do a complete inspection of the engine and make any needed repairs. Even pushing it as much as possible, it'll take 30 days."

"I don't think I can wait that long, Wade. It sounds like our friend might need help sooner as opposed to later."

"I agree, Will. What if I give you a loaner plane? I have access to a small private hangar at an airport just outside D.C. Because a big chunk of my business is in and around Washington, I've had the hangar for several years.

"I can call the airport manager right now and tell him you're coming. What kind of transport do you need?"

"Works for me, Wade. I need a small white van for transport. Before I leave, though, I need secure storage for some things I need to leave here. Can you help with that?"

"Would an 8' by 12' secure space in a bonded security company work? My cousin owns the place; all I have to do is call."

"That's great, Wade. If you'll point me toward the place and move the metal storage box from my plane to the loaner, I'll be back as soon as possible."

Since Wade's cousin had been waiting for him at the front entrance to the secure storage facility, things had gone very quickly there.

Two hours later, Will had securely stored his knapsack of money with the security company and was at cruising altitude on a direct heading back east to the D.C. area airport.

Chapter 14
RIP Dean

Virginia had not changed much during the five plus years Will had been operational. Even though Will had been raised and trained in Virginia, it did not really feel like home. It hadn't felt like home when he was growing up there nor when he was being trained there. It was just a place.

He knew his real home was Mobile, Alabama, even though he had spent very little time there as a child. For the past several years, he had been spending most of his downtime in Mobile trying to find some connection to his past.

So far, he had no luck reconnecting, but what could he really expect? He knew he had been born there and he knew his first name, but that was all. The reality was he would probably never know more. With no last name and no way to discover it, he'd have to be content with just living there.

At least he knew the name of the city where he was born.

Most of the kids in the orphanage where he grew up didn't even know that. He was luckier than many.

The airport was small and private with not a lot of activity. Taxiing up to the hangar area, Will was directed to a small hangar at the extreme southern end of the airport. The door was up and a small white van was sitting outside.

Will transferred the large metal box to the van then made arrangements with the airport manager to have the plane refueled and parked inside the hangar. Will had been given a key and assured everything would be done and the hangar locked.

On the outskirts of Reston, Will spotted a full-service motorcycle dealership. It didn't take long to buy a used machine in excellent shape plus necessary accessories including a small, lightweight loading ramp for the van.

Will had spent considerable time in the D.C. area during training and knew its traffic could be a nightmare. That was the reason for the bike. If you didn't mind angry looks and obnoxious horn blowing, you could weave in and out of traffic as you shadowed somebody in a car.

Wade had given Will the Dean's home address along with a different contact number than the Dean had given him. On the flight north from Texas, Will had decided to stake out the Dean's house as a way to pick up his trail. After that, he would keep a loose tail on the Dean. The bike would prove the perfect vehicle for following a man who was probably trying not to be followed.

The Dean's house was located outside of Washington, D.C., in an undeveloped, extremely isolated area of small farms and heavily wooded areas. When checking the address out on an area map, Will saw there were at least three major county roads leading into and out of the area.

He could only imagine the number of small roads coming into and exiting out of the immediate area.

The Dean had chosen his homesite well. Will had little doubt the acreage, home, and outbuildings were well protected by cameras and electronic warning systems. He had been taught to defeat such devices, but no doubt the Dean would know a few tricks that weren't common knowledge.

To get to the Dean's property, Will had ridden his new motorbike. It was a nice piece of equipment equally suited for the road or back country. He figured he would need both attributes.

Arriving just before sundown, Will had left the bike on the opposite side of a wooded area bordering the Dean's place. Traveling light with only a silenced High Standard 22 pistol, knife, night vision scope, several non-lethal restraints, and a small first aid kit, it still took over an hour to make his way across the wooded patch of ground.

As he quietly moved to within 20 yards of the wood's edge, he went to the ground and remained motionless. Will's scanning had detected the sound of crunching grass, probably less than 10 yards ahead and off to the left.

He was not the only person out and about in the woods. Someone had shifted position in an attempt to get more comfortable. Ordinarily, a trained sniper would not move, regardless of the discomfort.

Whoever was there, however, probably thought it was no big deal. Will felt there was little chance the Dean was home this early in the evening. The unknown person lurking ahead of him probably felt the same. Better to get into a more comfortable position while he could.

The presence of a second entity in the woods created a

dilemma for Will. Was the person a guard protecting this area of the grounds for the Dean, or was he a sniper looking for the opportunity to remove an obstacle from somebody's path?

Much to Will's surprise, the person quietly stood up and made his way toward Will's position. The only possible reason for such a move had to be an answer to the call of nature.

This was positive proof to Will the Dean had not yet arrived. He lay perfectly still as the person moved his way. Will smiled to himself; better lucky than good. Of course he was also very good, but luck made life easier.

Luckily, even snipers had to go occasionally. In a true combat or other critical situation, one would simply go without moving. A very uncomfortable option if the person had to stay in place for any length of time. It could also get smelly.

Just as Will was beginning to think the guy was going to step on him, he stopped and turned his back to Will. The minuscule sound of a zipper and subsequent rustle of fabric barely broke the wooded silence.

Before the sound of urine hitting the leaves stopped, Will silently rose behind the man. Because of his height, Will was able to lift the very surprised sniper off the ground in a viselike chokehold.

Once his adversary quit struggling, Will held him a few seconds longer to ensure he was really unconscious and not playing possum. He then quietly lowered the man to the ground.

Using the small flashlight he always carried, he quickly examined the man's face. Much to his surprise, it was his very own sniper training instructor, Mr. Bell. Will's dilemma was increased by this revelation.

He really liked and respected Mr. Bell; he certainly didn't want to kill him. But what if Bell had been sent to kill the Dean? Will couldn't allow him to go unscathed and have him come after the Dean later. A true conundrum, problem, dilemma—whatever word you chose.

A creative option was required. Will had several things in his small pack that could restrain without being lethal. He removed two of them, duct tape and superglue.

Again using the miniature light, Will located a small diameter tree, one he could get Bell's arms around. First, he used the tape to wrap Bell's fingers together rendering them useless for picking at the tape.

He then secured his arms around the diameter of the tree. His legs also went around the tree and were securely taped. Superglue was used to glue his eyes and lips shut. It would take a visit to a hospital to get the glue safely removed.

One last thing remained to be done. Will hated to do it, but Bell had to be taken out of action in a fashion that would keep him sidelined for two or three months.

If Bell were an innocent on security over-watch duty, he would fully recover. Even if he were there to do the Dean harm, it was probably an order from higher up. Whatever his reason, Will was not going to kill him, not when he had another option.

He reached in his front pocket and removed the knife he had lifted from a drug dealer years before. Kneeling on the ground and opening the knife one-handed, he used his other hand to hold the left leg of Bell's pants. The action was repeated on the other pants lag.

With a quick motion behind each ankle, Will severed both Achilles tendons. He quickly used superglue on each tendon to stop the bleeding. Then he administered a healthy dose of morphine to keep Bell asleep and comfortable if he woke.

As he was seeing to Bell's continued existence above ground, Will was thinking to himself. *If I were a true sociopath, I'd just have killed him; it would have been easier.* Somehow, that thought made him feel better.

With Bell out of action for the foreseeable future, Will still had a dilemma; were there others located around the perimeter of the property? If so, the Dean was still in danger.

His only option seemed to be complete withdrawal from the property and then make contact with the Dean ASAP. That was easier said than done, however.

Thanks to Wade, though, Will now had two telephone numbers with which to contact the Dean. With any luck, maybe one was a pager number. He decided to go on that assumption.

An hour later, he was at the closest store with an outside pay phone. Not wanting to appear clandestine in his actions, he parked the bike close by the phone booth and went into the store. Buying a Coke, he took his change and casually wandered back to the phone and called the number provided by Wade.

To Will's pleasure, the number yielded a pager messenger service. He left the number of the pay phone and the words, "Urgent you call, Wade."

He did not leave his own name in case others were monitoring the pager service. Will sat sideways on his bike's seat and waited. It didn't take long.

Will answered the phone on its first ring. "Hello."

"This doesn't sound like Wade, tell me who you are or I

hang up."

"If I were a crossword puzzle, I'd be a six-letter word describing somebody you might find in a library."

The Dean spoke with humor evident in his voice. "What a surprise, my favorite young *Reader*. I hadn't expected to hear from you for several more weeks. May I assume this is some sort of emergency?"

"I hope so, Sir, or someone is going to be extremely pissed at me. Please excuse my street-type utterance. I've been without intelligent banter for a while."

"That's alright, son. I am, after all, the one who is responsible for your current environs. It appears you are currently somewhat closer. May I inquire where? And don't worry about this call; it's secure and made from a small café on my way home."

Will told him.

The Dean responded. "I'm headed home now. The pay phone where you are is only about three miles from me. I'll be there in less than ten minutes. I'm driving a two-door, black Continental."

The phone went dead and Will hung up his receiver. The Dean arrived in a little more than five minutes. Cars like his were built for speed in a very comfortable package.

Expecting to follow the Continental upon its arrival, Will had his bike idling and ready to go as the Dean completed a U-turn through the parking lot of the small store. As he accelerated once back on the asphalt, Will was right behind.

The two quickly ate up the highway for several miles before the Dean turned left on a gravel road, accelerated and went a couple more miles before turning on what looked like a somewhat maintained dirt track. A mile or so down the dirt road, he pulled his car behind a small stand of trees.

Will followed.

Will dismounted his bike and walked quickly to the car. He opened the door and offered his hand to the Dean who was having some difficulty getting out. "May I help you out, Sir?"

"Yes, thank you, Will. As you can no doubt see, my body has experienced considerable deterioration since we last were face-to-face. I'll explain that later. But first, what are you doing here?"

"I'm here, Sir, because Wade is under the impression you are in danger. He asked me if I could help you. So, I left my plane with him to be modified, borrowed another plane from him, and here I am."

"I really wish you and my good friend Wade had stayed out of this mess. With that said, I am very glad to see you. May I assume there is nothing I can say to get you back in that airplane and fly south?"

"You may assume that, Sir. May I assume you are in serious trouble, and in no physical condition to carry out any necessary direct action?"

The Dean looked up at his favorite trainee. He knew Will viewed him as the father he had never known. Having never married and not having any children of his own, he had to admit he often thought of Will as his own.

Will had been so young when he came under the Dean's control, how could anyone not assume they had a strong psychological connection, much like that of father and son? The Dean had, after all, performed all the fatherly duties.

He protected and sheltered Will when he was too young to care for himself. He had seen to a top-notch education for the young orphan, and when it came time, he guided Will toward a career.

He had to admit, though, the career guiding thing might not hold fatherly water. Not many fathers would guide their sons toward a career as government killer.

It was now a moot point, however. The <u>R</u>edacted <u>E</u>xecutive <u>A</u>ction <u>D</u>irective had been cancelled. Will was the only *Reader* remaining alive. To make things worse, the Dean had been ordered to send a kill team and change that particular status.

"Will, the *Reader* Program has been deactivated by the Agency's Director. All files pertaining to its existence, all executive actions taken, and any personnel records, have been ordered destroyed. Since I was the program administrator, all the aforementioned were in my possession. They have been destroyed; no records of the program exist in any form.

"The final program removal directive was to have the remaining *Readers* eliminated. I reported to the Director that the final directive was moot. The last *Reader* had not reported back after the Hadad action. I told him it was likely you got trapped in the explosion and not made it out.

"He doesn't believe me, but I really don't care. It's not hard to extrapolate the next move after all field personnel are eliminated. The only thing keeping me alive is the Director's belief that I have been lying to him, which of course, I have."

"But why cancel the program, Sir? And then cancel the field agents? I can't begin to calculate the amount of time and money the Agency has in my training. All my executive actions have been sterile, with no connection to the Agency. I'm a ghost; not even you know how to find me."

"Ah ha, grasshopper, therein lies the bureaucratic rub and, for the moment, my life insurance policy. The Director knows I received a call after the Hadad action. I told him it was another agent, not a *Reader*.

"The Director is under the mistaken impression there are two of you left. I told him that was not the real situation.

"I have consciously not kept them up-to-date, them being the Director and his Assistant Director of Operations. At this point, they really don't know what to believe.

"The *Reader* Program is as dark as you can get in the Agency. It was not a matter of record other than what I had, and I have destroyed those records. The only physical aspects of the program that remain are you and me.

"I was chosen to head the program once it became operational for two reasons: my knowledge of those chosen for operational status and my age. Will, a program like this doesn't last forever; hell, it's lucky if it lasts five years.

"Agency Directors come and go. With them programs do the same. The impetus for the program's demise is a result of the very same. Changes are in the wind.

"Usually an outgoing Director will cancel dark programs like ours and personnel are transferred out or leave the Agency through natural attrition such as retirement. The new Director then comes in to a new slate of employees.

"If what we do were public knowledge, all those affiliated with the program could be prosecuted and sent to prison or worse. That's why knowledge of a program such as the *Readers* is so tightly controlled."

"What about all the instructors, Sir? Don't they know?"

"No, Will, they don't; they train dozens of agents every year. The Agency is huge, with agents all around the globe. A trainer's job is hard enough without trying to figure out where every individual trainee will end up."

Will was still not totally sure of what was going on, but

he had a strong feeling. "So, is all this associated with a change in Agency leadership? If so, why is this so different from other similar situations requiring all personnel be eliminated?"

"The stakes are exponentially higher this time, Will. The Director is in secret negotiations with the leading upcoming presidential candidate to be placed on the ballot in the number two spot. When that happens, he will be replaced in the Agency by his number two, the Assistant Director of Operations.

"It's just a matter of 'cover your ass' politics. Bury anything that can hurt you with the voters. If information about the *Readers* were to be leaked, the Director would not make the Presidential ticket, the Assistant Director would not become the Director, and their little house of straw would be burned to the ground. So, in their minds, we must go, and by that I mean go permanently, as in dead."

"Well, Sir, hating to be the one to state the obvious, but it sounds like two well-placed bullets would solve all our problems. You could go quietly into retirement and I could disappear back into the fog from whence I came. No muss, no fuss."

"As much as I would like to sic you on these two assholes, I don't want it to happen like that. If I do, the Agency will send massive resources into the field on a search and destroy mission to avenge their leaders. No, when they die, everything dies with them, including the one who killed them."

Will's face expressed the enigma of the Dean's statement. "Knowing you, considerable thought has gone into a solution. What can I do to help?"

"Before I explain my plan for this, there are a couple of

things you need to know. Time is of the utmost importance in this plan. I was beginning to think I wouldn't be able to pull this off in time until you showed up. Now I think we just might make it.

"Will, I'm dying; the doctors gave me six months to live seven months ago. So you see, I'm living on borrowed time, as the saying goes. The doctors now say I could go at any time. The cancer has already metastasized beyond the point of death for most people. They are stymied by my continued breathing. There seems to be no explanation other than sheer determination on my part."

Will's sadness was very evident as the tears formed in his eyes. "Sir, I am so sorry. In my naivety, I never imagined you wouldn't be around for the next 30 years. Are you in pain; what may I do to ease it?"

"What you can do, Will, is help me rid the Agency of these two arrogant, self-centered egomaniacs. I'm dead; that's a given. It's important for you to completely accept that fact. I am going to die and it won't be long. Once you accept my death, we can move forward. Can you do that?"

Taking a deep breath, Will pushed the Dean's death to the back of his mind; he would deal with the loss later. "Yes, I can, Sir; what is it you need done first?"

"First, I need for you to remove a certain squatter who has been occupying a sniper hide in the woods just south of my main house. He has been there for two days now. My motion detectors have been beeping in that quadrant since he arrived. He's just waiting for a clean shot."

"No problem, Sir; he has been neutralized already. When I arrived this evening, I decided to provide a little sniper oversight of your place until I got a feel for what was going on. I ran across our friend in the woods. Because he knew no one was at home yet, he got a little lazy."

"Did you kill him? If you did, I understand, but whomever was sent was probably fed a line about me selling information or something. He was just following orders."

"Relax, Sir, he's alive but will probably be out of action for a couple of months. When I identified his presence, I didn't know if he was sent to guard you or kill you. So, I decided on a less lethal course of action."

"Did you recognize him? Not that it matters much, but it could give me an indication of what level of personnel they feel comfortable using."

"Yes, Sir, I did. It was Mr. Bell, the sniper instructor from my advanced training."

The Dean could not help but smile. "Well, I see the student has become the teacher and the teacher the student. With precocious students, it's inevitable; it usually takes longer, though."

Both the men laughed. "What did you do to him, Will?" Will told him.

The Dean then spent the next 20 minutes explaining what he had in store for his other Agency colleagues.

As the two men started to say their goodbyes, the Dean put his hand on Will's shoulder. "Will, I'm very fond of you and don't want you to waste your life doing what I have done. When tonight is over, I want you to get back to Texas as quickly as possible, pick up your plane, and fly away.

"Your Will Villa identity is solid; stick with it. Find you a nice girl, settle down, and never mention this part of your life to anybody."

As Will digested the Dean's advice, he noticed the Dean writing something.

"Here, Will; this is a Swiss bank account and password.

There's enough money in the account for a very comfortable life. Don't get extravagant with your lifestyle, though. Buy a small business, something to justify income. Live well, but not too much so."

Will didn't know what to say. "Sir, I…"

"Don't say anything, Will, just promise me you'll leave this life behind. Be happy and get the family you've never had. That's all I ask. Goodbye, Will."

…As Indians say, "The Dean had planned a good death."

Everything was planned and since Will had shown up, the Dean decided to implement the plan that night. After all, he might not have another 24 hours.

The Dean proved to be not only a meticulous planner but also skilled in plan execution. One final phone call set everything into motion.

At midnight, two large black vans made their way to the rural home of the Dean. Moving cautiously, they rolled to a stop and waited. The grounds were ablaze with light emanating from half a dozen large lights mounted on high poles placed strategically around the house and outbuildings.

The occupants were instructed to show up at midnight sharp in dark colored vans. Instructions specified four occupants in one van, two in the other. They were told to exit the vans upon arrival and wait five minutes. All occupants had to be known to the Dean.

At the five minute mark, the two occupants from that van started to move toward the woods south of the house. The other four men waited.

Shortly, the two men returned from the woods carrying Mr. Bell between them. After he was carefully placed in the van, they drove away to find medical assistance for the sniper instructor.

Once the first van was out of sight, the four men standing outside the second van dispersed. One headed for the barn; two headed for the house; and the fourth swept the grounds.

As the man entered the barn, the Dean spoke from the shadows. "Hey, Marty, it's me. I'm sure you were told to search the barn and make sure I'm alone. Please do that now, but at no time are you to get closer than 30 feet from where I'm standing. Do you understand?"

"Yes, Sir, I do."

Ten minutes later, all four men were once again standing by the van. A short, wiry-looking man took the lead. "Rich, you and Marty secure the back door. Remember, no one in. Rick, you and me got the front."

The small leader of the group then brought a handheld radio to his mouth. "All's clear here, Sir. We've cleared the grounds, house, and barn. Come on up." ·

Within minutes, a black Towncar made its way up the drive and stopped. The two agents opened both front doors for the Director and his Assistant. Getting out warily, they looked around and then back at the small, wiry man. The Director was looking closely at the barn. "You sure there's nobody here but us and him?"

"Yes, I'm sure. I've got two men on the backdoor and the two of us are going to secure the front. If anything happens, we're in there immediately."

The Director and Assistant Director turned and started for the barn's entrance. The large barn doors were closed so they directed their attention to a small one standing open.

The Assistant Director, Tony Glen, carefully opened the door and took a quick look inside. The Director, Shawn

Gleason, had instructed him to enter first and make sure the Dean was there. He was.

The Dean was standing in the middle of the barn by a makeshift table which appeared to be merely an old door laid atop a rectangle of hay bales. The table was empty except for a thin file folder and a Browning High Power semiauto handgun.

Keeping his eye on the gun, the Assistant Director motioned with his hand for the Director to come into the barn.

The Director noticed the gun immediately. "What's with the gun? I thought this was going to be a friendly farewell meeting."

"Oh, it is. The gun is just to keep us honest. Feel free to put your gun on the table. Just one of you, though; let's keep everything equitable."

"Tony, you're the one with the gun. Put it on the table when you sit down. That way, when we sit down, we'll just be well-armed friends sitting down for a chat."

The Dean motioned to the three chairs placed at the table. Let's take a seat. The two CIA directors sat across from him. Both CIA men were looking at the folder in front of the Dean.

Noticing their interest, the Dean took the folder in his right hand. "This is what you two guys came for. In this folder you'll find the current names of the two operatives in question, their current locations, basic descriptions, and contact methodology.

"Before I give you the folder, I need you to call the four men outside and tell them to back off. They need to wait at the entrance to my property. That's a half mile from the barn.

"Once you get the folder, I'm leaving through the back door of the barn and disappearing into the woods. Follow at your own risk. Before you do, however, remember what I did to your man in my woods.

"If I can do that to the Agency's best sniper, guess what I'll do to those you brought along tonight. Not one of them has been in the field in ten years."

…back in the woods

Will was situated in the woods with a mobile device monitoring the Dean's motion detectors spread throughout the property. There had been no activity detected.

The Dean's phone call issuing final directions, including the sniper in the woods, had put the Agency on notice. Obviously, electronic observation devices were in use.

There was not enough time to find another sniper and get him inserted. They'd just have to trust the Dean. Knowing him as both men did, they knew that could be bad juju.

Will was located in the edge of the woods directly in line with the small door and about 40 yards away from the barn. Immediately on the other side of the door was the makeshift table.

In his hands was a LAW rocket, extended and ready to fire. Will was glancing at his watch. The Dean had asked him to wait five minutes after the guards withdrew, and then move to the back of the building and shoot the rocket through the back door.

The reason the Dean was glad to see Will was the difficulty in detonating an excessively large amount of C4 explosive. C4 was not real easy to explode. It typically required a detonator or small explosion to create the big bang.

The Dean had a really big bang planned. The makeshift table the three men were currently occupying had a secret. The hay bales holding up the table were only one layer thick. The remaining space under the table was packed with explosives. He had several pounds of C4 plus anything else he had that went boom.

Using a timer was not precise enough for the Dean. What if the men entered after the timer was set, then one or more left? That wouldn't work anymore than a handheld detonator. What if the men noticed it? A bullet fired from his handgun wasn't much better. It might not penetrate the barrier hiding the C4.

No, those were too iffy; he needed human judgement in the equation. The Dean wanted the explosion to happen with them sitting at the table. His most talented recruit would take care of the issue.

Will knew there was going to be one hell of a bang. When he and the Dean were deciding the most expeditious method of igniting the explosives, they decided a LAW rocket was just the ticket.

The Dean informed Will of his explosive cache under the table. In addition to C4, there were grenades, three LAW rockets, several thousand rounds of ammunition, and numerous ignition devices.

Will had seen the explosive material when they were getting a LAW for him to use. "Damn, Sir, there's enough boom, boom stuff here to level the barn and probably your house next door."

"Yes, there is, Will; so make sure you're far enough into the woods to protect yourself. I'd also recommend you stuff something into your ears and wear sunglasses. It's going to be loud and bright. The flash will be bright enough to induce temporary blindness."

As Will glanced again at his watch, the Dean was looking at his; 10 seconds to his nirvana. Smiling at the two men across the table, he slid the folder over.

Director Gleason intercepted the sliding folder and opened it. "What the hell…"

He never finished the question. Just as his hand was stopping the sliding folder, Will's finger was squeezing the LAW's trigger.

He had not allowed himself time to dwell on what he was doing. If he had, he probably would have had trouble squeezing the trigger. The Dean was the closest thing to family he had ever had. Now, he was about to kill him. Maybe he really was a sociopath.

Deep in his heart, though, Will knew he was doing the right thing. The Dean was living on borrowed time and wanted to accomplish something of note with his death.

The Agency he had devoted his entire adult life to was being used to further political agendas as opposed to helping keep the country safe. The fact the Dean was still alive, against all doctors' opinions, was a testament to his desire to remove the political cancer eating away his beloved agency.

What better way to enter the afterlife than by taking two arrogant political assholes with you. And to put icing on the cake, the person sending them on their way was a young man of whom he was very fond.

The life of an Agency lifer was often a lonely life. The ones who chose to marry and have a family hardly ever were successful in the endeavor. Usually, their families paid a high price for daddy's chosen profession.

The Dean had decided early on in his career to forego the

marriage route and spare some decent woman and potential kids the heartache. Thus, a recruit like Will, who came into your life at an early age, often became the son you never had.

These were the thoughts going on in the Dean's head as the rocket's blistering presence became his last conscious awareness. He died with a smile on his face and the satisfaction that his agency would live on.

Chapter 15
Doppelgänger

After the trip to Virginia, Will had flown back to Texas and spent a few weeks waiting for his plane's work to be completed. He and Wade had spent a great deal of time talking about the Dean and helping each other through the grieving process.

Later, after picking up the money left in secure storage and saying goodbye to Wade, Will filed a flight plan for the Caymans. He had a little banking to take care of.

The flight to the Caymans was very pleasurable for Will. The new plane was a dream to fly. The engine had been rebuilt and the interior modified to Will's specifications.

The money was secreted in the furtive compartment in the baggage storage area along with his weapons and a couple other items. The interior space of the plane was designed to seat eight people; Will had that reduced to zero. Initially, he had told Wade to leave a few seats but had reconsidered.

He didn't anticipate transporting a group of people so the space was now used for a small living area. Even though he intended to keep his promise to the Dean to get out of Agency business, old habits would probably die hard.

Will always felt the most exposed when in a rented motel room. With the new configuration of his Cessna, he had a place to sleep and a small lounging space.

With the small toilet and shower that had been installed by the previous owner, Will felt he could fly anywhere he chose and have a comfortable place to stay when he got there.

The new accommodations allowed him to never be farther from escaping an emergency than a short takeoff. He could then go anywhere his plane's 1500+ mile range would take him.

Right now, that was the Caymans for a little banking and a few days on the beach.

...The Cayman Islands

The plane had performed flawlessly on the flight southeast. The flight was 1200+ miles and about six hours flight time. Because of the Cayman's location south of Cuba, Will had to be careful to avoid Cuba's airspace. No big deal, really; just fly a little farther south before turning east.

The Cayman Islands, originally named 'caiman' by Sir Francis Drake, had started to develop its reputation as an international banking center in the early 1960's and had prospered since.

Its main attraction was pretty much a total absence of taxes and, of course, privacy. Because of its close proximity to the United States, a Cayman bank was often the first stop in the movement of money offshore, much like what Will was doing.

After landing in George Town on Grand Cayman, Will ordered fuel for his plane. While the fuel truck did its thing, he arranged for hangar space with 24-hour access.

Will paid for the fuel and five days' rent on the hangar space. He then rented an open-topped jeep and headed for the bank, money in a large knapsack.

As the Cayman's banking industry grew and started creating a positive international reputation, it was making a move to eliminate large cash deposits. Luckily for Will, that particular policy was not yet in effect at his bank.

Because he had been in the bank on numerous occasions, Will's deposit went effortlessly. He then wired most of the deposited funds to one of his European accounts.

The account set up by the Agency would be left as is. He would never use it again. The $10,000 in the account would be left. Will knew the account was private and, without the password he had established for it, could not be accessed.

But in his mind, better safe than sorry. It was, after all, the only link he had to the Agency. Even though improbable, it would never be used against him.

Will then asked for the use of a phone in a private location. First, he called his attorney in Miami and cancelled the pending trade of his Airstream camper. With his acquisition of the Cessna, he no longer needed the small plane.

Will also made arrangements to transfer the ownership of the Cessna to his Brussels Corporation. He wanted no assets in his name. Even though he believed what the Dean had told him about the security of his name, it never hurt to continue his habits of invisibility.

The last thing Will requested was for Conny, his lawyer, to wait two weeks, then dispose of two vehicles and his Airstream which were all in his storage facility. That left only the van and some supplies, which were also there. He'd be picking them up personally in a few days.

After this, Will would no longer have any connection to Miami, with the exception of his lawyer and answering service.

The next call was to the Dean's Swiss bank. Using the password he had been given, he checked the balance.

"Holy shit" were the words that slipped through his lips. The Dean had obviously been putting away money in the account most of his career.

With the Dean's money and his own, Will would never have to work another day in his life. If his identity were ever compromised, he could simply get in his plane and fly away. With a 1,500-mile range, the Cessna was his greatest insurance policy.

Feeling completely free of any encumbrances for the first time in his life, Will decided to ignore his caution about rented rooms and celebrate a bit.

Dialing the extension of the banker with whom he always worked, he asked if the bank could recommend a nice hotel on Seven Mile Beach and possibly reserve a suite for the next five days.

The banker was more than happy to accommodate Will's request. A secretary showed up shortly with the pertinent reservation information.

Will drove the rented jeep a short distance to the hotel. It was smaller than expected and well-guarded.

As Will approached the front entrance, a well-dressed

doorman appeared as if by magic. He was very polite and had a world-class smile on his face. It was obvious, however, Will would not be allowed entrance without conversation.

The man spoke with a British accent. "Good day, Sir. May I be of assistance?"

This was obviously not your run-of-the-mill beach hotel. Will decided to put forth his best persona. "Yes, thank you for asking. I'm Will Villa; I have a suite reserved for five nights."

"Why, of course, Mr. Villa. I was informed you were on your way. Welcome to the Sir Barker. May I attend to your luggage?"

"No, thank you; it's in my plane at the airport. I'll get it later. This was a spur-of-the-moment decision. It's so beautiful here, I decided to take a mini-vacation and catch a little sun."

The doorman escorted Will inside and transferred his service to an equally impressive bellman with a similar accent. Will was soon in his suite gazing out a wall of windows at the panoramic view of Seven Mile Beach and the adjoining ocean.

Will was tired from his flight and also hungry. The room service menu occupied a prominent position on the small dining table sited by the window. He ordered a meal then headed to the bathroom for a quick shower.

...A good meal and six hours of sleep later

It was early evening by the time Will ventured out. His first stop was the airport and his plane. He was going to need more clothing.

An hour later, Will was once again walking out of the Sir Barker. This time, though, he was in fresh clothing and once again hungry.

Before leaving he had stopped at the Concierge's desk and inquired about restaurants on the beach. He was told there was an excellent nightly seafood buffet about a mile down the beach.

The suggestion proved to be an excellent one. The buffet was on the beach side of a large four-star hotel. Will stood in a small queue waiting to be seated.

He immediately scanned the dining area for points of exit as he had been trained to do. In addition to scanning for exits, he cast an eye over the crowd in a non-conspicuous manner.

Both exercises were probably moot with his newly found freedom, but as he had surmised earlier, old habits die hard.

About a third of the way across the large outdoor dining area sat two very attractive young ladies, both of whom were staring at him and smiling.

Just then the maître de caught Will's attention. He was a young man about Will's age. "I see you caught the attention of those ladies. They're in here a couple of times a week. They're airline stewardesses and fly in regularly. Want me to seat you by them? Might get lucky."

Will looked at the man smiling at him. "Uh, no thanks. I'm at the end of a long day of flying. Maybe later; I'll be here for a few days."

Laughing under his breath, the man directed Will to a table close to the buffet yet still within sight of the young women. "Suit yourself, but if you change your mind, they're still checking you out."

Will sat down with his back purposely toward the

women. It wasn't that he didn't like women; he did. It was just that in his newfound role in life, he needed to proceed cautiously until he developed more of a comfort zone.

A waiter soon approached Will and inquired as to whether he wanted to eat from the buffet or order from a menu. He also inquired about a drink request.

Will chose the buffet and ordered a dark rum on the rocks in deference to his Cuban surname. "I'll be right back with your drink, Sir; please proceed to the buffet at your leisure. Please take your time. Here on Grand Cayman, we're never in a hurry."

Looking around at the crowd and then out to the ocean, Will sensed movement behind him. Fighting the reactions beaten into him by the Agency, he turned very casually. Walking behind him and now standing at his table were the two women.

Just as the waiter returned with his rum, one of the women spoke. "Hi, may we join you?"

Will had to put his brain into overdrive. If he refused them, he would, no doubt, draw attention. After all, what young single man would decline? Even if the man were married, it would still be rude to decline the friendly young ladies.

Will stood and extended his hand toward two empty seats. He displayed his most award-winning smile just as any man would, no doubt, do under the circumstances. "Please, have a seat."

The waiter stood, waiting for Will to help the women sit down. "Your drink, Sir. Would you ladies like something?"

Before the women could respond, Will graciously waved his hand at them. "Please bring these two beautiful women anything they want."

The women were obviously used to such gallant behavior from men and did not hesitate to order. "We'll have two virgin margaritas."

The two women were both probably in their young twenties and radiated youthful exuberance. One was very blonde with big blue eyes, and the other, mirror opposite. She had dark hair and piercing eyes, almost black in color.

The dark-haired girl was staring intently at Will as the waiter left to get their drinks. "If you're wondering about the virgin drinks, we're flying out in three hours. We're stewardesses so no drinki-drinki before work.

Staring even more intently and positioning her face so Will could see her more clearly in the soft light, the dark-haired girl spoke with a questioning look on her face. "Justin, don't you remember me? I know it's been a couple of years, but I recognized you as soon as you walked up to the line earlier."

Will looked closely at the beautiful young girl; he knew for a fact he had never seen her before in his life. "Who do you think I am?"

The girl laughed. "You asshole, quit jerking me around. I'm Maggie Sumpter from Mobile, Alabama, and you're Justin Boché. You dated my sister for three years in high school. I've seen you a thousand times and you've seen me just as much."

Will was totally flabbergasted and it must have shown on his face. His subconscious registered the importance of this, but his conscious mind was spinning too quickly to process the information. All he could do was issue a stammered response. "Well, I uh, uh…"

"Okay, shithead, enough is enough. You're Justin Boché from Mobile. You're 25 years old. You and my sister broke up when you were drafted and sent to Viet Nam. You came back, went to Auburn and got a degree in accounting. You still live in Mobile last I heard. Now fess up and quit kidding around."

Will had regained his composure by now and subconscious and conscious minds had synced. He realized this serendipitous encounter was important. Making a special effort, Will replaced the confused look on his face with one of playful intent.

Reaching into his hip pocket, he removed his wallet and placed it in front of the girl. "Well, they, whoever they are, say everyone has a doppelgänger somewhere in the world. I am, no doubt, Justin's."

The blonde girl responded for the first time. "A what?"

"A doppelgänger," Will repeated. "You know, a twin, double, look-alike."

Will turned to the other girl and motioned to the wallet. "Open my wallet and check out the driver's license."

The dark-haired girl picked up the wallet and removed the license. "It says you are Wilbert Villa and are 27 years old. It's an Alabama driver's license."

She stared at Will with a combination of shock and embarrassment. "I am so embarrassed. You look just like Justin; y'all could be twins. The only difference is he's two years younger than you. This license is real? You're not still messing with me?"

About that time, the waiter arrived with the women's drinks. The dark-haired girl took a big gulp from the virgin drink as if it really contained alcohol.

Will held his hands up in the universal sign of defeat. "I promise you; I'm telling the truth. I'm Will Villa, a Cuban born in Miami and raised in the Washington, D.C., area...."

He related his made up biography complete with the cultural incursion into Little Havana. "You know the really weird thing about all this, though? I live in Mobile and have for several years. I travel a lot because of my job, but my employer transferred me to Mobile a few years ago to provide a corporate presence.

"I own a boathouse on the bay where I keep my boat. I live in an apartment upstairs in the boathouse when I'm in town."

The dark-haired girl laughed out loud. "Here I am quizzing you, and we haven't even formally introduced ourselves. As I so rudely blurted out earlier, I'm Maggie Sumpter from Mobile, Alabama, and this is Susie Miller from Grand Junction, Colorado."

Will playfully nodded at the girls and replied, "Nice to finally meet you."

Maggie jumped right back into the conversation. Like many Southerners, she wasn't shy about asking questions. "So, where exactly on the bay is your boathouse?"

"It's up toward the north end. If you've heard of the Panther Run Marina, my boathouse is just north of there."

"So, you're a ghost writer who travels a lot? You live in Mobile, but aren't there much?"

"That's right, Maggie, at least it was. I'm tired of the years of travel. Getting in my plane and flying to some country and holding up in a hotel for six to eight weeks getting the information I need for a book is not as glamorous as it sounds. As a matter of fact, it's not glamorous at all.

"I just recently moved to a new position in the company. Since I started the corporation's athlete ghost-writing genre, it has grown into a major cash source for the company. We now have seven writers plus me doing it.

"Therein lies my move. The corporation has created a ghost athlete division, and I'm becoming its first dedicated editor.

"I'll no longer travel; the writers will fly into Mobile with their draft manuscripts and hold up in a hotel while I edit and help them structure the final product.

"Hell, who knows; I might actually stay in town enough to meet my twin. Wouldn't that be something?"

The two young women were enjoying their drinks and hanging on Will's every word. Will decided to proceed cautiously and pull a little more information from Maggie. "So, Maggie, this twin of mine is named Justin Boché. What kind of name is Boché? Sounds like an ethnic slur or something."

Maggie was quick with a response. "Justin is from a Cajun family, so I guess it's French."

"So, are there a lot of people named Boché in Mobile?"

Maggie stopped to concentrate. "You know, I don't think so. The only ones I ever knew of was Justin, his mama and daddy and his grandparents. They're obviously a bunch of Cajuns in Mobile, but not named Boché."

The three of them spent the next hour and a half enjoying the buffet and getting to know each other better. Maggie promised to contact Will the next time she was in Mobile. He said he would really like that.

It was dark by the time Will left the restaurant and headed back to the Sir Barker. Walking along the beach deeply in thought, he categorized the evening as one emanating from the mind of Alfred Hitchcock or some similar writer. It truly was stranger than fiction.

Will had been trained over the years to never accept coincidences. Actions coming together in such random fashions were hardly ever random.

He could not believe it was just a coincidence there was a man his age living in Mobile who just happened to be a mirror image of himself. No, that was not random; there had to be more to it, more information to find.

Well, he had wondered what he would do with all his free time in Mobile; now he knew. Somewhere, his doppelgänger existed in Mobile. It shouldn't be that hard to find him.

Will spent the next couple of days doing the things a young single man on vacation might do. He spent time on the beach, drove all over the island, went scuba diving and spent the evenings at the restaurant from his first night.

Because of its proximity to Cuba, Will was not surprised to find a couple of Cuban bars. Even though he was only faux Cuban, he had grown to like the culture and the people.

Will figured being a fake Cuban was better than being an unknown nothing without roots or culture of one's own. So, with those type thoughts in his head, the fourth night on the island brought a change of routine.

The place he chose to eat and have a drink was the Café Cuba. When inquiring at the hotel, he was told it had a reputation for excellent authentic food but had been the location for numerous altercations among the patrons.

The very proper British staff of the Sir Barker had strongly suggested he forego such an establishment and choose something along Seven Mile Beach. Will naturally ignored their advice.

Café Cuba was located on a section of waterfront not likely to draw your everyday flower shirt and Bermuda-wearing tourists. It reminded him of his chosen watering hole in Key West.

Viewing Café Cuba from the outside, you could see it extended onto the water, with the building supported by large treated wooden pilings. Walking into the bar, Will, as always, scanned for exits.

Two exits were very evident. First was obviously the door through which he had entered. The second was the open deck portion of the bar extending over the water. It would be a risky exit at best since it would involve jumping into the unknown waters below.

Just beyond the bar and to the right was the swinging doors leading into the kitchen. No doubt there would be at least one exit through them.

The inside of the restaurant appeared clean and uncluttered. Tables were generously spaced with ample walking room between. Will estimated about half the tables inside the place were occupied; the deck appeared more crowded.

Walking up to the bar, Will caught the attention of one of two bartenders. Speaking in Spanish, he inquired about a table on the deck. He received a positive response and headed that way.

Walking through the inside diners, Will drew admiring glances from several young Latino women; Cubans, he surmised.

Stepping onto the deck, he was intercepted by a middle-aged waitress and directed to a small table located in the back left corner adjacent to the deck's rail.

He sat with his back to the corner facing the front. All in all, not a bad strategic seat. If a person of ill intent came at him, it would have to be a direct frontal attack.

On the opposite side of the deck was a small space for musicians and an adjoining dance area capable of handling a half dozen couples. Obviously, Café Cuba was more about drinking and eating.

Will felt very comfortable in the restaurant and started his evening with a dark rum on the rocks. After the better part of an hour just relaxing to the music, he ordered a hearty Cuban meal and a beer.

By the time Will finished eating, the inside of the restaurant had mostly cleared out. It had been occupied primarily by families who headed home after their meals.

The deck, if anything, had become more crowded with a rowdier crowd seemingly more interested in drinking and listening to music. Three couples were currently on the dance floor showing off their footwork to the beat of a lively Latin tune.

Will's table had been cleared and he was enjoying an after-dinner cup of coffee. He'd have to relay to the Sir Barker staff how pleasant his evening had been.

During the entire evening in Café Cuba, Will had not heard a single word of English, only Cuban Spanish. It was just that kind of place.

Much to his waitress' pleasure, Will had left a very generous tip. He smiled at her and received a smile in return as he moved from his table across the deck toward the front of the establishment.

It was about then he heard the first words of English. "You call this weak-assed, Mexican Donkey piss beer? We told you to give us beer, not this low-grade crap."

The gifted linguist uttering his evaluation of the beer was one of a trio of very large, very rough-looking men standing at the bar. Both bartenders had moved to the section of the bar occupied by the men.

Given the accent bouncing around the room, the trio of

complainers were Irish, no doubt seaman on one of the many ships arriving daily to keep the island stocked with food, liquor, and whatever.

Will was ignoring the three men as he passed on his way to the front door. The biggest and loudest of the three, however, was not ignoring Will.

Stepping up to Will with a bottle of Cuban beer in his hand, he extended it to him. "Here you go, buddy; tell us how you like this horse piss." All three men laughed.

The bartenders looked on with concern. "Please, do not annoy the young man; I will provide you with a different kind of beer. Maybe an American Budweiser?"

The man turned his head toward the bartender. "The only thing I can think of worse than this Mexican beer is American beer."

The man turned his attention back to Will. "I asked you if you liked this piss."

Will held the man's stare long enough to make the other man nervous. "First of all, it isn't Mexican beer, it's Cuban. And secondly, yes, I think it is an excellent beer."

Smirking at Will, the man winked at his buddies. "What you know? An English-speaking Mexican."

Will stared at him again. "You're not very smart, are you? The beer is Cuban, just as most of the patrons, including myself, are. Why don't you guys take your business elsewhere?"

The man winked at his friends again. He turned and raised the beer bottle to pour it on Will. "I'll show you elsewhere."

Will knew exactly what the man had planned. Before any beer had made its way onto Will, he struck the Irishmen with a six-inch jab just below his Adam's apple. Using the extended second knuckle of his middle finger, he had suddenly made it very difficult for the large Irish man to breath.

Falling to the floor holding his neck, the man was desperately struggling for his breath. His efforts could be heard all throughout the restaurant.

Turning to face the two remaining men, he pointed at the man on the floor. "Look around you; there are a lot of angry faces in here. Unless you want the kind of trouble your friend found, I'd suggest you get him out of here."

The two men looked out in the restaurant at the crowd. Several men were moving toward them. The two looked back at Will. "Your friend is not seriously hurt; I pulled my punch. He'll be alright in about an hour."

Will walked through the front door without looking back. Nothing like a couple of drinks, good food, and some lightweight entertainment to enjoy the evening.

There was one thing, though; maybe he should reevaluate what he planned reporting back to the Sir Barker staff.

Miami…

Will flew back to Miami and headed straight to his storage facility. He loaded all remaining supplies into the van and drove directly to his bunker.

There were still enough operational supplies to last for at least a year. Will decided the best place for them was the bunker. It wasn't like you could take them to the dump.

The trip to the bunker took a couple of hours. Will maintained his speed just under the speed limit so as not to attract any attention.

Explaining to a local Highway Patrolman his reason for

having numerous weapons and explosive supplies wasn't something he wanted to do. Will knew oftentimes a professional such as himself was discovered by something as innocuous as a speeding ticket.

The trip to and from the bunker proved uneventful. Once back in Miami, he had one last chore before flying to Mobile.

There was still the issue of the van. He needed to trade up for a vehicle more suited to a young, successful book editor. He needed something stylish but not over the top.

Appearances might now be more important. He would no longer seek anonymity; he would seek to become a part of the community, albeit a low-key member.

Life as Will Villa was about to take a hard turn onto a more traditional road. He no longer was a deadly contractor for the Agency. He was just a somewhat brainiac English major who worked in a very boring business editing books.

The only exciting thing about his life was the occasional required home office trip to Belgium. He was only halfway interesting because his home was an old boathouse.

Easing into the new lifestyle would proceed slowly. He would make friends deliberately, choosing both professional and working-class people.

His new persona would match his occupation. He would appear self-confident but somewhat of a loner. Socializing would be carefully gauged against any chance of compromising the new Will Villa.

Then, there was romance. Will's driver's license said he was 27, but he was only 25. He'd had a girlfriend at the orphanage and a brief relationship with Maria, his neighbor in Miami.

That relationship faltered when he started spending most

of his spare time living in the Airstream. The last he heard, she had gotten a promotion to head of legal for another corporate location within her company.

Other than those two brief romances, Will's experience with women had been provided during Agency training. The Agency left nothing to chance.

They had a term, *Honey Trap*, for female spies who were trained to use sex in the completion of their missions. Men were also trained and often referred to as Romeos.

The men had to be charismatic, sexually skilled, good listeners and project themselves into any situation as "the center of attention." Because Will was very attractive and extremely intelligent, the Dean felt such training would, no doubt, be useful to Will during the course of his career.

Will was, therefore, extensively trained in the various skills necessary to effectively set a *Honey Trap*. He had to admit he rather enjoyed the training, especially lab sessions.

Will looked forward to his new life, one where you could make mistakes and not die for them. But probably most of all, he looked forward to having honest relationships with people.

Sure, he would still be living a made-up life, but what other kind of life did he have? It had been made up for him from the beginning. He was really just 25 years old, and already he'd had four made-up names.

Will's life contained only two truths; everything else was made up. Truth number one: he came from Mobile, Alabama; and truth number two: his first name was William. Even his age was an educated guess.

William, no surname, of Mobile, Alabama, age 25 give or take, was being reborn. His real life was just beginning. Whoever and whatever he was had yet to be determined.

Will's final stop before heading home to Mobile was a local Dodge car dealership. Even though he didn't want anything flashy, he did want something fast. He knew speed might be useful to him in the future.

To Will's surprise, it seemed most speed came with flashy. He chose a Charger SE with 400 HP engine and four barrel carburetor. In addition to a manual transmission with four-speed Hurst shifter and pistol-grip handle, he added power steering.

For a guy who didn't want flashy, he got it. But more importantly, he got speed, lots and lots of speed.

The last part of Will's car buying agreement was delivery of the car to a Mobile dealership. A quick call to his attorney, Conny, and Will was done. He'd have the car in a few days.

Will took a knapsack out of the van and caught a taxi to the airport. His plane had been gassed up and was ready to go.

The flying distance from Miami to Mobile was 586 miles. Flying time in the Cessna should be about a couple hours or so, depending on wind. Will should be home in Mobile by dinner.

Chapter 16
Family

Before leaving Miami, Will had placed a call to Mobile inquiring about long-term hangar rental. He had been told there was a small, one-plane hangar capable of handling his Cessna available.

The owner had agreed to meet Will at 6 pm to talk about the terms of a long-term lease. As the Cessna taxied up to the designated hangar, a large, swarthy-skinned man with a protruding belly stepped through the open overhead door and waved Will's plane inside.

Seeing the hangar through the cockpit windows, it appeared clean and well-squared away. Killing the engines, Will exited the aircraft and approached the man who had waved him in.

Will extended his hand which was warmly grabbed by the man. "Justin, I've known you most of your life. Why is it I never knew you were a pilot? Is flying something you learned in the military? Wow, what a great looking Cessna;

yours?"

When the man slowed to take a breath between questions, Will took the opportunity to jump in. "I'm sorry, Sir, my name isn't Justin. I'm Will Villa. To my knowledge, we've never met before."

"Come on, Justin, quit foolin' around. I've been going to crawfish boils with your family since you were in diapers. I'd know you anywhere. How're your mama and daddy been doing? I haven't seen them in a couple of months."

For the second time in less than a week, Will took out his wallet and handed the man his driver's license. "This guy Justin and I must really look alike. This is the second time in less than a week I've had to show another disbeliever my license. I assure you, I am not Justin; I'm just a real close look-alike."

The man stood clutching the license and looking back and forth from it to Will. "I'm sorry, Mr. Villa, but I'd have bet my house you were Justin. It's really kind of spooky how much y'all look alike.

"I'm sorry for the mistaken identity. My name is Billy Sochcer. I own this hangar and another much larger one down the way a bit. I know Justin and his family through a local Cajuns' Social Club we all belong to.

"But enough of that. I used this hangar for years until my business just outgrew it. I own an air service company; you know gas, service, plane repairs and such. If we can agree on a lease, I'll give you a 10% cut on any business you do with me."

The deal was made and Billy agreed to have the plane refueled tomorrow morning. Will gave him a cash deposit on the hangar and promised to have the remaining year's lease payment wired tomorrow.

The lease was set up in the Belgium corporate name and Will promised to have his lawyer call tomorrow to finalize the paperwork.

With the paperwork in place, Will asked if he could use a phone and call a taxi. "Well hell, Will, I'm headin' home myself. Why don't I give you a lift?"

"I'd appreciate that, Billy, if it's not too much out of the way. I live in a boathouse up on the north end of the bay just up from the Panther Run Marina."

"That's not much out of the way; I'd be happy to run you home."

"Thanks, Billy."

The men walked over to a Ford truck and got in. "So, Billy, tell me more about Justin Boché. That is his full name, isn't it? I met an airline stewardess on Grand Cayman a few days back who made the same mistake as you. She said she and her sister had gone to school with him."

"You're right about his last name. Like I said before, I've known Justin and his family since he was a baby. It's just him and his mama and daddy; there aren't any other kids. That's kind of unusual for Cajuns. Me, myself; I've got six.

"Anyway, Justin was always a good kid; he was quarterback for his high school football team and he's real smart, too. After he got back from Viet Nam, he got a college degree in three years. He's an accountant now. I use him for all my stuff like that.

"Let's see; what else? Oh yeah, he's married and has a couple of kids. His office is in an old converted house downtown, a real nice setup. Last I heard, the family lives in the main house and Justin's office is in some kind of outbuilding."

"Do you know if Justin is looking for new business? My tax status is changing and I need a good local accountant to keep me out of trouble. If you're satisfied with him, I probably would be too."

"Oh, I'm real satisfied with him. He handles my bookkeeping and taxes. He's in the book; why don't you give him a call tomorrow?"

"Thanks, Billy, I think I will. Just up here on the left is my boathouse. I sure appreciate the ride."

Will got out of the truck and retrieved his knapsack from the back. "Thanks again, Billy. See you around the airport."

Will watched Billy pull out of the small parking lot and turn onto the street. *I've got to meet this Justin Boché, maybe in a couple of days,* he thought as he unlocked his door. *Maybe in a couple of days.*

…More like a week later

Will had picked up his car and was on his way downtown. He had a 4 pm appointment with Justin Boché.

Since he had an hour before his appointment, he decided to take the Charger for a little test drive on the interstate. Entering the on-ramp, Will downshifted. The 400 HP engine leapt forward like a greyhound chasing a stuffed rabbit.

The Hurst shifter was as smooth as anything he had ever used. The four barrel carburetor kicked in about the time he merged onto the highway. He hit 90 before he shifted into fourth gear.

What a car! If he ever needed to make a quick getaway, this was the car to save him. Before long, he had left all the traffic behind.

Will slowed down and worked the car through its paces.

It was really fun to drive. Maybe he'd take it for a road trip before long.

Justin Boché's house/office proved easy to find. There was a small, tastefully done sign by the entrance drive. The "outbuilding" turned out to be a small gatehouse with room for a couple of cars to park on the side. Obviously accountants didn't hold massive meetings.

The main house sat about 20 yards behind the gatehouse. As houses went, it was a medium-sized, plantation-styled home. All in all, a very nice place. His doppelgänger was doing quite well for himself.

Will had made a joke with the ladies on Grand Cayman about a look-alike. He had also joked with Billy, his hangar landlord about Justin.

He knew most people had others who resembled them. But was that all this was? He figured when he met the accountant, the guy would be tall and dark with a passing resemblance.

What if it were more than just a resemblance, though? Could this guy somehow be related to him? He hadn't really given it much thought.

He was born in Mobile, however. It would make sense he had relatives in the area. Could this guy be a look-alike cousin? Or, heaven forbid, a brother. Either of these were possibilities.

If the aforementioned bore out, how would he handle the encounter? Would he hug him, with tears in his eyes, and reveal his long journey back home?

Or would he just laugh it off and blame everything on a quirk of nature, saying all brown boys looked alike? What was the best way to handle such a situation?

After all, wasn't the real reason he came to Mobile was to

find a connection to his past? Deep down, if he admitted it to himself, wasn't he really looking for family?

He was obviously curious; who wouldn't be? But what about the consequences of telling people the truth. Would it make people happy or would the revelation possibly ruin lives?

Will had been thrown away by his parents. Even if he could find them, what made him think they wanted to hear from him now?

No, if he thought he might be related to Justin Boché, he'd keep the suspicion to himself. Will saw nothing good coming from the disclosure.

Knowing would be enough for him. He had no desire to upset lives; there was no upside to such an action.

So, just as he had been trained to do; he'd deny, deny, deny. That would be best for all concerned.

Will stepped from his car and started for the door. As he approached the entrance to the accountant's office, a newer model station wagon turned into the drive.

As the car slowed, he smiled at the woman and two little girls inside. Seeing him, the car stopped just past where he was standing.

No sooner had the car stopped, the back doors flew open and two little girls came running toward him. They were, quite obviously twins, about four years old with black hair and dark eyes. "Daddy, Daddy," they shouted loudly as they ran up to him.

By then the mother, who looked like a grown-up version of the twins, climbed from the car and walked toward Will. "You girls, leave your daddy alone; he's got a four o'clock appointment and probably needs to get inside.

"His appointment's car is in the lot. He's probably

waiting inside. As the beautiful young woman walked closer, she had a quizzical look on her face.

"Did you get a haircut? Something's different about you. Is that a new shirt; I don't think I've seen it before."

By now, the little girls were tugging on Will, trying to get his attention. "Daddy, Daddy, guess where we've been."

Will stood there dumbfounded. He was frozen in his astonishment at the encounter.

About that time, no doubt in response to hearing his family outside, Will's doppelgänger came through the front door. As he looked up and saw Will, he physically stumbled on the oyster shell drive. "Who the hell?"

He couldn't get any other words out. His mouth became an unmovable opening in his face.

Will found his composure before any of the other four discovered theirs. The twins were looking back and forth between the two men as was their mother.

The accountant's gaze was locked on Will. Will stepped forward. "Mr. Boché, I'm Wilber Rodríguez Villa; my friends call me Will. I'm your four o'clock appointment."

Justin stepped toward Will. "I'm Justin Boché; please call me Justin." The time necessary to get those few words out seemed indeterminable. Time had stood still, or so it seemed.

Will laughed a belly laugh. "Are you guys as uncomfortable as I am? Why don't we get out of the sun and talk about the elephant on the driveway?

"Justin, you and I look kind of alike. I think your little girls are confused. Maybe we should all talk about this."

Justin's composure was returning. "I think that's a good idea."

About then, his wife spoke. "Look kind of alike? You

two look like friggin' identical twins. How on earth is that possible?"

Justin motioned back toward the main house. "I don't know about you, Will, but I could use a drink. Why don't we all walk up to the house and try to figure out if we are related in some fashion. We've got to be cousins or something."

Justin's wife, Marty, took charge once they entered her domain. "Justin, why don't you take Will into the library, and I'll be in in a little bit. I need to get the girls cleaned up before supper."

Marty was no doubt being polite so Justin and Will could have time to talk. She ushered the girls up the stairs as the two little twins giggled and kept pointing at Will. Only the twins knew what was so funny.

The library turned out to be a fair-sized room with bookshelves on three walls and a wet bar on the other. Justin walked over to the bar. "What's your drink, Will?"

"I'll have rum, dark if you have it. You have a very nice home, Justin, and a beautiful family. I'm sorry; I seemed to have startled you and them.

"I was told by Billy out at the airport we looked alike, but I just assumed you were a tall dark guy with similar features. He's why I called you. He recommended you; said you were a good accountant and a good guy. He never told me you were so damned good-looking."

Justin laughed. "Right back at you; you're one good-looking guy."

They both laughed as Justin handed Will his drink. "So, Will, are you my long-lost brother or something?" The question was another attempt at levity, although laced with an undertone of seriousness."

"Were you adopted, Justin?"

"No, I wasn't. How about you, Will; were you adopted?"

"Well, Justin, it's been my experience that Cubans who arrived on shore in small boats with little possessions had little tendency to adopt other mouths to feed.

"No, I was born in Miami and raised in the Washington, D.C., area. I'm an only child raised by my grandmother after my parents died."

Will gave Justin his bio minus occupational information. He also showed Justin his driver's license.

"So, Will, you've been in Mobile for a few years based on the expiration date on your license. It's a wonder we haven't met before now."

"We probably would have except I have been traveling abroad extensively for my job. I bet I haven't been in Mobile half the time."

"Will, how is it we look so much alike? Marty was right; we look like identical twins. It's kinda spooky."

"You know how there are always look-alikes for Presidents and movie stars? If you look long enough, Justin, and hard enough, I guess everyone can find a twin.

"We just did it by accident. I do admit, though, we look an awful lot alike. The next time we get together, we better wear name tags."

"That's a good idea. I'll just label you Cuban and me Coonass. Of course, you know I'm really better looking, right?"

"Hell, I don't know, Justin. I've started to think of you as the ugly twin."

They both laughed. Together less than an hour and they were already acting like brothers. Even though both brothers had the thought, it went unspoken between them.

"So, Wilber Rodríguez Villa, what can I do for you? I assume you need accounting services or you wouldn't be here."

"Yes, Sir, I do. For several years now, I have been an independent contractor employed by a Belgium Corporation and performing 100% of my work internationally, primarily among Spanish-speaking countries.

"I now find myself as an independent contractor working for the same corporation. The big difference is my work will primarily be completed in Mobile from now on.

"It's been years since I have filed an income tax return. I need help setting things up so I don't run afoul of the law."

Will filled Justin in on the ghost-writing scenario and the rest of his back story. He was lucky; when the Dean developed his background, he had included past tax returns. Will's background could be followed back to birth if necessary.

Will freely offered information about an offshore bank account where he had been keeping fees and royalties from previous books. He did, however, neglect to mention his ownership of the corporation and additional offshore banking activity.

When questioned about physical assets, Will responded he had none save personal effects. Justin was surprised at the corporation's generosity with its housing and transportation benefits.

Will explained the considerable success he brought to the company. Benefits and elimination of most international travel had been parts of his recently negotiated contract.

He could, of course, supply all accompanying paperwork by way of the corporation's lawyer in Miami.

Justin did not see any major issues with establishing Will

as an independent contractor. He took time to review with Will the IRS's test for independent contractors.

Justin thought it would be a good idea to meet again in a week to discuss any further requirements. Will agreed.

Justin had refilled Will's and his drinks when Marty walked in. "Okay, boys, it's time for supper."

Will didn't realize he had spent almost three hours with Justin. "Marty, I don't want to impose on you guys. I probably should get back home."

"Oh no, you don't, buster. If you think you're leaving this house before the girls and I hear y'all's story, you're sadly mistaken."

Justin looked at Will. "It's no use, my twin brother from a different mother; Marty runs the house and all within. Unless you have a medical emergency or note from some authority, you will be our guest for supper. You Yankees up in D.C. call it dinner."

"Okay, okay." Will held his hands up in mock surrender. "If you promise not to torture me excessively, I'd love to stay."

Justin and Will got up and followed Marty a short distance to the dining room. The twins were already seated. They had dressed up for the occasion in matching pink patterned dresses. As he walked in, the girls giggled in unison and said, "Hi, Mr. Will."

"Hi, uh?"

Marty quickly spoke up. "They're Jess and Tess. Don't try to tell them apart. Justin and I have trouble most of the time. They will answer to either name, just to mess with you."

"Hi, Jess and Tess. You look very pretty this evening."

The girls whispered something while they watched the

three adults sit down.

Dinner was on the table; it consisted of crawfish étouffée, fried okra, and cornbread. Dessert was a delicious bread pudding with rum sauce (faux in deference to the twins).

The girls took off immediately after dessert. To that point, conversation had been about where Will lived, what he did for a living, how he liked living in a boathouse, and a dozen other trivial subjects.

"Okay boys, now give me the good stuff; what have y'all figured out." Marty possessed one of those delightfully direct personalities present in many Southern women. It was impossible not to be taken in by her charm.

Justin shrugged his shoulders at Will. "To start with, Will is two years older than me. If we are twins, it was an extremely lengthy and difficult delivery. It was made even more so by him being born in Miami and me at Mobile General Hospital."

"Is that all y'all've got?" Marty obviously wanted more.

Will added his piece of the story. "Let's see; what else? Oh, I remember, Justin is Cajun and I'm Cuban. I was raised and educated in the Washington D.C., area, and Justin was raised and educated in Alabama."

Smiling at Justin, Will asked, "Did I miss anything?"

"Well, my not-so-good-looking twin, there is one similarity. We were both raised as single children."

Marty chimed in, "You had a brother, Justin; so even that's not the same."

Will looked at Justin for an explanation. "I did have a brother, but I didn't know him. He died when I was just a baby."

Marty was looking from Justin to Will to Justin again. "You guys may not be brothers, but you already act like you are. And I should know; I have six of them.”

Will backed his chair away from the table. “Marty, the food was excellent. Next time, it’s on me. I’ll treat you to some good Cuban fare. I better get home; I’ve got an editing deadline in a few days.”

“Not before I document this crazy coincidence.” She quickly rose from her chair and retrieved a polaroid instamatic camera.

“You two ‘twins from different mothers,’ as you so eloquently explained, stand over by the wall. I’m going to take a couple of pictures. No one will believe me if I don’t.”

Sitting so long in one position had caused Will’s left leg to stiffen up a bit. The occasional stiffness was about the only lingering effect he had from the polio. Limping slightly, he joined Justin by the wall.

Marty looked at the limp with concern. “Are you okay, Will? You’re limping.”

“I’m fine, Marty; just an old childhood injury that stiffens up when the weather decides to be onerous.”

Marty spent the next few minutes snapping shots from different angles. She then insisted they wait for the photos to develop.

“There you go.” Laughing, she handed one of the photos to Will. “This is for your scrapbook.”

Marty and Justin walked Will out into the refreshing night air. Justin extended his hand. “It’s nice meeting you, Will, and thanks for the business. I look forward to getting to know you better. I’ll see you next week.”

As a general rule, most Southern women don’t extend their hands to shake. Marty, instead, leaned over and kissed Will on the cheek. “There’s more to this story than meets the eye. See you later, Will.”

…later that night

Justin was watching television as Marty walked into their bedroom. "The girls are down and sound asleep. Now, buster, you and I are going to have a talk about your newest client.

"Look at these photos; there's no way in the world, on God's green earth, you will ever make me believe you and Will aren't somehow related."

Justin had turned off the television and was staring intently at the photos Marty had thrust at him. "I know, Sweetheart; it's weirder than anything I've ever encountered in my life. But you heard what he said; there's no way we can be related."

Marty had retrieved one of the photos. "There's a way if everyone involved in this isn't being completely honest."

"Are you talking about me, Marty? You know everything I know. I have to admit, though, Will and I had this immediate connection like I've seen with brothers before."

"You're right about the chemistry or connection or whatever you want to call it. Anyone seeing you two together would pick up on it immediately. There's definitely something going on here, and I want to know what.

"Tell me about your twin brother, William. What is the family explanation of his birth? Do your parents ever talk about him?"

"No, they don't talk about him at all. It's almost as if he never existed. I did ask them about him when I was a young teenager.

"Everyone in the Cajun community knows I had a twin,

but I never heard anyone mention it except once. You know my friend Dalton from high school? Well, one night we were over at his house playing Elvis records.

"I was messing around playing the air guitar and making Elvis gyrations with my hips. Dalton made a snide comment about me looking like Elvis.

"He said Elvis and I were a lot alike; we both had twins who died. Dalton thought the comment was a lot funnier than I did."

"Okay, Dalton had a morbid sense of humor. What does that have to do with you talking with your parents?"

"I'm getting to that part. I went home, and that night at supper I repeated Dalton's comment. Telling them the comment had made me realize that, even though I knew about my twin, William, I didn't really know anything about what happened."

Marty looked on anxiously as Justin continued. "The question made my mother turn really red in the face and both Mama and Daddy just looked at each other. I believe the situation was what is often referred to as a pregnant pause.

"Tears came into my mother's eyes as my father turned to me. I could see from their reaction to my question they were reminded of something sad.

"My father began to speak:

'Justin, William is not a subject your mama and I like to talk about. With that said, though, we knew you would eventually ask us about the details of his death. It's time you know.

'You and William were born just a couple minutes apart. We were ecstatic about our beautiful identical twins.

'For the first six months, everything was perfect, one might even call it idealistic. You and Will, that's what we called him, were healthy and happy babies.

'You would lie in the crib side by side and speak gibberish. It was as if you had your own language. The only time you cried was when separated.

'We thought our family was perfect; then Will began to change. He started crying for no apparent reason. Seldom did the crying stop for the next three months.

'During y'all's nine-month check-up, we asked the doctor what was wrong. After examining Will very thoroughly and consulting a specialist, he gave us the worst possible news. In the late 40's, it was every parent's most horrible nightmare.

'Will was diagnosed with infantile paralysis, more commonly referred to as polio. The doctor said you and Will had to be separated immediately. If not, you would likely be infected as well.

'At that point, the doctor gave Will the worst prognosis any parent ever heard. In all probability, he would die very soon; and even if he didn't, he would never be able to live any kind of normal life.

'Will was immediately removed from contact with the three of us and placed in an isolation ward. The doctor strongly recommended we commit Will to a polio hospital where he could get the treatment he needed.

'Three days later, he was sent by ambulance to a Virginia facility for continuing care. Needless to say, we were not allowed to go with Will. As a matter of fact, we were not even allowed to visit.

'We were told Will continued to get worse in the facility. He had no cognitive skills and was totally paralyzed.

'We were informed we could visit, but it would be dangerous and a complete waste of our time. There was a chance we might even catch polio. Out of concern for all our health, we chose not to visit.

'Will died two years later and we held a small private service for him. You were too young to remember all this and we were so sad, we chose not to talk about Will.

'That doesn't mean he has been forgotten; he hasn't. He has always lived in our hearts and always will. Hopefully he will continually be in yours, too.'"

Justin had tears in his eyes. "And that's the story of my identical twin whom I never got to know."

Marty looked at her husband with sympathetic eyes. "Wow, what a story. Why haven't I ever heard this story before? I've known you since high school."

"My parents emphasized to me the private nature of Will's story and the need to keep it in the family. They said nothing could come of discussing it except sadness.

"The only reason I'm discussing it now is because you asked. It was never a secret I intentionally kept from you; it was just a reminder of something I didn't want to remember."

"I can see why you kept it a secret, but maybe it's time to further explore what happened to your twin."

"Why do you say that? Don't tell me; you think my new client 'Will' and my dead brother 'Will' are the same person, don't you?"

"Tell me, Justin, what do you think? Before you answer, though, let me throw out some facts of an empirical nature.

"First of all, you two are identical in appearance. I know many famous people go and find look-alikes. But when you put the two people side by side, they are never identical. You two are exactly alike.

"Secondly, what about the limp? No doubt his statement about it being a childhood injury is correct; he just neglected to say how early in his childhood.

"Thirdly, he was raised in the D.C. area, as in next door to Virginia. The same Virginia where the polio hospital was located.

"There's also the almost inconceivable coincidence of Will showing up for an appointment. I know what he said about the referral, but it's all just a little bit too convenient, don't you think?

"And last, but not least, both are called Will. That's just too freaky to write off.

"Plus, none of this deals with all the misconceptions about polio. When I was pregnant with the twins, you know I was paranoid about something being wrong with them.

"During the pregnancy, I read everything I could get my hands on even remotely associated with childhood diseases. Polio was covered in many of the publications I read. It may no longer be epidemic, but it still occurs.

"As I recall, a total lack of cognitive function was never discussed in relation to polio. And paralysis, that was typically associated with kids who had to be in those iron lung breathing machines.

"If Will had that kind of problem, he'd have shown breathing problems during those three months before diagnosis.

"You know what we should do? We should invite your parents to dinner this weekend and casually work your new client into the conversation.

"As a matter of fact, I called them while the girls were in the tub. They'll be here at 5:00 Saturday evening."

"Marty, you didn't? Have you been out in the sun too long? What are we supposed to say to Mama and Daddy at supper? Oh, by the way, we just met my long-dead twin Will, and guess what; he's alive and well.

"What's he like; you ask? Well, he's now Cuban; he doesn't seem to have polio anymore. Oh yeah, one other thing; he's two years older than me now and lives right here in Mobile.

"And what do you expect their response to be? 'Oh, how nice to catch up on his life; we'll have to have him over to dinner. By the way, how are the twins enjoying preschool?'

"I can't imagine any problems, can you? By the way, what are you serving?"

"Don't be an ass, Justin; we're not going to say any of those things. We'll just have our usual conversation and casually work in your new client and his look-alike appearance.

"We'll show them the pictures and see how they react. You know your mother can't hide her feelings. If there is anything to my suspicions, we'll know by her reaction."

"And if there is something, how do we deal with Mr. Wilber Rodríguez Villa?"

"One thing at a time, Dear, one thing at a time."

…Saturday supper – the aftermath

Grammy (Madge) and Papa (Gary) Boché had excused

themselves earlier than usual from supper and headed straight home.

Not really knowing what to say, both were quiet on the short ride. Once settled into their comfortable den with drinks in hand, Gary was the first to broach the subject. "What do you think? The two of them are definitely identical in appearance. You think that's possible without them being related?

"I've seen look-alikes before, but never like this. It's spooky as hell. Could he really be William?"

"I don't know for sure, Honey, but the limp certainly adds credence to the possibility. But how could it be conceivable?

"Dr. Jennings told us William was going to die; even the specialist in Birmingham agreed. I remember that morning at the hospital like it was yesterday; how could I not?

"We had to make a choice no parents should ever have to make: abandon one child so that another might live. I've relived that morning a thousand times in my dreams.

"I can still see William reaching for me as they took him away. The look in his eyes was haunting.

"If Justin's new client is William, I'll know as soon as I see him. A mother would always know."

Gary was studying his wife's expression with concern. It was as if she had already decided the client was their William. "Slow down a little, Sweetheart; the chances of William being alive are so remote as to be impossible.

"Before we get ahead of ourselves, let me do a little checking. We need to have a few more facts before we jump off into the deep end of the pool."

...The Boathouse

It had been several days since Will had supper with Justin and Marty. He had kept himself busy around the boathouse. Since it was his full-time home now, it needed some serious attention.

The first thing he had done was hire a maid service to spend a couple of days in the small apartment getting everything spotless.

Prior to the maids' hiring, he had the whole place painted in soft Caribbean pastels. He wanted the place to reflect his Cuban roots.

Even though the Agency thought him dead and he could be whomever he wanted to be, he knew his best path forward was one of continuity.

The Dean had been very careful in developing his Cuban persona and keeping it confidential. To abandon that now and try to create another would be very difficult.

In addition to his Wilber Rodríguez Villa passport, Will had five different passports in his possession, ones the Dean had also created for him. Two were American, one Spanish, and the other two for countries in Central and South America.

He had been instructed by the Dean to keep at least two passports unused in case he needed to disappear at some point. As with all other advice from the Dean, it had been followed.

All six passports were now in a waterproof ammo can secreted in an out-of-the way nook under water below the boathouse. If needed, Will could retrieve them without being seen.

Will was now sitting in the apartment admiring his new home. If he were going to live here full-time, he wanted to make it comfortable.

Bob's wife had done a great job designing and furnishing the place. Other than some paint and the feminine-looking curtain by the bed, he left it as it was, one 400-square-foot space with everything he needed.

Not bad for an orphan with polio who had been thrown away by his parents, parents he thought he would never know. That had all changed once he saw Justin Boché.

If he and Justin were not twins, then someone should notify *Ripley's Believe It or Not*[®]. Look-alikes were one thing; he and Justin were something else.

One evening and the two men had an unexplainable chemistry. It was like they had known each other since birth.

Will felt in his bones that, despite the almost 0% probability of finding his family, he had done so. Now what?

He decided to just continue acclimation to his new home and let things play out. He had not asked Justin about his parents or other siblings; he'd let Justin bring up the subject.

For now, he would hang out at his boathouse and the marina and try to establish some sort of normalness in his life. Fate would plot its own course.

Will decided to stroll down to Panther Run Marina. He and Bob had become friends since becoming neighbors of sorts. Will had had several nice meals sitting with Bob and Nadine on their deck overlooking the marina. Not a bad life.

Panther Run Marina was a beehive of activity as Will walked up to the office area where Bob could usually be found. Bob was in a somewhat animated, if not heated, conversation with two young men about Will's age.

His first impression of the two was that of spoiled, trust

fund babies. "Look, old man; as soon as I get home tonight, I'll send you a check for what I owe you for gas and supplies." The speaker winked at his companion. "Now, take that lock and chain off my boat; I'm not telling you again."

Bob was trying to stay calm, but it was apparent he was losing the battle. "Look, Jimbo, you've fed me that line the last three times you took your boat out. If you want to take the boat out today, I'll need 1,350 dollars cash. End of discussion."

Jimbo poked his finger into Bob's chest. "The key, now, old man, or I'll kick your ass and take it."

Jimbo turned to his buddy. "Jeff, go in the office and see if you can find the key. I'll finish with this old shrimper."

Will stepped between Jeff and the office door. "Bob, you want this pencil-dicked frat boy in your office?"

Bob smiled at Jimbo then glanced toward Will. "Not in this lifetime."

Jeff, no doubt taking a clue from Jimbo, poked his finger into Will's chest. "Out of the way, spic, before I kick your Cuban ass back where it came from."

Will looked down at the finger still pushing into his chest. "That would be one hell of a kick, frat boy; I'm from D.C. Now move that finger."

"Move it yourself, greaser, if you think you can."

Grabbing the offending finger with his left hand, Will broke it in one, seemingly easy motion.

Jeff immediately yelped with the initial surge of agony from the pain. It's amazing how much pain can emanate from one small appendage.

Jimbo quickly forgot about Bob as he jumped between his distressed friend and Will. "Hey, asshole, what'd you do to him?" He immediately grabbed the right side of Will's shirt and attempted to pull him forward.

Obviously, Jimbo thought such tough guy behavior would intimidate Will. He was attempting to pull Will to him when he, too, experienced great pain.

As Jimbo had grabbed Will's shirt, Will responded. Sweeping his right hand inside Jimbo's, he delivered a hard hammer fist to the frat boy's nose.

The crunching of gristle and sinew could be heard by anyone standing close by. Bob laughed. "Good shot, Will. They teach you that in college?"

Will turned to Bob with a grin. "Naw, got that one from a gangbanger friend back in the hood. What's the problem with these two tough guys?"

Bob was looking at both boys now writhing on the ground in pain. "The only place these guys have any chance of being tough is maybe over at one of the country clubs.

"Jimbo, there, has had a boat slip for about a year. His daddy got it for him and paid a year in advance, which I might add is almost up. Ever since showing up, he's been a pain in the ass of one kind or another.

"Up until now, it's been loud parties and too much drinking. He's also hard to collect from for gas and supplies. I finally had enough; I chained his boat to the dock and added a big-assed lock for good measure.

"Must have hurt his feelings. You walked up just as he was lodging his complaint. Hope he likes his answer."

Both men let out a belly laugh. "What should we do with them, Bob?"

"I've got a cousin in the PD; he patrols this area. I'll give him a call and get him to come over. I won't lodge a complaint as long as Jimbo pays his bill and moves his boat."

"What are you going to say about their injuries?"

"I'll say I did it when they tried to assault me. My cousin will believe it; he and I fought our way through half the bars in town during our rowdy years."

"Thanks, Bob. My company would not appreciate this sort of publicity. I'll see you later."

"Thanks for the assist, Will. Come by after supper and I'll give you a shot of that dark rum you're addicted to. You can tell me more about your ill-spent youth."

After leaving the Marina, Will headed back for the boathouse; he had some thinking to do. He had responded to the incident with the frat boys without thinking. That couldn't happen again.

In the future, Will would have to react more like a common everyday kind of guy. He couldn't go around taking out two young healthy men without breaking a sweat.

Most guys his age would probably have engaged in fisticuffs or some form of wrestling when challenged in such a fashion. His reaction had been swift and extremely effective.

Bob was no doubt a bit curious but had chosen not to comment. He did say, though, he wanted to talk about it later over a drink. Will would have to come up with a believable explanation.

…Appointment with Justin

Justin was coming out of the main house as Will pulled into the small parking lot. The accountant walked over to the car as Will got out. "Nice ride, bro. Had it long?"

"No, I haven't even gotten used to driving it yet. It can

get away from you if not careful; the big engine is really something."

"I have to tell you, Will, from what you explained about your company benefits the last time we met, you must be a very valuable contractor: a small yacht, the boathouse, and now this Charger."

Will was smiling as he contemplated his response. Justin was a very astute accountant who was, no doubt, somewhat suspicious about the expensive perks. "As my accountant, you need to know more about what I really do for my employer."

He filled in the blanks for Justin using his ghost-writing history, Spanish-speaking athletes and the way the deals were set up. "So, after completing my fourth book, I had accumulated enough money to quit working.

"If I just quit, however, I would be walking away from significant contacts in the Spanish-speaking athletes' market. Plus, what would I do with myself?

"About that time, I had been approached by Brussels General Services, Inc., a Belgium-owned company. They had somehow heard about what I was doing.

"The company has a publications division and was interested in the market I had discovered. They made me an offer I couldn't refuse.

"In exchange for my contacts and future deals I negotiate for them, I receive a very lucrative benefit package plus salary. Please remember, however, the corporation owns the boat, boathouse, car, and a small airplane.

"To date, all accumulated assets have been generated offshore. I own nothing in this country. If my contract is terminated by the company or me, I have first right-of-refusal on the assets at current market value.

"It's really a sweet deal. The really big thing for me was no more international travel. I meet new clients here in Mobile and also handle the editing duties of my contract."

"And you just kind of lucked into the whole career because you're Cuban and speak Spanish. Damn, you are one lucky guy.

"As to the whole asset and income situation, you obviously received some very sound advice along the way. Your only concern at this point is declaring your income and reporting on a quarterly basis.

"I'll handle that for you plus any incidental issues as they arise. If you decide to move any of your offshore assets to this country, please let me know. I will help you with any tax issues.

"Are there any other business concerns I may help you with? Oh, before I forget, keep good records on your expenses; we'll need them at tax time."

"No, Justin, that covers everything I can think of. I assume I can call you if I have questions."

Will stood up in preparation for leaving. Staring up at him, Justin seemed surprised. "Where you think you're going? We may be through with business, but we're not through by a long shot."

Will sat back down laughing. "Okay, what else we got to do? You want to know why I have such a dynamic personality and it appears you survived charisma bypass surgery? Or is it the 'I'm better looking than you' thing?"

Justin was smiling, although with a serious undertone. "Maybe we can work on your perceptions of reality later. Right now, I want to tell you about my supper guests this weekend.

"Marty invited my parents over while we were discussing

business last week. She's convinced you and I are somehow related; she believes you're my long-thought-dead twin brother."

"What do you think, Justin? You know, considering we had different parents and we're different races, can we really be twins? If so, we need to alert the scientific community and media immediately. We have truly made an unbelievable discovery."

"I know, Will. I'm with you, but my wife can be like a dog with a new bone. She's not going to turn loose until it's been gnawed beyond recognition."

"I detected a hint of Marty's determination at supper. How can we convince her it's just one hell of a coincidence? Did your parents' supper conversation help any?"

"Help, hell! After my parents left, Marty's determination moved into overdrive. You have to know my mother to understand. She has zero ability to hide or even disguise her feelings.

"When Marty produced the photos she had taken, my mother turned extremely red and couldn't speak for a couple minutes. My father's reaction was a bit more controlled, but not much.

"They commented on the similarity although both denied we are identical. Within thirty minutes of seeing the pictures, my parents both feigned fatigue and went home much earlier than is their custom.

"Their reaction certainly didn't help my attempt at explaining the whole thing as an unlikely coincidence. Who knows what kind of investigation Marty has been attempting since then?"

"Justin, maybe I could help if you told me about your twin and what happened to him. There has to be some fact associated with him we can use to convince Marty."

Justin spent the next few minutes relating the story of his twin just as he had previously done with Marty. As before, he concluded with the funeral service and an admonition not to speak of his brother in the future.

"That's a very sad story, Justin. There's probably nothing there to convince Marty her thesis is incorrect except the funeral service. Let me ask you a question of clarification.

"Was there a body present at the private service? If there were and your parents and family saw it, then you should have several witnesses to support our coincidence theory.

"If there were no body, then the thesis of Marty's investigation can be neither proved nor disproved."

Will smiled at who, he was now convinced, was his twin. "I tell you what I'll do, though. Since I never had any siblings and you no longer have a brother, we'll agree to be brothers from different mothers until Marty can prove us biologically related."

As inane as the suggestion was, Justin seemed somehow relieved. "That sounds like a plan, with one caveat; we both agree I'm the best looking."

"Okay, okay. I'll concede your movie star good looks, as long as you concede my superior social skills and winning personality."

Both men stood laughing and extending their hands to seal the deal. "How about my parents? Do you want to meet them?"

Will had anticipated this question/request during their conversation. "I don't think that's such a good idea. Obviously, just seeing a photo representing what might have been if William had survived was enough to bring their pain rushing back to the surface.

"I think it would be a good idea, though, if you could surreptitiously find out about the presence of William's body at the funeral service. That could get Marty to back off her quest."

Justin had a concerned look on his face in response to Will's statement. "Or it could shift her quest, as you call it, into high gear. An absent body and she will never stop looking for an answer."

"That's just a chance we take, I guess." Of course, Will already thought he knew the answer. If he were a statistical analyst, the predicted probability they were brothers would, no doubt, be about 99%.

Before this meeting, Will had been surmising what he would do if Justin were his brother. Now, after hearing the story of young William, there was no doubt.

How many baby boys named William were picked up at the same time from the Mobile Hospital by a polio hospital in Virginia? Especially ones that looked identical to William's twin.

No, the surmising of "what if" was replaced by the reality of the two men being twins. Even though there was no coincidence relating to their looking alike, there was a big coincidence of Will encountering two different people in a matter of days who mistook him for Justin.

Now, Will needed to take some time and game theory the "what if's." What if he admitted the truth; what would be the resultant effect on those involved?

If he continued to deny the truth, how would that impact him personally? If he were completely honest with himself, he'd admit finding his family was the real reason he moved to Mobile.

Now that he had found his family, could he mentally "unfind" them and move on? He'd have to give the situation some serious thought. Maybe there was middle ground upon which he could stand.

The two men walked out of the office and out into the sunshine. It was truly a beautiful day.

"So, Will, how about you and me go fishing in a couple weeks? I know some great spots."

"That sounds like a plan, Justin. How about I give you a call? I've been planning a boat trip for a while. It's all gassed up and ready to go. I'm heading around the coast and over to New Orleans.

"There's a new prospect I want to contact. I'll give you a call when I get back. It'll probably be at least eight to ten days, maybe even more. I'm not much into schedules these days."

Slapping Will on the back, Justin headed back into his office. As an afterthought, Will yelled, "Tell Marty and the girls I said hello."

Chapter 17
Reunion with Mr. Bell

Conny, Will's lawyer, had left a message with his answering service. He needed to see him; nothing serious, just something he wanted to discuss.

Since he told Justin he was planning a busines trip, Miami was as good a spot as any. Conny had not said it was an emergency so Will decided to take a couple of days and meander along the Gulf Coast.

Toward the end of day three, Will eased his boat into the wake-free area of the marina. He had chosen one as far away from the last moorage he had used as possible.

Some might consider his behavior a tad bit elevated on the paranoid scale; it had been several years since he first procured the boat in Miami.

Will's view on the topic was simple: why take the chance someone might remember him? Changing marinas was no more trouble than using the same one, and it was a lot safer.

He didn't really think anyone was trying to find him, but

why take chances. If he lived to be a 100 years old, part of him would always be on alert. It had, after all, been ingrained in him since childhood.

To change now would require extensive reprogramming; why would he do that? Will could think of no reason to do so.

The next morning, Will secured his boat and began walking until he came to a small motel. A taxi was just dropping off a fare. Will jumped in and rode away.

A change of taxis later (paranoid, right?), Will arrived downtown in the general area of Conny's office. In a building across the street from Conny's building, he spent time surveying the area.

During training, Will had excelled at basic tradecraft. He was very proficient at identifying surveillance and avoiding/losing the watchers.

Why was he doing that now? Why not? He had plenty of time; better safe and all that.

Twenty minutes later he was at a pay phone in another building with a different vantage point. He asked Conny to meet him at a coffee shop a couple of blocks away.

Will was sitting at a table in the rear of the shop and watching the front door. He saw Conny enter and stop to look around.

Spotting Will, Conny waved and started back to the table. Will stood as Conny reached the table. "Thanks for meeting me here, Conny. I really appreciate it."

"No problem, Will. I needed a little fresh air anyway. It's been one of those crazy mornings.

"It's been a while since we last met. I guess that's the advantage of phones and answering services. I almost didn't recognize you; you're not that young college kid I met years ago.

"Based on the business I've taken care of, I'd say the last five or six years have been profitable for you. As I can remember, you've accumulated two properties, a nice boat, an even nicer plane, and, more recently, a kick-ass car.

"The ghost-writing business must be going quite well."

"It is going very well; well enough, in fact, I can be choosier in the selection of projects. That, and the royalties flowing in have made me very financially comfortable.

"I'm trying not to travel so much, though; travel has gotten old. One hotel is pretty much like another. The only difference is the view out the window.

"That's why you've heard from an accountant in Mobile. I'm trying to settle down and live a more normal life.

"Is there some kind of problem with him or some other aspect of my business?"

"No, not at all, Will. As a matter of fact, your account with me is one of my most profitable when compared to others, based on time I have to spend sorting out legal issues.

"You are an excellent account and I really appreciate your business, which brings me to the reason I wanted to talk.

"I believe someone is trying to locate you."

Will's face, no doubt, registered his surprise. "That's news to me. I can't imagine why anyone would be looking for me. There's no family left and I've always been a loner; I'm not the kind of guy to leave a bunch of friends in my wake."

"I didn't think you were. You strike me as a very successful, yet private, young man. The fact we have met only three times during our business relationship is testament to your privacy."

"So, Conny, what has led you to the conclusion someone is looking for me?"

"A little backstory to help you make sense of what I think. If a person wants legal help relating to the international corporate community or foreign financial advice, they can go to any lawyer in town for help.

"What they don't understand, though, is that your average, run-of-the-mill lawyer has only cursory knowledge of such things. When the average Joe Lawyer has a client needing international help, said lawyer has to contact somebody like me.

"I, or one of the other half-dozen specialists like me, perform the necessary work, bill Joe Lawyer, and the client never realizes his lawyer contracted out the service.

"The point of my explanation is, if you want to find a person who is banking offshore, there's a good chance they are using one of us.

"Now, back to my wanting to see you. About a week ago, I had a guy show up in my office waving a Federal badge from some obscure agency, purportedly a division of the Treasury Department.

"First of all, I've never heard of such a division and secondly, this guy didn't strike me as the bean counter type.

"Before I continue, let me tell you something about my past. After law school, I did a stint in the military. Because of my education, the Army thought I'd be a good fit with their intelligence branch.

"Jump forward a bit, and I find myself in Vietnam working with special operations types. Some of the operators were not military; they were CIA types.

"I got to where I could identify them by their walk and the way they talked. They really stood out from your regular

Army guys.

"Back to a week ago and my visitor. I'd bet dollars to doughnuts the guy who came to see me was one of those guys.

"He said his name was Mr. Bell and he was doing preliminary investigative work into a money-laundering ring led by a young man. The only information he had was the young man was between 22 and 30 years old with a swarthy complexion. The suspect stood over six feet tall and weighed in excess of 200 pounds.

"He added the young man had an athletic build and was extremely well-spoken. He'd probably want to move money offshore, probably small amounts initially but increasing in volume over the years.

"I informed Mr. Bell I did not accept clients wanting to move money offshore unless they were large corporate accounts. Even then, I vetted them through the IRS and reported all major transfers.

"Mr. Bell then asked if I provided services for other attorneys, to which I responded, yes. He left a local contact number and asked me to contact him if I had any information cross my desk concerning such a young man.

"Will, in my opinion, this guy is a shooter, not some office drone. I don't know if you're who he's looking for or not, but I thought I'd give you a head's up.

"You're my client and my first responsibility is to you. To my knowledge, you are completely legal in your business transactions and have violated no U.S. laws.

"When you first came to me, you made it very clear you wanted everything done legally and wanted to learn international banking rules. That's the reason I took you on as a client.

"You obviously had stumbled upon a money-making career and wanted to make sure everything you did was legal. I admired your resolve and obvious intellect.

"If this guy is after you, it's not to review your tax return. I'd suggest you reconsider your permanent location to Mobile and head for Europe while maintaining an extremely low profile."

"Thanks, Conny, I really appreciate your concern and advice. Whomever Mr. Bell is chasing certainly sounds an awful lot like me. But let me reassure you, it is not me.

"As a matter of fact, if you will share Mr. Bell's contact information, I'll give him a call. If I don't, he may get on my scent and start to make a nuisance of himself. I'd just as soon head him off if I can."

The contact phone number Mr. Bell had left with Conny was the switchboard at a medium-priced hotel in the South Beach area of Miami.

Because of the time Will had lived in Miami, he knew exactly where to make his first stop. As in several of his previous jobs, he thought a good, used motorcycle might be his best option for transportation.

He had developed a list of dealerships around town where such transportation could be procured. He had never used the same one twice.

South Beach was one of those areas described by real estate agents in the 70's as "up and coming." Still somewhat affordable, it had been discovered by young people and wannabe celebrities.

Rolling through the beach area, Will saw no less than a dozen young men who fit his physical description. Fitting in around here should not be very difficult.

Before heading to Mr. Bell's hotel, Will headed to a "hot

cot" motel he knew about farther down the beach. Located in a considerable less touristy section of town, it consisted of small, stand-alone cabins, each with a one-car attached garage.

The Bay View Motel was popular for a short rendezvous. The convenience of shielding your car for an hour or two of illicit activity kept the place pretty busy.

Will was an anomaly at Bay View; he paid in advance for five nights. He now had a base of operations close to Mr. Bell's location with the added benefit of a place to hide his motorcycle if needed.

On the way to Bay View, Will had headed back to the Marina and picked up a few clothes and several other necessities. It was now time to go check out Mr. Bell.

Mr. Bell was staying at the Pink Surf Hotel. Pink Surf; what the hell was "pink surf?" Will had heard of red tide but never pink surf. Maybe red tide turned pink when encountering the shoreline.

He didn't really care; it was merely an idle curiosity to occupy his mind while he waited for his target to either arrive or leave.

Will was ensconced on the second floor of a three-story parking garage across the street from the hotel. It no doubt served to accommodate overflow traffic from the hotel.

The Pink Surf had its own parking lot adjacent to the front entrance. In many places, hotels hid their parking in the rear; not beach hotels, however. Beachside space was way too valuable to allocate for parking.

From his vantage point, Will could easily see eight vacant parking spaces in the lot. Given its convenience and ease of access, he figured Mr. Bell would choose to leave his preferred conveyance there.

Surveillance was hardly ever an easy activity. Will smiled at his TV memories of the good guys sitting in hotel rooms looking through giant binoculars at the bad guys.

He, however, was viewing the parking lot through a ventilation/light slot, one of many designed into urban parking structures so parking clients would not asphyxiate from exhaust fumes.

Will had parked his cycle next to a large van. He was hidden from passing vehicles by the van under which he was laying. No comfortable motel rooms for him.

Also, unlike on TV, the target doesn't show up in a timely fashion. Six hours after slithering into his makeshift hide under the van, Will watched as a nondescript, light green Chevy Nova pulled into the hotel's parking lot.

The Nova pulled into a vacant space close to the front doors. The driver slowly exited the car and stood for a few seconds. He was, no doubt, surveying the parking lot for potential trouble.

Mr. Bell swung his glance past the parking garage without pausing to examine it in detail. Will knew that didn't mean Mr. Bell had not looked at it carefully; he had.

Will had not been looking directly at his target; he had been using peripheral vision; Mr. Bell had emphasized the technique repeatedly.

Many people, even untrained ones, still had their animal instincts intact. Direct observation could often set off some primitive defense mechanism response in even the most innocuous person.

Most people feel it at least occasionally. How many times have we all heard a friend say, "It feels like someone is watching me."

Will never took chances, even those purportedly

connected to primitive caveman. You definitely don't want Mr. Caveman showing up with his big club.

Seemingly satisfied he was not in somebody's crosshairs, Mr. Bell took a large bag from the Nova's trunk and headed toward the front door. No doubt it contained some sort of weapon that could reach out and touch somebody.

Will noticed Mr. Bell's gait was not that of a normal man his age. He obviously had some sort of injury associated with his ankles.

Will smiled as he watched Mr. Bell limp slightly as he walked. The limp was probably much like Will's; it only made an appearance after fatigue had made an entrance.

In Will's case, fatigue was brought about by lingering effects of the polio he contracted as a baby. Mr. Bell's was, no doubt, the manifestation of having both Achilles tendons sliced by a sharp knife.

Will wondered whether or not there had been any lingering effects from having his eyes and lips superglued shut. Mr. Bell could possibly be holding a grudge for such actions, if he, in fact, knew who was to blame.

He obviously didn't totally buy into the story of Will's untimely demise. The Dean said the Director didn't really believe Will had died in the Memphis explosion. Maybe he shared his doubts with Mr. Bell.

If he did, then Mr. Bell probably deduced it was Will in the woods that night, especially since he had been left alive. What possible reason was there to do such a thing?

Leaving him alive was a serious tactical mistake. Only someone who knew and maybe considered him a friend would do such a thing.

If he believed it was Will in the woods, then it followed that he didn't think the Dean would allow Will inside that barn. Then, of course, there was the unexplainable ignition of the fatal explosion.

If ignited from inside, there would have been secondary explosions from the initial blast source. One gigantic explosion, like the one that night, seemed to be the result of all munitions exploding at the same time.

One detonator fired by hand or even timer just could not get the job done. Sure, it would create a killing blast and then a second or so later reach the other munitions and set them off.

But that had not happened. Everything in the barn went up at the same time. For that to happen, the igniting action had to be more powerful than a single detonator stuck in a block of C4.

The only explanation was an ignition device capable of blowing apart the barn all on its own. Say for instance, a LAW rocket fired into the barn. Now that would explain one big-assed explosion.

Will was postulating the possibilities for Mr. Bell's presence as he watched the older man limp into the hotel. But why was he hunting Will?

If he guessed it was Will in the woods that night, he should be grateful he was spared. Could he be so pissed, though, he wanted revenge?

Or did he want something else? Maybe he wanted out himself; possibly he wanted Will's help.

Will couldn't just kill Mr. Bell. It would certainly be easy enough. His Thompson Contender with a suppressed barrel could handle the job when he came back to his car.

There were two problems with such a direct action, however. What if Mr. Bell just wanted help? Killing him didn't seem a reasonable response.

There was also the secondary problem created by the publicity of such a kill. Conny would probably read about it in in the local paper and make the assumption Will had done it.

The assumption would, of course, be accurate. From the first would come the second assumption regarding the illegal nature of Will's activities. Such an assumption could create serious logistical issues.

It could lay open all his activities for public review. He didn't need that. Even though everything was technically legal, he wanted to avoid the problem.

The best course of action seemed to be a plan allowing him to talk with Mr. Bell. If he misjudged Mr. Bell, though, meeting him face-to-face was exceedingly dangerous.

Will decided to head back to his hot cot palace and get a few hours' sleep. Maybe a plan would reveal itself to him.

The Bay View was perfect for Will. People didn't stay at the Bay View's of the world to make new friends; they usually had more immediate needs to satiate.

Will didn't have those kinds of needs, but he did have a need for privacy. The current journey upon which he was embarking had no room for passengers.

He had hoped this part of his life was over and he could pursue a more normal existence. Other people seemed able to accomplish it; why couldn't he?

Will had to admit, though, nothing about his life had ever been normal. Why should the Gods of the universe change it now? He was what he was, and it was never going to change.

He could put a beard on it, maybe slap a couple coats of paint over the really ugly parts and sand off some of the rough edges; but the core of what Will was would remain with him forever.

What had he been thinking when he moved to Mobile? Finding his family was a fool's errand and could only hurt those with whom he connected.

When this current situation was resolved, he would disconnect from Justin, Marty, and the twins. There was no reasoning in the world allowing Will to justify putting them in danger.

He was not going to facilitate dragging them into his world of violence and pandemonium. They had done nothing to deserve such a fate.

Will decided to surveil Mr. Bell for a couple of days to see if he had a team. If a team were present, the best course of action would be exfiltration and living to fight another day.

He would not do that, however; the chance was too great Mr. Bell might be able to trace him to Mobile. Will would take the fight to him here, on familiar ground, where he held the tactical advantage.

By 6:00 the next morning, Will had resumed an observation point across the street from the Pink Surf Hotel. By 6:30, he had the answer to his team question.

A white, nondescript van with a plumbing logo on the sides slowed on the street and turned into the hotel parking lot. It stayed on the street side of the parking lot as far as possible from the Nova.

After parking and checking all doors to insure they were locked, the man headed toward the front entrance. Such behavior was a dead giveaway something of value was inside.

As the driver got to the front door, he turned and glanced back at the van. That was when Will was hit by the proverbial lightning strike.

Will knew the driver; he was one of the other two graduates of the Lost Boys' Academy. He had been one who could not meet the blood graduation requirement.

Since he wasn't a shooter, there could be only one reason he was here: the Lost Boy could identify Will on sight. He, no doubt, had other valuable skills to the Agency or he would not be here, but his biggest value was more personally oriented.

No more than 15 minutes after Lost Boy arrived, a third member of the team arrived. Will recognized him as one of the two men who had tried to follow him when he first left the training facility and headed to Miami for good.

So far, the team consisted of Mr. Bell, Lost Boy, and the Follower. He, too, could identify Will by sight. No more team members showed up; at least Will could not identify any more.

Whatever was going on in the hotel broke up less than an hour later. Mr. Bell was the first to leave; about 15 minutes later the Follower exited the hotel and drove away.

Will was sitting across the street on his bike when the Lost Boy also exited 20 minutes later. The team was being very cautious, obviously staying in three different hotels with each going a different location in their search.

The good part of all this was they were probably still casting a wide net in the attempt to locate Will. The bad part: they were seriously hunting him.

Everyone on the team knew him by sight, and if they were good at their jobs, they would eventually get on his scent. Since most Agency personnel were very good at their jobs, it was just a matter of time.

A matter of time, that is, unless someone interfered with

their obviously well-orchestrated search. Will figured he was as good a someone as anybody else.

The Lost Boy didn't give the motorcycle and its driver a second thought as he pulled into the morning drive-time traffic. It wouldn't have helped if he did; Will was concealed from head to toe.

The helmet, with darkened visor, made his face impossible to see. It was joined by a leather jacket over denim jeans and heavy biking boots.

After seeing the three members of the kill team, Will knew immediately the Lost Boy was the weakest link. Physically, he had been in the bottom half of the Academy class; intellectually, however, he had been second to only Will.

Given his attention to securing the van, Lost Boy was probably one of the Agency's highly touted surveillance experts. The van was undoubtedly loaded with sophisticated listening and communication equipment.

Will followed the van through the congested traffic of early morning. As always, the bike proved very adept at keeping sight of it yet maintaining a safe distance.

The van headed to the docks where it parked in view of the marina where Will had originally picked up his boat for the Key West job. Not a bad strategy.

One of the three team members must have been involved in procuring and mooring the boat. A skilled agent would never come back, but one never knew.

The follower was probably at the airport where Will picked up the plane for the Memphis job. Mr. Bell knew him well enough to guess he may not have gotten rid of the valuable vehicles.

Minus any hard data, Mr. Bell was working the lawyers

and the other two were staked out at the two locations just in case Will was stupid or over confident enough to violate basic tradecraft skills.

At any rate, the team had little to lose until something more solid came along. Will had the passing thought of just walking away; the team didn't have a clue where he was. They didn't really know if he was alive; they were merely operating on a hunch.

The thought faded quickly; Will refused to live with the thought a team was out there somewhere. Yeah, he could walk away; but if he did, he'd probably have to deal with them in the future.

No, he'd deal with the team now. Having an initial advantage of knowing they were after him and who they were was significant. He would leverage that while he could.

After observing the van for a couple hours, the side door slid open. Lost Boy quickly jumped out and headed for a public restroom. He had slowed only enough to lock and double-check the van.

Lost Boy must not have enjoyed the experience of pissing in a jug. Will followed the man into the public john. He was still wearing his helmet.

The surveillance specialist was now surveilling the inside of a crapper. With the noises emanating from within the stall, Will figured the task would take long enough for him to also take care of a little business himself.

He left the facility and moved back toward the van. Lost Boy came out a few minutes later and followed.

Just as he unlocked and slid the side door open, Will stepped quickly from the rear of the van and grabbed the man's arm. "Looking for somebody? Maybe I can be of assistance."

Will forced the smaller man into the van and closed the door. The equipment Will was expecting to be crowded into the van was missing.

There were a couple of cameras with long-range lenses and a steel trunk not unlike the kind Will had used in his van. The trunk was secured to the floor and locked.

The one thing surprising Will about the van was a set of straps secured to one sidewall with an accompanying set secured to the floor. In addition to the straps, a medicine cabinet was secured to the wall immediately behind the passenger seat.

The van looked like it was designed more for interrogation than surveillance. *Gee, I wonder who they want to interrogate.*

As Will looked up and over at Lost Boy, the other man displayed a guilty look and would not maintain Will's stare. "Get over here. I've got a few questions for you, but first we're going to find a little more solitude."

The man remained silent as Will secured him to the sidewall via the straps. Satisfied the Lost Boy was going nowhere, Will opened the back doors of the van and jumped out.

He returned pushing his lightweight bike. With a little huffing and puffing, he was able to get the machine loaded into the van. It was a tight fit with the man strapped to the wall, but it fit.

Ten minutes later, Will was making headway toward the airport. He loved airport long-term parking garages. People hardly ever lingered because of their schedules.

He pulled into the garage and drove the circular path leading eventually to the roof. Once on top, Will parked in a corner slot as far away from the stairs and elevator as possible.

He turned to face his passenger. "It's been a long time, Gene. That's probably no longer your name, but it'll do. Remember me?"

Gene, aka Lost Boy, finally made eye contact with Will, who was no longer wearing the bike helmet. "I knew it was you as soon as you grabbed my arm, even with the helmet visor covering your face.

"I had my doubts about you being alive, but I joined up anyway. I had nothing to lose. We were all beginning to think we were on a snipe hunt. Two weeks here in Miami and nothing to show for it. Lucky me!

"I always admired you, Will; Bell said that's still what you're called. I didn't join the team with the idea of hurting you. We just needed some information; that's all."

"Let's talk about that for a while. My impression is you are a kill team. Who all is on the team? Lie and I will kill you right now.

"Consider this a qualifying question. I already have a great deal of information from following you several days. I just don't have the whole story."

"You know I'm not a shooter; I'm a surveillance geek, and that's all. I'll tell you whatever you want to know.

"I know you're probably going to kill me, but I don't want to be tortured; I've never been strong like you. All I ask is you make it quick."

"Okay, Gene, I can do that. How many on the team and who are they."

"There're only three of us; Mr. Bell I've already mentioned, myself, and Joseph, another surveillance guy like me. That's all, I swear.

"We're not really a full-blown team; we're unsanctioned. As a matter of fact, Bell is disabled and retired; Joseph was a mandatory retirement because of age; and me, I'm just tired, tired of traveling around the world and viewing it through a van window."

"What made you guys come after me; what's the point of finding me?"

"It was Bell's idea. The three of us have worked together numerous times and know each other quite well. You probably know the Dean is dead.

"Bell was there that night. He's convinced you were there, too, and you're the one who cut him up. He said it had to be you; anyone else would have just killed him.

"He also said, of all the snipers he has trained, you are the best and probably the only one capable of sneaking up on him. He's convinced the explosion at the barn that night was caused by a rocket.

"He told us the after action report said there were no secondary explosions, just one great big bang. Bell thinks you ignited the explosion somehow, maybe a LAW rocket or the like."

"That still doesn't explain why you guys are hunting me down. What's that all about?"

"It's money, Will. Pure greed. None of us have enough money to retire the way we would like to retire, even the other two guys. Their pensions might get them a used, single-wide trailer house in Florida, but not much more."

"I understand that, Gene, but how am I associated with securing a better retirement for the other two? You, I don't understand at all. You're young enough to start a new career and put in 30 years."

"You're right about me; just lazy I guess, but also burned

out on life with what I've seen and been involved in. You probably know what I'm talking about."

"Yeah, I do; this business can really get on top of you. Until you guys came a-calling, I was pretty much retired.

"Enough polite talk. Explain the plan after you located me."

"Pretty simple, really. We've got enough lethal and non-lethal firepower in that trunk there to take you. At least, that's what Bell said.

"After getting you strapped into the constraints here in the van, Joseph would get the information we needed. He spent some time in the interrogation unit of the Agency.

"The medicine case you see up front has a full array of chemical interrogation supplies."

"Okay, Gene, you've talked around the subject. What exactly do you want?"

Will had removed his knife from his pocket and opened it. A trickle of blood was visible where he pressed it against Gene's neck. "No more bullshit; what?"

"Please don't do that, I'll tell you! It's the bank number where you transferred the Dean's stash. Everyone knows field operatives all stockpile money away, just in case they have to run.

"Hell, the Dean had been at it a long time. Bell said he probably had millions stashed offshore in some Cayman or Swiss account."

"What makes Bell think I had access to the account? I wouldn't think it the kind of information an old spy like the Dean would share.

"If he did, it would be with a child or some other relative. It certainly wouldn't be with one of his trainees."

"Based on what Bell said, you were more than just a

trainee to the old man. The Dean was a lifelong bachelor with no living family left. Bell said he'd give it to you because he viewed you like a son.

"Everybody knew the Dean was past due. He had already outlived the cancer prognosis. Bell figured he called the head-shed guys there that night to kill them while committing his own suicide.

"If he did and you somehow showed up, Bell's thesis seems likely. He's convinced, however, the Dean called you to help out."

Will wandered up front to the medicine cabinet which proved easy to jimmy open. He looked at the array of chemicals available.

His initial training after leaving the Lost Boys' Academy had included basic pharmacology. The Agency provided several chemical options for not only interrogation but also dispatching targets.

There was also a very special chemical concoction designed for use when killing a person wasn't a viable option. Oftentimes, information was needed from an uncooperative innocent.

Once the chemical interrogation had been completed, turning the person loose to report what had been done wasn't something the Agency could allow.

The chemical mixture was referred to as "The Time Machine." Once injected by The Time Machine, it was as if a time machine had transported the innocent back in time.

Depending on the unique physiology of each innocent, they would be mentally transported back in time anywhere from one to three years.

For most, their memory of the past 12 or so months was completely erased. It wasn't immediate, though.

For the first couple of weeks, they couldn't remember their own name or any other personal information. Then, all of a sudden, everything was back except the lost years. There was no case history of the lost memory ever being recovered.

Will palmed The Time Machine hypodermic and stepped back to Gene. He held it up. "You know what this is?"

"I'm not sure, but I think it looks like The Time Machine. The print is too small for my eyes."

"You're right, Gene, it's The Time Machine. I doubt I would have received this accommodation, but because of our past relationship, you will."

"Thank you, Will. Both Joseph and Bell argued saying you were much too dangerous to leave alive. You may not believe me, but I argued against killing you.

"You probably don't know this, but I failed the final exam activity back at the Academy. I couldn't bring myself to kill. That's why I ended up in surveillance.

"Honest, Will, I didn't want you dead. The money was important, but not as much as your life.

"I figured they might kill me, too, because I argued so strenuously with them. I caught them a couple of times looking at each other in a funny way.

"My only ace in the hole was their ignorance of international banking. But, even that wasn't a sure thing for me."

"One last question before you start your time trip, Gene. Where are you and Joseph staying?"

"Bell thought it a good idea that we be spread out. It would increase our chances of finding you. He's in the Pink Surf Hotel; Joseph and I are staying on the western edge of town in a small house.

"Joseph grew up here on a small farm that grew oranges and other fruit. When his parents died, they left him the farmhouse and about ten acres of land.

"We decided to stay there in case we needed something other than the van for you."

He gave Will the address and directions to the farm. "Thanks, Will. I would say I'll never forget what you did for me, but we both know that's not true."

The men offered meek smiles in response to the dark humor. Will injected Gene and sent him back to the past.

The next day, a local Florida daily newspaper reported an unidentified man found wandering North of Miami in Fort Lauderdale. The individual was reported to be suffering from amnesia. Officials had no idea who he was or where he was from. The man carried no documents of any type.

Will left the van in long-term parking at the Fort Lauderdale airport. If he needed it, he knew where it could be found.

Later in the day, an hour before sundown, a motorcycle ridden by a man in leather and jeans with a darkened helmet visor rode past a rundown house on a few acres just west of Miami.

The place looked like no one had paid attention to it for some time. Weeds were making a valiant effort to overtake the sandy yard, and the house was in desperate need of a coat of paint.

Adjacent to the house was a detached carport with room for one car. The small structure was currently occupied by a mid-sized Ford sedan, no doubt a rental.

Will could detect no activity as he cruised by the farm. Joseph was probably inside waiting for Gene.

Joseph would probably hang out awhile and head out

again. The nature of surveillance meant anyone could be anywhere at any time. Gene might show up or might not.

Will found a secluded spot among a stand of cottonwood trees, no doubt an old homestead. The countryside was full of them. He was able to conceal his bike and still observe the house.

It didn't take long for Joseph to give up on Gene and head out. Will stepped back within the shadows of the trees as the Ford sped by.

He figured Joseph was, at a minimum, headed out for supper. He might even indulge in a few drinks with his meal. Will figured he had a couple hours minimum before his target returned.

Will waited 30 minutes to make sure Joseph did not return to the house. There were other reasons to leave home other than drinks and dinner out. He could be running a quick errand before preparing dinner in.

Will made his way down to the small house without revealing himself to passersby on the road. He stealthily approached the house from the rear.

Squatting at the edge of the yard, he was able to scan the house and adjacent ground. Will's eyes immediately came to rest on a large propane tank.

The tank sat about 20 or 30 feet from the house as they often do. People like Will viewed an open propane tank as a bomb waiting for ignition.

He stood up and listened to insure his presence had gone undetected. Satisfied he had gone unnoticed, he moved quickly to the back wall of the house.

By looking back at the propane tank, Will estimated where the buried gas hose entered the house. Moving to that spot, he lowered his body to the ground.

As with most older structures in the countryside, Joseph's house sat about 12 inches off the ground on several strategically placed solid concrete supports.

The entire perimeter was then enclosed with some type of barrier to keep out dampness. On each side of the house, a small, screen-covered vent was typically located to facilitate airflow, crude but effective.

Will was lying beside the house where he projected the propane hose entered. It took him fifteen minutes to unearth the hose and excavate the dirt under it. He could now, by feel, examine the hose's entrance upward into what he guessed was the kitchen.

Located about 18 inches from the hose's entrance point under the wall was one of the screened vents. Using his knife, Will removed the screen from the vent.

With that accomplished, he moved back down to the hose entrance. By putting his hand through the excavated opening, he could get the knife under the house where he carefully sliced through the propane hose as it came out of the ground under the kitchen.

Being very careful not to make contact with any spark producing rock or metal, he warily removed his hand and knife.

Will then took time and pushed the excavated dirt back into place. Standing and looking down at the spot, he could not determine anything had been done.

Making his way back to the stand of cottonwoods proved uneventful. Will's hiding place was approximately 40 yards from the vent he had modified. He settled in to wait.

Sometime shortly after midnight, the rental Ford showed up. Joseph's gait seemed to be wobbling as he got out of the car and headed toward the front door. Maybe he had more drinks than dinner.

Whatever the issue, it was working in Will's favor. Continuing to watch Joseph proved a bit entertaining. First, he stumbled going up the porch steps; then he dropped his keys while trying to unlock the front door.

Obviously, the man was drunk. Mr. Bell wouldn't be happy given the seriousness of the mission.

Obviously mad at the door for its obstinate behavior, Joseph slammed it violently after entry. The sound easily carried to Will's hiding place.

His intention was to create an explosion that might be viewed as an accident. Propane was the perfect vehicle. It was an extremely flammable gas which was involved in rural house fires on a regular basis.

Since propane vapors are heavier than air, they can accumulate in low-lying areas such as under the floors of houses built off the ground. When the underneath space is confined by dampness barriers, the leaking propane would simply accumulate at the lowest point.

While waiting for Joseph to return from dinner, Will had assembled his T/C rifle and attached a 22 magnum barrel. To the barrel, he attached a sound suppressor.

The disassembled rifle fit perfectly into the backpack Will was wearing. When he had last been on his boat, he chose the 22 magnum barrel because the sound could be suppressed to almost nothing.

Not knowing exactly how he might need to use the rifle, Will brought several types of ammunition. One type was tracer rounds.

Tracer rounds consist of bullets built with a small pyrotechnic charge (explosive powder) in their base. Ignited by the burning gun powder, the pyrotechnic composition burns very brightly, making the bullet path visible to the naked eye

Tracer rounds may also ignite incendiary elements on contact from a marginal distance. This secondary use was why Will chose to use them.

During the several hours Will had been waiting for his adversary to return, the leaking propone hose had probably emptied the tank. The heavier than air flammable gas had, by now, infused every available crevice underneath the house.

Any ignition source would obliterate the structure and any person or thing inside. The only clue to the fire being deliberate was the sliced hose. The extreme heat would melt that clue away immediately.

All these things passed through Will's mind as he heard the door slamming. The Thompson Contender rifle seemed to effortlessly ascend to his shoulder. The screenless vent appeared in his scope.

Will's heartbeat had slowed as it always did in a shooting scenario. His finger added ever increasing pressure to the trigger.

The round made the trip downrange with almost no sound. The only hint of its passage was the incendiary trail left by the pyrotechnic charge.

The bullet passed through the vent opening carrying the ignition source with it. Within the blinking of an eye after leaving the rifle barrel, ignition was achieved.

Explosion and complete obliteration of the house were simultaneous. One fraction of a second the house was there, and then it was gone.

Burning embers of the wooden structure were strewn a hundred yards in all directions. Engulfed by the initial explosion, the carport and ensconced rental car blew shortly thereafter.

Obliteration of the two structures was absolute. A pile of twisted metal marked the spot of the Ford.

Needless to say, annihilation of Joseph's body was utter. Evidence of the body would be nil and next to impossible to verify. Forget positive identification.

The house had no sooner exploded than Will was on his bike and headed to his hot cot motel. He needed some rest before launching phase three of his plan.

…Breakfast at the Pink Surf

Will walked into the Pink Surf at 6 am; he wanted time to check the lobby for exits and possible ambush points. The place was your run-of-the-mill, moderately expensive beach property.

Stepping into the dining room, he requested a table for two in the rear close to the kitchen door. After being seated, he ordered a carafe of coffee and two cups plus a tray of pastries.

Just as Will had expected him to do, Mr. Bell walked into the restaurant at 6:30. He did not glance in Will's direction nor scan the rest of the room for danger.

Will was surprised at the lackadaisical approach of his former instructor. He thought it could be a manifestation of the physical injuries received at Will's hands.

It could also be merely the familiarity of eating here for several mornings. Will's suspicious mind jumped in a different direction, though.

Perhaps Bell had caught a quick glance of Will and decided to feign sloppy tradecraft. Erring on the side of caution, Will went for the latter explanation.

Catching the attention of his waitress, Will asked her to inform the hostess he wanted Mr. Bell to join him.

Bell pretended to be shocked when the Hostess redirected him in Will's direction. Will kept both hands on the table as Bell walked up.

Sitting to join Will, Bell also kept his hands on the table. "Well, well, if it isn't the boy wonder himself. It's a miracle: you're not dead. I knew the Dean was blowing smoke up my ass.

"I could just feel it in my bones. Especially after that night in the woods. That was you, wasn't it? You made a big tactical mistake; you should have killed me."

Will was taking in Mr. Bell's demeanor; he had also taken special note of his physical challenges when the hostess was bringing him over. His old instructor was not motoring well.

It was obvious that night in the woods had taken its toll. Sliced Achilles could do that if not properly rehabbed. Mr. Bell was probably 30 pounds heavier and looked 20 years older.

He also had the look of the heavy drinker. Even with the physical changes, Mr. Bell still somehow had the look of a guy who had been there and done that, as they say.

Will knew the man was still a serious threat. His body may have gone south, but his mind was probably the same.

Their profession was a thinking man's profession. Sure, an athletic body helped, but it didn't take a great deal of athleticism to pull a trigger.

"Yeah, that was me in the woods; you got a little sloppy, didn't you? Were you in the bag or something?"

"In the bag, my ass. I may have had a couple drinks, but

it was the most boring job in the world. I didn't think anyone could slip up on me like that.

"You were the only guy I ever trained I thought had anything close to my skills, and I thought you were dead. You know you got lucky, right?"

"Please, Mr. Bell, lucky? Hell, a Boy Scout with a BB gun could have taken you. If you remember, I didn't have to stalk you at all. I spotted your hide almost immediately and was thinking how best to approach.

"Then, to my amusement, you just stood up and walked right over to where I was crouched. I actually had to stifle a yawn as I was taking you out."

"Stifle a yawn, my ass; you just got lucky because my bladder wasn't what it used to be. I have to admit, though, I was very surprised to wake up.

"Slicing the Achilles was a good touch. You knew it would be months before I'd be back on my feet. But the superglue, that was just mean. Where did you learn that, anyway?"

Will was watching Mr. Bell with interest. If he didn't know better, he'd think the older man was nervous, maybe even a little scared.

Being bested at a skill you had worked a lifetime to perfect could do that to you. "I learned the superglue trick in a spy novel; worked pretty well, didn't it?"

"You could say so; it took the doctors two days to figure out how to get my eyes open without blinding me."

Will noticed Mr. Bell kept throwing quick glances at the restaurant's entrance. "You can quit looking; they're not coming to your rescue. As a matter of fact, there're not going anywhere, ever again."

Will had lied about Gene, but he didn't want Mr. Bell to

get the idea he was getting soft. He wanted his imagination to run wild conjuring in his mind possible scenarios.

"You should really have gotten better help, Mr. Bell. It took almost five minutes for me to deal with each of them. That just leaves you.

"I don't suppose I could take your word you'd just drive away forgetting about me and promising not to tell anybody about me. Could I."

"You wish, you arrogant shit. You think because you got lucky in the woods that night, you are now better than me. I may be a little older and a few pounds heavier, but my trigger finger still works as good as ever. You'll discover that soon enough.

"Don't worry, though; I'm not going to kill you. I still intend to get the Dean's money from you. After I finish, I'm going to leave you with bullets in both knees and pelvis.

"You'll live, but for the rest of your life, you'll think about me every day when you are struggling around in a wheelchair. I don't want you dead; I want you suffering."

Will repositioned his right hand on the tabletop and Mr. Bell jumped slightly. Will laughed. "A little nervous, are we Mr. Bell? May I get you a Valium with a shot of whiskey to wash it down?"

Mr. Bell could not hide his anger; it was immediately obvious by his facial expressions and voice. He moved his hand slightly toward the edge of the table. "Maybe we should just finish this right now, right here."

"I don't think so, Mr. Bell; there's still the imagined money to consider. I understand Federal disability retirement falls a little short in the lavish living department. Of course, maybe a used, single-wide trailer behind a gas station is all you really need."

"You've really got a mouth on you kid; I don't know why the Dean took to you. Must have been dementia or something."

"Okay, Mr. Bell, enough chest puffing. I concede; you're a big, bad, tough guy. Maybe, you'll even concede I have a respectable skill set myself.

"We can take umbrage with each other all morning or we can get on with it. How do you propose we proceed? I want you to go away, and you want to cripple me.

"That's why I'm here today. I had hoped we could reach an amicable agreement. I was willing to share the money with you, but I now see there is more to it. You also want revenge.

"You're really pretty stupid, aren't you? You're just an old drunk who teamed up with a couple non-shooters to try and take me.

"What were you thinking? Maybe you thought I'd quiver in my boots at the thought of you and your reputation. Did you forget I've outmaneuvered you once already?"

All of a sudden, Bell's demeanor morphed into that of an aggressive predator completely in control. "I knew your arrogance would get the better of you, asshole.

"Did you really think I'd come after you with only Gene and Joseph? I knew you'd take them out as fast as a drive-through burger. They were the distraction.

"I knew you'd eliminate them and come find me so you could gloat. 'So, here you are,' said the spider to the fly."

Will's face immediately became a feigned mask of confusion and fear. "What are you talking about?"

"What I'm talking about is you underestimated me. I planned on you killing my two Agency cohorts. I also planned on you showing up here.

"I didn't know how or exactly when, but I figured today or tomorrow. You're now in my little trap.

"I'll give you a choice: surrender and follow me up to my room, or try to leave."

Will was faking the regaining of his composure. "I think I'll choose the leaving thing. You're too old and beat-up to stop me by yourself."

"You're right, Will; I can't stop you by myself, but my four friends from the Cuban Mafia might be able to help. Every one of them outweighs you by 20 pounds and is a lot meaner than you.

"There're two in a car out back and two more parked by the front door. Either way you go, you're trapped.

"I don't want you too scared, though. I told them to shoot you in the legs; I need some information, remember."

Mr. Bell was standing by now and staring at Will with a taunting little smile. Will stood and retrieved his cycle helmet from the floor. "You figured this out all by yourself, did you Mr. Bell? I'm so impressed and really, really scared."

Just as Bell was about to respond, Will hit him hard in the mouth with the motorcycle helmet and ran through the kitchen door.

The two Cubans in the back alley saw the helmeted tall man appear in the alley. He immediately ran behind a dumpster, then reappeared almost instantly on a lightweight motorcycle.

They immediately pursued with tires squealing on the alley's paved surface. The passenger had a walkie-talkie raised to his mouth, no doubt alerting his colleagues.

About this time, Mr. Bell was being helped to his feet by a waiter. His mouth was bleeding profusely, and there was a noticeable gap where two of his front teeth had been.

Shoving the waiter aside, he had his walkie-talkie to his ear listening to the rapid conversations bouncing between the two sets of his men.

The car from the alley was right on the cycle's tail. The second car was pulling away from the curb as Bell ran out the front door. The car screeched to a stop and he jumped into the back seat. "Let's go; I don't want to lose that son-of-a-bitch."

The passenger had turned and was looking at his boss. "Damn, Boss, what happened to you? You're bleeding like crazy, and it looks like a couple of your teeth are missing."

"The little prick sucker punched me with his helmet. When we catch him, I'm gonna shove it up his ass.

"Get on the walkie and find out where the others are. I don't want to lose them."

The other car came online. "He's about a block in front of us, and the traffic is light. We're heading out of town on Dixie Highway about two miles away from the hotel.

"He just turned into that large industrial warehouse area. You know the one that was abandoned when the hurricane blew most of it down a couple of years ago."

The passenger in Bell's car hurriedly responded. "Yeah, we know the one; we're a couple of minutes behind you. Keep on him; we'll help box him in."

The cycle sped through the destruction of the abandoned warehouses. He circled through the area as if he were toying with his followers. By now, the second car had caught up and was also in close pursuit.

The cycle wove its way through the area and toward an especially large building on the back edge of the complex.

The building was one of the few still standing. It was

huge by anybody's standards. It easily occupied 100,000 square feet and was accessed on the front by two large overhead doors, one blocked by debris.

The cycle entered the building and immediately slowed to a crawl as it navigated huge mounds of rubble and assorted equipment, some the size of small buildings. The place was like a maze designed by lunatics.

The back doors were completely blocked except for an opening just wide enough to walk the bike through. Inside the two cars had come to a halt. They could still hear the cycle but could tell it wasn't speeding.

The cars were parked about 20 yards inside the open front entrance. The five men had exited and were listening to the sounds of the motorcycle.

Driver one was pointing toward the rear of the building. "He's back there somewhere. It sounds like the engine is idling; he must be walking it through the junk. If he makes it, we'll never catch him; he could go in a dozen different directions."

About that time, the entrance, through which the two cars had passed, exploded. The five men and two cars were showered with all manner of debris, some small and other large enough to kill.

The explosion was far enough away that most damage was superficial. Most was not all, however. The passenger in car one did not get up to join the others.

As the four others stood and surveyed the damage, one noticed his friend had not moved. "Hey, Carlos, you okay? Get your ass up."

Carlos didn't move so the other three quickly moved to where he was covered by light pieces of metal, probably from the overhead door.

One of the men removed a larger piece of the metal covering Carlos' head. "Shit! Look at that. A piece of metal cut his throat; it almost cut off his head. He didn't have a chance."

The remaining men jumped in unison as the sound of a motorcycle passed the now blocked entrance at full throttle. Mr. Bell retrieved a larger piece of overhead door and covered the dead body. "Well, there he goes. The first thing he was taught was to always have a backup plan.

"At one level, I'm proud of him; at another, I'm pissed I let him suck us into this trap. Now you guys know why I needed some heavy muscle.

"This guy is smart and extremely dangerous. But he'll still be out there when we get out. He won't be easy to fool again. Let's see if we can move enough of this crap to get the cars out."

The remaining four men walked to the junk pile now blocking the door. Just as the first man reached the pile and bent over to start, he fell face forward.

Before anything untoward registered with the other three, a second Cuban dropped close to his fallen comrade. By now, Bell's instincts had clicked in and he was diving for cover.

The remaining Cuban was not so lucky. His escape journey was halted in midstride. As he dropped facedown on the floor, Bell was scrambling for a more secure position.

He achieved the protection of a small disabled forklift. "Is that you, Wonder Boy? Maybe I should have paid more attention to the Dean's opinion of you.

"He always said you were the brightest trainee we ever had. I'll admit it; I underestimated you.

"This obviously took a little time to set up, how did you

figure things out?"

Will's voice drifted down from an elevated position. "I've never underestimated you, Mr. Bell; you were an exceptional operator. Even though you've diminished somewhat physically, I never thought, for a minute, your mind had.

"After I took care of your initial team, I got to thinking. The whole thing was too easy. An operator of your experience would never leave a contact number leading back to a physical location.

"Then, when I was reconsidering the situation, you show up just nonchalantly parking your car and walking into the hotel. I knew something was wrong.

"Gene and Joseph were just bait. The real kill team had to be hiding in the shadows. Once I came to that conclusion, the rest was just planning.

"I needed to get the whole team in one place at the same time. I took the chance you had not shared my background with the rest of the team. Not tactically smart on your part.

"I knew about this place from my time living in Miami. It's still newsworthy occasionally as the city tries to decide how to handle such an eyesore."

"That wasn't you we were chasing, was it, Will? You ran a look-alike in on us didn't you?"

"I did, but it was a grand well spent. The hardest part was finding a guy my size who could ride well enough to fool you.

"I wanted to be well situated before you guys arrived. I took a shortcut while my double took you for a bit of a ride.

"Once the parade left the hotel, I came straight here and armed the explosive. I couldn't do it in advance and endanger some homeless person or kid messing around."

"What now, Will? That was what you asked back at the hotel, wasn't it? Where do we go from here?"

"We do what guys like us do. Only one of us will walk away.

"Shall we have at it?"

Mr. Bell could not get to high ground as easily as Will. The damage to his feet and lack of adequate rehabilitation, prevented most climbing and jumping from pile to pile of junk.

The two men would throw a few shots at each other and then move. The secret to staying alive in a shootout was usually movement.

When designing his trap for Mr. Bell, Will had anticipated the outcome. Even though Mr. Bell was limited physically, his reflexes and other instinctive behaviors were still top notch.

Engaging in an extended shootout with such a highly trained operative might not turn out in Will's favor. Such an old warhorse might have some secret techniques up his sleeve.

With this in mind, Will had placed not one but two explosives in the old dilapidated building. All his shots and movement the past few minutes had been choreographed to position Mr. Bell exactly where he was currently concealed.

"Hey, Boy Wonder, I can do this all day long. You may have the high ground and more agility, but I've been in the game a lot longer.

"How about we split the Dean's money and I forget you exist? I give you my word. You don't really want to kill me anyway or you would have done it in the woods that night.

"I'll give you an account number and you transfer half the money. I'll trust your word on the deal."

Will knew about what Mr. Bell's word was worth; just ask Gene and Joseph. Looking across the expanse of the warehouse, he now knew exactly where Mr. Bell was hiding.

To Mr. Bell, it seemed like the perfect place; he was well protected on all sides and there were no good downward angle shots. He was perfectly placed where Will would have to come to him.

"Think about my offer, Will. It's your safest bet. I'm in a very defensible position. To get at me, you'll have to expose yourself.

"You're a good shot, but I'm just as good if not a little better. I give your chances of success at 75 / 25, in my favor. Take the deal and we both walk away with something."

If Will thought for a moment Mr. Bell would keep his word, he'd give him the money. He didn't really need it. His own preparation had been more than adequate for a comfortable existence.

"Here's my deal, Mr. Bell. Kill yourself and avoid the agony of an extended death." As he talked, he was loading a tracer round into his rifle.

"What do you say? A single gunshot will suffice as an answer. I'm listening."

"You're a real smartass, aren't you? Let's see how you do against a trained opponent. Come get me, if you can."

Will raised his rifle and aimed about a foot over Mr. Bell's head. He had concealed a block of C-4 behind what appeared, at a casual glance, to be cardboard rubbish.

He slowed his breathing and started to apply trigger pressure. As usual the gun fired without Will's conscious knowledge. The tracer's pyrotechnic did its job.

Almost concurrently with the slight pressure Will felt on

his shoulder, the explosive made its presence known. Mr. Bell had no time to react or be surprised.

Cautiously working his way over to what had become Mr. Bell's last sniper hide, Will scrutinized the damage. His target had absorbed most of the directional blast, just as it had been designed.

Squatting down, Will touched his former instructor's neck in search of a pulse. Mr. Bell's eyes fluttered in an attempt to look up at Will. "The student truly had become the teacher and the teacher the student, just as the Dean said."

Will worked his way to the rear of the structure and pushed his bike out into the bright sunshine. He wondered to himself. *How many more Mr. Bells are there at the Agency?*

Will knew he had been born of an organization built on suspicion and mistrust. What made him think he could just walk away?

His life had never been simple; why should it be so now? Will had not really been collecting good karma based on his actions of the last few years.

Chapter 18
Moving On

Will left Miami much as he had arrived, anonymously. The look-alike he had hired never saw his face; Will kept it concealed behind the shaded visor of his motorcycle helmet.

The men who were hunting him had all been cancelled in a most permanent fashion. Even if found and identified, the Agency would work with local law enforcement to cover things up.

Even though Mr. Bell was operating off the reservation, the Agency could still be tied to the whole thing because of his previous affiliation.

Leaving Gene alive might come back to haunt Will, much like Mr. Bell had. He considered the statistical probability of such an occurrence almost 0%, though.

The Agency would wonder who did it, but they could never be sure. The best candidate for "The Time Traveler" was Mr. Bell. With no further data to discount the theory, it would be filed away and forgotten, just as Mr. Bell would be.

…Back in Mobile

The fallout of the Miami situation had been the realization, by Will, he could not just morph into Joe Citizen in Mobile and live out his days in peace. If he tried, the consequences might reach out and engulf his newly found family and friends.

Will could not allow that to happen. He was what he was, and they were what they were. Their relationship was analogous to a burning candle floating in a bucket of gasoline.

At some point, it was inevitable; the candle would ignite the gasoline and all participants would be destroyed. His family and friends deserved a better fate.

They had not asked him to enter their lives; he had forcibly inserted himself. It was now time to undo the insertion.

Disassociation might prove to be more difficult than it appeared on the surface, though. Justin and Marty had some pretty serious suspicions.

He'd have to deal with those. They weren't just going to disappear; they would require some serious neutralization.

Will took a long and circuitous route back to Mobile. He needed a plan, and it required flawless execution. His family's and friends' lives might well depend upon it.

…Plan of Disassociation

During the many hours alone on the Gulf, Will had

reached some conclusions which would become major components of his disassociation plan. The first had to do with his growing number of physical assets.

He came to the conclusion possessions were an Albatross around the neck of effective disappearance and ultimate invisibility. Possessions equaled baggage.

Will planned on staying in Mobile no longer than 30 days. Within that time period, he would liquidate all physical assets minus the airplane.

The plane would be needed to disappear from Mobile. He'd liquidate it later.

Will decided to pull into the Panther Run Marina instead of heading to his boathouse. He could see Bob puttering around on the dock.

Will stopped his boat by the fueling barge. As was habit with all his vehicles, he kept the fuel tanks topped off and ready to go. Never knew when you might have to leave in a hurry.

Bob made his way out to the fueling barge as Will temporarily tied up. "Hey, Will, I was beginning to think you got lost or something. Everything okay?"

"Yeah, everything's alright, Bob. I just took the long way home after spending a few days in Miami. I had some serious thinking to do."

Bob started the fueling process then walked over to where Will had stepped up on the barge. "That sounds kind of serious. Anything I can help you with?"

"As a matter of fact, there is, Bob. I detoured to Miami because the owners of the company I work for were in town and wanted to see me. The two of them had a very interesting proposition they wanted to discuss.

"There was a third minor owner who had recently died

and left his shares in the corporation to his aging wife. Because of her age and deteriorating health, she wanted to sell her stake.

"They offered me the first right of refusal on the stock. Her minor share plus stock I already own would be enough to guarantee me a position on the company's board of directors.

"I don't know how much you know about these kinds of things, but it's a really big deal. I'd go from contract employee to third largest shareholder in the company.

"My salary would increase significantly, and I'd participate in all corporate decisions."

"That sounds like a great deal, Will. What's the catch? There's always a catch."

"You're right. The catch is, I have to live in Brussels, Belgium. That brings me to how you can help.

"I need to unload the boat and boathouse. Do you know professionals who can help me do that?

"Also, I've got quite a few things to deal with before I leave. I'll need someone to show potential buyers the boat and boathouse. If you'll find people to sell them and then show them for me, I'll give you $5,000 on each when they sell."

"Will, you know I'll do both of those things for you, but you don't have to pay me ten grand. I'll do it for nothing."

"I know you will, Bob, but I'm not going to accept your help unless you accept the money. Besides, it's company money, not mine."

Bob held out his hand for Will to shake. "In that case, I'd love to take the money." Both men laughed.

...

It had been a week since that day on the dock with Bob. Bob had wasted no time getting everything under way.

After Will had meetings with the two salespeople, it was in Bob's hands until offers came in. The boat sold within a few days; it was in very good shape and priced to move.

The boathouse was also priced to move but had no serious offers yet. Will was sitting downstairs in the boathouse with the overhead door open.

He was talking on the phone with Justin. They had spoken a couple of times since Will got back into town but had not seen each other. "Okay, Will, I did what you said. Everything relating to you and/or your new business has been removed from my files and shredded.

"Your presence on the IRS's radar has been reduced to whatever it was before we met. The only thing not disappearing is my bill for expert services rendered.

"Are you real sure you want to become a Belgiumnite or whatever they call themselves? You're also getting yourself involved in a socialistic economy.

"The tax rates are exorbitant. Tax, social security contributions and other deductions often amount in total to more than half of an employee's monthly salary.

"That's one hell of a bite. Hopefully, all their government services are worth it."

"Don't worry, my ugly brother from another mother; they have tax-cheating assistance over there just like you offer here. I'll be fine.

"How're Marty and the girls? You taking good care of them?"

"Naw, not at all; but as long as they keep selling homemade pralines on the streets, I let them stay here. They do have to pay room and board, though.

"By the way, Marty told me to tell you she was planning on you for supper tomorrow night and excuses were not acceptable. Be here at 5:30, or we're both in big trouble."

"Well, I did have a hot date, but I can reschedule; I'll see you then."

"Hot date, my ass, and as for as rescheduling; as long as you pay her going rate for undesirables, she'll show up.

"Don't be late!"

Before Will could get the last word in, Justin hung up.

When Will showed up for supper the next night, the first thing he noticed was the extra car in the driveway. "No, no, no," was all he could mutter as he walked to the door.

The door opened before he could knock. Jess and Tess were once again dressed to the max. To a woman, having beautiful little girls must be the ultimate game of dolls except they were real walking, talking dolls.

The twins were wearing identical blue dresses and white shoes. Looking at them standing in the doorway smiling was surreal.

Then it hit him. People seeing Justin and him together must have the same feeling. It had to be fascinating yet weird at the same time.

"Hello, Uncle Will."

"Uncle Will, is it? You know I'm not really your uncle, right?"

They spoke in unison as if they shared one voice. "We know, but Mama said we could call you Uncle if we wanted to. Is it okay?'

"Of course, I don't mind at all. Who else is here? There's another car outside."

Again, the one combined voice answered. "Grandma and

Grandpa Boché are here. Mama said they wanted to meet you."

I bet they do, Will thought to himself. He had deduced it would probably be hard to exfiltrate Mobile without a meeting.

If he were truthful with himself, he'd admit he really wanted to meet his parents. Leaving without ever having met them would be hard if not impossible to do.

Following the twins into the living room, Will experienced a very unfamiliar emotion—fear. Who were these people? Could he control his emotions upon meeting them?

Would they jump to conclusions as Marty had? How could he convince them he was not their son? Could he devise a story good enough to deceive them?

He had to, and it had to convince Marty and Justin. When he left Mobile, he had to leave them behind for good. If not, they might be in danger. He had to be simply a look-alike who wandered through town one time.

The best bet to get through dinner was not making a big deal out of it. Laugh the whole thing off as a joke perpetuated by the universe, God, Mother Nature, or any other deity available for blame.

Grandma and Grandpa were standing as Will walked into the room. The proverbial pin dropping would have sounded like dynamite going off. The silence was unnerving in its totality.

Marty quickly jumped in before the whole scene imploded. "Will, these are Justin's parents, Madge and Gary Boché. Madge and Gary, this is Will Villa."

Will smiled at the very formal introductions. He shook hands with the Bochés and accepted a glass of dark rum on the rocks from Justin. He nodded in appreciation at, what he immediately noticed, was a very generous double shot of the strong liquor.

After all the adults were seated, the twins came and sat as close to Will as possible. Perhaps they sensed his discomfort. Most people thought twins were somehow psychic. He didn't discount the belief.

Will, himself, had not experienced the phenomenon with Justin. Of course, maybe that's what the double shot of rum was all about.

To break the ice, Marty jumped back in. "Isn't it amazing how much Justin and Will look alike? Even though Will is two years older, they're as hard to tell apart as Jess and Tess.

"The first time the twins and I saw him, we started talking to him. We thought he was Justin.

"It's just too spooky, isn't it?"

Madge was looking intently at Will. She seemed to be examining him from head to foot. Her face was flushed and her eyes were moist. It was quite obvious to everybody in the room what she must be thinking.

Gary was taking Will in as well although he was doing a better job of maintaining his composure. "Will, your resemblance to Justin is beyond belief. I hope you can forgive Madge and me if we seem emotional.

"As you have probably heard, we lost Justin's twin to polio as an infant. To see the two of you together like this is a reminder of what we lost and what could have been.

"Tell us about yourself, Will. Do you have any siblings? Are your parents still alive? It's just such an amazing thing, we're interested in your life. Do you mind sharing it with us?"

Will was looking on in concern. The emotion evident on Madge's face could boil over at any time. "I don't mind telling you my story. It's pretty boring, like most people's are. I'm a Cuban by nationality. I've never lived there, never even been there."

Will decided to give the Bochés a piece of information they could use to rationalize the fact that Will could not be their child.

"I am an American citizen by birth, even though barely. I tell everyone I was born in Miami of Cuban parents shortly after they arrived in this country.

"Sorry, Justin and Marty; I fibbed just a tiny bit. I was not actually born on American soil, but I was born within its territorial waters.

"My mother was due at any time when my grandmother and parents left Cuba. According to my grandmother, my mother started having labor pains almost immediately. Luckily, they were the fake kind, not the real deal.

"To my parents, it was very important I be born on American soil. They didn't want me ever forced to return to Cuba.

"About 10 miles off the Florida coast, our little boat lost power and started to sink. To add to the difficulty, my mother had gone into real labor.

"As my family was about to be forced to abandon the small craft, an American Coast Guard cutter showed up.

"By the time my parents and grandmother were all safely aboard, my mother was in a bad way. To make a long story short, my grandmother and a Coast Guard medic delivered me on board the American ship.

"That's probably why I live on a boat. I guess it got into my system."

They all laughed politely at Will's feeble attempt at humor.   Will then relayed the rest of his made-up background like he had initially for Marty and Justin.

He concluded with what had become his drill by now. "Of course, I don't think Justin and I look that much alike; I'm a lot better looking."

The laughter was more genuine this time and less forced. Madge's emotional meltdown had receded, and she was smiling with the rest.

Attention then shifted to the twins who were doing something silly as kids are inclined to do when not receiving enough attention.   They had abandoned Will and were attacking their grandfather.

Justin's parents became very relaxed and seemed persuaded the whole look-alike scenario was just a fluke of nature.

The rest of the evening became a very pleasant supper among family and friend, with all present seemingly enjoying the experience.

A couple hours later, Will was on his way home, convinced he had successfully pulled off the evening. He had concluded the evening with his most recent fabrication involving his relocation to Mobile and subsequent business opportunity in Belgium.

He promised to try and get by to see Justin and his family before he left. He, of course, had no intention of doing so.

He had not had a chance to ask Justin about his brother's funeral and whether or not there was a body. At this point, the question seemed moot.

The next day he got an offer on the boathouse and would close in a few days. The only thing left to sell was his car.

The local dealership made him a fair offer, and he had

decided to take them up on the deal. Only one more thing to consider.

A few nights later he was relaxing in the boathouse looking at a world atlas. With all the activity associated with his plan of disassociation, he had not given a lot of detailed thought to his next location.

The only decision he had made was it would be a Spanish-speaking country, probably Spain. With his skin color and fluency in Spanish, he should be able to blend into the new country without great difficulty.

Finding him there would also be quite the chore. He had a passport with new name and well-vetted background. The Dean had provided him with several passports, three of which provided identities traceable back to birth.

Upon arrival in Spain he would become the only son of an oil field developer of Mexican heritage who had grown up in the southwestern United States. His parents had been killed in a plane crash the first year after he graduated college.

He had attended and graduated from Texas A&M with a degree in teaching. Since then, he had bounced around the world teaching English as a second language. He was currently between jobs and living off his inheritance.

Narrowing down his country of choice to Spain, he was now searching for an appropriate city. He wanted to live on the coast and in a city big enough for him to completely disappear. Marbella seemed to fit the bill.

…Two weeks later

Will had made a circuitous trip hopping from location to location, then backtracking a couple of times as he made his way to the Spanish Rivera. Saying the beautiful area was gorgeous seemed disingenuous; it was several descriptive adjectives beyond such phraseology.

To confuse any potential searchers, he had sold the airplane in Paris then taken the train to Rome where he purchased a small caravan (European for camper).

Taking his time and enjoying the scenery, he made his way to Southern Spain and the city of Marbella.

Now, this was a beach town! *Yeah, this would do just fine.*

Lying on the beach several days later, Will's mind wandered back to his family. They had been lost as quickly as they had been found.

He vowed to not forget Justin and the rest of his family. Will would never endanger his family by staying in contact, but they would always be with him.

Perhaps fate would reunite them someday. Karma could be like that.

A New Beginning

ABOUT THE AUTHOR

Jerry Moorman grew up in a small cotton-farming community in Mississippi. He often describes himself as "just an ole country boy from Mississippi." Maybe that describes his inner essence, but he is also a retired Professor Emeritus of Business research. His writing style often reflects both sides of his persona.

In addition to numerous academics books and publications, he has written three other novels and one award-winning book of poetry:

- Jungle Sniper (out of print)
- Coahoma Street
- Killer Tuition
- A Body Less Perfect (poetry)

www.ingramcontent.com/pod-product-compliance
Lightning Source LLC
Chambersburg PA
CBHW030658120726
47905CB00001B/261